Revenge!

A Natalie McMasters Mystery

I0676265

The Natalie McMasters Mystery Series by Thomas A. Burns, Jr.

Stripper! (2018)

Revenge! (2018)

Revenge!
A Natalie McMasters Mystery

Thomas A. Burns, Jr.

Published by Tekrighter LLC 2018

Revenge! A Natalie McMasters Mystery

Copyright © 2018 by Thomas A. Burns, Jr.

All rights reserved. No part of this book may be reproduced in any form or by any electronic or mechanical means including information storage and retrieval systems, without permission in writing from the author. The only exception is by a reviewer, who may quote short excerpts in a review.

Cover designed by Thomas A. Burns, Jr. with Corel PaintShop® Pro 2018

Front cover image is a free stock photo from https://www.pexels.com

This book is a work of fiction. Names, characters, places, and incidents either are products of the author's imagination or are used fictitiously. Any resemblance to actual persons, living or dead, events, or locales is entirely coincidental.

Thomas A. Burns, Jr.

Printed in the United States of America

First Edition: August 2018

ISBN 13: 978-0-692-16324-5

ISBN 10: 0-692-16324-7

Dedication

To my son Seamus, an Eagle Scout, college senior and a damn good bass guitarist, of whom I am very proud.

Table of Contents

Acknowledgements

I want to thank the following people who were instrumental in the completion and publication of *Revenge!*

My beta readers Craig Chapman, Ilia Davidovich, Peter J. Reilly and my wife Terri Burns provided many helpful suggestions and encouraged me to see this project through.

My book launch team comprised Brian Scott, Craig Chapman, Ilia Davidovich, Kalli Bunch, Mike Paris, Paul Crockett, Paul Rusnak, Peter J. Reilly, Skip Dyer, Susan Rice and Terri Boykin, all of whom were invaluable in getting Revenge! off to a good start.

"And if you wrong us, do we not revenge?"

WILLIAM SHAKESPEARE – THE MERCHANT OF VENICE

Chapter 1.

When you kill someone, it changes you. Totally.

My name is Natalie McMasters. I'm twenty, short and blonde (OK, it's bleached) and I'm way cute. And I've killed three people.

Two of them, I shot. The third one, I stabbed and burned to death. I killed them because they would have killed me and my gf Lupe if I hadn't killed them. For a while, that justification allowed me to sleep at night. But then the nightmares came back.

"What are you not telling me, Nattie?" Rebecca asks.

Dr. Rebecca Feiner is my campus counselor. Her high cheekbones, copper skin and slanted, nearly black eyes suggest she has native American blood. She wears her ebon hair in a bun at work, but I've seen her with it down and it falls nearly to her waist in a smoky cascade. She's a thirty-something, about five eight and the white doctor's smock she's wearing does little to hide her curves. She is absolutely one of the most gorgeous women that I've ever seen.

I'm lying on a stainless steel and black leather daybed in her office. The sickly-sweet aroma exuding from a vase of hyacinths on her desk overwhelms the old building musk. I intently scrutinize the blue flowers to avoid meeting her gaze. I've been seeing her since last year after my best friend was murdered and I decided to find her killer. I found him, all right.

"I'm concerned that we can't seem to get you off the prazosin." Rebecca says. "Outwardly, it seems that you've gotten your life back on track. You're back in school. You're in a stable relationship with Lupe, whom you tell me you love very much. You're not working as a private detective or a stripper anymore and no one's stalking you or trying to kill you. But every time we stop the prazosin, the nightmares come back. So what are you not telling me? What happened to you after you were kidnapped?"

I'm still not meeting her gaze and I know she notices. I force my eyes away from the flowers to her face.

"Nothing," I lie calmly. "The kidnapper took me and Lupe to the basement of the strip club. He was going to rape both of us. But before he could, a fire got started and burned the place down. I managed to get myself and Lupe out, but he didn't make it."

She fixes me with those dark eyes of hers. "Did he rape you, Nattie?"

"No." *It's not rape if I let him do it.* "I've told you everything that's been going on with me." Inside my head, I scream, *I'm not telling you I've killed three people!*

A frown mars Rebecca's elegant face.

"I can't help you if you won't be honest with me, Natalie."

She's gone from Nattie to Natalie. A bad sign.

"If he did rape you, there's no shame in it. It wasn't your fault. But you can't heal from it if you won't talk about it."

I fleetingly consider telling her that I seduced my kidnapper to gain our freedom, but I'm afraid of what else I might let slip if I open that can of worms. "But I have been totally honest with you," I say.

Her frown becomes a glare and she closes her portfolio with an audible crack.

"Then I guess we're done for today," she snaps.

I know there's at least twenty minutes left in the session, but I don't say anything and neither does she. The silence becomes painfully acute as I get up to go.

I put my hand on the knob to open the door, then turn and say, "I guess I'll see you next week."

"Why bother? Coming here isn't going to do you any good if you won't tell me what's going on with you."

"So you're cancelling the session?"

"No. You're cancelling it. I'm just not going to allow you to lie there and stonewall me. If you can tell me the truth, come on in. But if you won't talk to me, I'll have to ask you to leave again."

The only other person besides me who knows what happened is Lupe, because she was there too. She knows what I did. But she'll never tell.

Rebecca's office is in the Counselling Center, on the old part of the State University campus. I've been a pre-law student at State for the last two-and-a-half years. I've also been working for my Uncle Amos Murdoch while I'm in school. He is the founder and proprietor of the 3M Detective Agency. He hired me as his assistant. Most of his current business comes from dogging insurance scofflaws, waiting for them to do something for the camera that shows they're not hurt as badly as they say. The pay ain't great but the work ain't hard - most of the time I can study in the car while I'm on stakeout. He even got me a private detective trainee's license from the state, of which I was prouder than I liked to let on.

A few months ago, my good friend Becca was murdered and Uncle was attacked and left for dead. Becca was an online exotic dancer who could have been my twin. I took her place to draw her killer to me and ended up working undercover in a local strip joint. I found the killer and broke up a major drug ring, but I also got a good case of PTSD in the process. That's why I'm still seeing Rebecca. When Uncle found out about the stripping, he fired me. He told me I could see about a job with him when I had my law degree if I still wanted one. I didn't know it when he hired me, but it was his strong sense of family that was responsible for the job offer. That's also why he fired me when he had reason to believe I might get hurt.

I go out of the front door of the Counselling Center onto a red brick porch that overlooks a sunken courtyard the size of a football field, rimmed with stately oaks and a border of multicolored chrysanthemums. It's nearly lunchtime on a gorgeous fall day on campus. Even though the morning was chilly, it's now well over eighty because we're in the South but the fresh autumn breeze keeps the humidity down, so it's not as oppressive as it would be in the summer. I slip off my hoodie and tie it around my waist.

Because Rebecca cut the session short, I've got some time to kill. My next class is on new campus, so I head that way.

As is usual on a day like this, the courtyard is full of students. Some are going from one class to another or back to the dorm. Others are playing Frisbee, lolling about on the grass or on beach towels, sleeping, reading or snuggling. A flash of anger wells up in my chest. How dare they be so carefree?

I turn my back on them as I climb the long concrete staircase that leads out of the courtyard. Why am I so angry? I did nothing wrong. The men I killed were murderers and would have surely killed me and Lupe if I hadn't stopped them. I have no reason to feel guilty. And I have little reason to fear arrest. The fire destroyed all of the evidence, so the chance that cops will ever trace anything to me is vanishingly small.

Why won't I tell Rebecca what happened to me? I've finally accepted that I was raped in that basement, even though I was the one who initiated the sex. I didn't kill my rapist for revenge, I only did it to stop that pervert from killing us. Lupe and I have talked about it and she told me that wasn't my fault. But I'm still ashamed I had to let him screw me. Lupe was a victim of multiple rapes by cartel thugs when she lived in Mexico, but she seems to have put that behind her. Why can't I?

I reach the top of the stairs where the street runs along a ridge, separating old campus from new campus. I look down into the cement courtyard in front of me, the so-called New Commons. It's ringed with contemporary concrete and steel buildings. The university logo, done in orange and blue bricks, stands out hideously in the center of the courtyard in front of an equally hideous building called the octagon. I can't imagine two colors that go together less well. The New Commons is also full of people, but almost none of them are lollygagging. The concrete benches are not welcoming and who wants to fall on hard pavement chasing a stupid Frisbee?

I make my way to the library on the opposite side of the New Commons, where there's a snack bar/coffee shop/cafeteria on the ground floor. I push open the glass door and the smells of coffee that's sat too long, sour bread and greasy burgers slap me in the face. It's a good thing I'm not really hungry because I think I might catch something if I ate here, but it's still a good place to kill time before my next class. I get me a plain black coffee and find an empty table in the back. I'm in no mood for company.

I pull out my phone and thumb the button. 11:09. Thirty-five minutes until my next class. I could use the time to study, but I'm just not in the mood.

I let my eyes drift around the spacious room. It's about half full — the lunch crowd is still in class. A buzz of conversation fills the air. The glass and stainless steel tables are bolted to the floor so the students can't inflict chaos on the arrangement. Most of the tables are occupied by groups, but a few other loners like me are scattered about. TV sets are hanging from brackets on the ceiling at regular intervals and public service announcements are scrolling on the screens — club meetings, special lectures, concerts and the like. My eyes are automatically drawn to a screen, against my will.

...National syndicated columnist George Markarious will be on campus to discuss the failure of the current U.S. economic policy to address the needs of...

The screen suddenly flickers and goes black, but only for a second. When it comes back on, I see two naked women, entwined on a bed, engaging in an enthusiastic sixty-nine. It doesn't seem to be a porn flick - the perspective doesn't change and the room on the screen is dimly lit, so it's difficult to make out details. There's something disturbingly familiar about it, though. Wait a minute, I know that heart-shaped bed…

The girl on top raises her head from between her partner's legs to take a breath, giving the camera a full view of her face. OMG! It's me!

Chapter 2.

I want to crawl under the floor! I struggle into my hoodie and pull it up to hide my face like a criminal about to be perp-walked out of City Hall and slink into the courtyard. I'm oddly grateful - the crowd is way too fixated on the steamy scene on TV to even notice, much less recognize me.

I know that video of Lupe and me! It was made on webcams in our bedroom by the guy who raped me without my knowledge. He swore at the time that he'd done it just for his own lols and he hadn't shared it online. Obviously, he lied. Why am I not surprised? But I'm also shocked to see it on campus TV. Who has done this horrible thing to me? And why?

I briefly consider returning to Rebecca's office and telling her what's happened, but I wouldn't know how to start. I'm not ashamed of what I did, but I feel incredibly violated that it's out there for the world to see. My actions were an expression of my love for Lupe and never meant for anyone else's eyes. This is almost worse than rape!

I need to tell Lupe what's happened. This affects her as much as it does me. I'll have to cut class, but big whoop.

The bus ride to the student parking lot seems to take forever. I know it's just my imagination that everyone, especially the guys, is staring at me, judging me.

I finally get in my little red Z-car and head for home. I have to keep wiping the tears out of my eyes while I drive. Finally, I pull into my space in the parking lot of our townhouse complex in front of the little bronze plaque with my name on it. Good! Lupe's car is here too.

As I approach the front door, mewing comes from the azaleas. A small, mostly white Siamese cat scampers out and runs up to me. Despite my distress, I can't help but smile. It's Xin Niu!

Xin Niu used to be Becca's cat and she continually reminds me of my very dear friend who is no longer alive.

I hold out my arms and Xin Niu leaps into them, purring loudly as I enfold her. How did you get outside, girl? The tension drains out of me as I nuzzle my cat.

I fumble for my keys while holding six pounds of feline, then unlock the door and go inside. The ever-present aroma of chilies and corn welcomes me. Xin Niu jumps out of my arms and runs off. Lupe pokes her head out of the pass-through between the kitchen and the dining nook.

"*Hola!*", she says. "Nattie, you are home early." Then she sees my face. Her welcoming expression vanishes and she lapses into her native tongue. "*Cariño! ¿Qué te pasa?*"

I throw myself into her arms, bawling. She coos to me in Spanish, kissing my face and comforting me like a little girl.

When I've cried myself out, I tell her what's happened.

"I do not understand," she says when I've finished. "That *hijo de puta* is dead! How could that video even be still around?"

Lupe is damn smart, but she's not very technically savvy. I explained to her that the video might have been disseminated on the Internet, but she obviously didn't understand the ramifications of that.

"Somebody's gotten hold of it," I tell her. "Maybe one of my ex-fans from the strip club who knows I go to State thought it would be funny to put it up on campus TV."

Lupe and I met at the strip joint where I was undercover. The damned place burned to the ground, but its influence on my life obviously lives on.

"*Cariño.*" Lupe uses her pet name for me. "I am sorry that this happened. But think of all the things we did on stage every night in that place. Everybody saw them! But we did those things because we had to. There is no shame in that."

"This is different, Lupe. What was on that tape was private. It was just between you and me."

She smiles fondly. "I remember that night. It was not our first time, but it was when I knew for sure that I loved you. Nobody can spoil that for me, no matter what they do."

I look at her dumbstruck. She had never told me that before.

"Do not worry about what other people think of you!" said Lupe. "This is America, where a girl can live how she wants. All that matters is that we love each other, Nattie. Let them say whatever they want to about us, it will not change that."

See why I love this woman? She has a way of getting to the heart of things! I throw my arms around her neck and kiss her.

My cell phone is playing Moment 4 Life. That's my ringtone for an unknown caller. I dig it out and hit the button.

"Hello?"

"Is this Natalie McMasters?"

"This is she."

"This is Margaret Sheerer at the Office of Student Conduct. I'm calling to tell you that Associate Director Simonson would like to see you in his office as soon as you can get here today."

WTF? "I don't know…"

"Miss McMasters!" Ms. Sheerer interrupted me. "If you want to remain enrolled at this University, you will get yourself down here as soon as you can. At what time today can I tell the Associate Director that you will see him?"

I look at the clock above the pass through. It's a little past twelve-thirty. "I can be there by two o'clock." I tell her. It's only a twenty-minute drive to campus, but I'm in no hurry.

"You have a class at one-ten today." Holy shit, she's looking at my schedule? "Can't you come then instead of going to class?"

"I'm at home," I tell her. "I wasn't planning on going to class this afternoon."

"Hmmph." The disapproval in that snort speaks volumes. "Be here at one-ten. And don't be late!"

"But what's this about…" The phone goes dead in my hand.

Lupe notices my distress, so I tell her what the call was about.

"But why would the Student Conduct Office want to see you? You did not do anything wrong!"

"Maybe that's not how they see it," I reply. "If I want to stay in school, I have to go straighten this out."

I grab my backpack. As I reach for the doorknob, I hear feline chirruping at my feet.

"Oh no you don't." I reach down and scoop up Xin Niu, then carry her over to the sofa and give her to Lupe.

"She's been getting outside," I tell her, "and that's not good. There are always a lot of cars in that parking lot. She could get run over."

"I catch Eduardo taking her out a coupla times," Lupe says. Eduardo is Lupe's eight-year-old son. He and Xin Niu are nearly inseparable when he's not at school. "I tell him to quit or I whip him," she says.

"Don't do that. Just tell him she could get hit by a car. That will stop him, the way he loves her." I stroke her head as she lies in Lupe's arms and she purrs. "Problem is, she's gotten to like the great outdoors. We'll just have to watch her when we come and go."

It's normally a twenty-minute drive to school, but traffic is light and I make it in less time. On the way, I reflect on the situation. I didn't even know that State had an office of Student Conduct. Surely they don't think that I put that video up on purpose for all the world to see? As a matter of fact, how in the hell do they even know it is me in the video? The visual quality is far from great - I totally didn't think I was even recognizable. I have had a lot of media coverage in the last year, though. Maybe I'm more famous, or infamous, than I realize.

The Office of Student Conduct is in a squat, modern two-story building on the edge of campus. It also houses the Registrar's office, where I've been before to handle enrollment issues. I'd never even seen the OSC office, for the very good reason that it's on the second floor where nobody would go unless they had to. There's a long hallway at the top of the stairs that smells like old socks. It's lined with fluorescent fixtures that brightly illuminate a hideous two-toned orange and royal blue cinder block wall, with a lone door at the other end. I wonder who designs these college buildings? Maybe they take the plans from failing student papers when the semester is over.

I trudge all the way down to the door. It's made of that ugly blonde wood you see nowhere but in institutions. It has a useless rectangular window of wired glass that is about five times taller than it is wide that allows me to see nothing of the room on the other side. I press down the door handle. It doesn't budge. WTF?

I take out my phone and thumb the button. It's 1:00. I'm a little early, but they know I'm coming. Why is the door locked? I draw back my arm and clench my fist to pound on it, then I notice the call box unobtrusively mounted on the wall next to the doorframe.

I push the button.

A tinny voice answers. "Yes?"

"It's Natalie McMasters. I'm supposed to see Dr. Simonson at one-ten."

The raucous buzz that fills the hallway is so loud that it makes me close my eyes. I open the door and enter.

The room is lit by glaring fluorescents that make the orange and blue cinder blocks seem even brighter than in the hallway. The revolting flowery scent of perfume fills the too-warm, stuffy chamber. A woman at a desk in the center of the room who is presumably the source of the odor looks away from her computer and glares at me. There's a couple of windows to the outside but they're duplicates of the one in the door, so they can't be opened to air the place out.

I assume the woman is Ms. Sheerer. She's a fifty-something and wearing a dress your meemaw would be embarrassed to give to Goodwill — all ugly flowers and lace. She sports a pair of gold-framed glasses on a chain that goes round the back of her neck and hair so stiff and blonde that it has to be fake. She's gazing over her spectacles at me like I'm something the cat dragged in. I become painfully aware of my battered backpack, my too-tight Opeth t-shirt and my scruffy jeans.

"You're early," she accuses. "Mr. Simonson will see you in nine minutes." She waves me toward an uncomfortable-looking beige sofa on the wall across from her desk, then goes back to her monitor. A copy of the *State of State*, the student paper, lies on a low table made of the same blonde wood in front of the sofa along with multiple issues of the University magazine. Neither of one is my idea of interesting reading. I shed my backpack and put it on the table, earning another glare, but I leave it there anyway and sit on the hard sofa.

The minutes seem to creep by as the second hand slowly ticks around the face of a large, circular clock on the wall above Sheerer's desk. The clock has an image of the college mascot, a centaur with a crossbow, in the center. I try not to look at it, but it draws my eyes like a magnet. I remember a discussion in one of my classes about getting rid of the crossbow, because it promotes violence. Someone else brought up the point that the centaur itself might have to go, because it's cultural appropriation. God, how I wish that shit like that was all I had to worry about!

I can feel the sweat starting to bloom in my armpits and run down my sides, pooling up around my waist band. I squirm on the hard vinyl cushions, earning yet another dirty look from the witch at the desk. Yep, an early arrival was totally a bad idea.

The centaur clock says one-ten on the dot when the old witch picks up her phone and presses a button. After a moment she says, "Ms. McMasters is here, Mr. Simonson.", then hangs up. She motions to a door across the room. "You can go in."

I move to the door, which buzzes as I approach. It's locked too? I wonder how he knows I'm there? I push down the handle and enter.

A rush of cool, spice-scented air washes over my face as the door closes behind me with an audible click. This room couldn't be more different than the one I just left. There's a soft carpet under my feet and the walls are paneled in dark wood. Two of those stupid narrow windows admit daylight on one wall and there's a large photo of University Gate between them. The other office walls are lined with shelves that hold books, photos, trophies and other mementos of the occupant's career. There's a large picture of the university seal with the centaurine archer rampant on the wall behind the heavy, ornate desk where Simonson sits. I instinctively move towards the overstuffed leather sofa on the wall perpendicular his desk, but he says, "No, please sit there," pointing to an uncomfortable-looking orange plastic cafeteria chair that faces him.

Simonson is fiftyish and wears a tan suit, a white shirt and an orange and blue striped tie. He's got thin brown hair, sunken cheeks and a little toothbrush mustache that doesn't do anything for his looks. He's ogling me up and down like I'm back in the strip club. Again, I regret my tight-fitting clothes.

"So, Natalie. I hear you've caused quite a commotion on campus this morning," is his opening salvo.

That's how it's going to be, is it? And who gave you permission to call me by my first name, asshole? I shift in the uncomfortable chair to find a position that doesn't hurt my butt and the chair wobbles because one leg is obviously shorter than the other. "I wasn't aware that I'd caused anything, Mr. Simonson," I say demurely.

His computer monitor is set off to one side so he can face his victim in the plastic chair. He types a few keystrokes (a short password?), clicks the mouse, then swivels the monitor so I can see the screen. Yep, it's my sex tape all right!

"Do you deny that this is you in this video?"

"Nope."

He seems a bit taken aback that I didn't expand on my answer. I'm just following the advice that Uncle Amos once gave me. When you talk to the cops, don't say anything you don't have to.

"And you'll agree that something of this nature would be highly offensive to some members of our University community?"

"I guess so."

An uncomfortable silence reigns for a while as he waits for me to break. It doesn't work.

"Then how can you say you're not aware of the commotion you caused." he says finally.

"Because I didn't cause it. The creep who put up that video did."

The smirk that appears on his face tells me he was ready for that one. "Do you really expect me to believe that, Kira?"

Oh shit! Kira Foxxx was my stage name when I worked at the strip joint and online.

"I know that paying back your college loans can seem daunting," he continues in a sarcastic tone, "but disseminating pornography across campus to revitalize your online exotic dance business isn't the way to go about earning money to do that."

I'm speechless for a few seconds, then realize that I've got to respond to this accusation. "I didn't put up that video, Mr. Simonson. I don't know who did. And you can't prove it was me." As soon as that last was out of my mouth, I realized that it was the wrong thing to say.

"Do you know what Title IX is, Kira?"

"My name is Natalie."

"OK Natalie, do you know what Title IX is?"

I think for a minute. "I'm not sure."

"Title IX of the Education Amendments of 1972 is a federal law that prohibits discrimination on the basis of sex in any educational program or activity that receives federal money." He sounds like he's reciting by rote. "The principal objective of Title IX is to stop federal dollars from being used to support sex discrimination in educational programs and to provide effective protection to students, faculty and staff against such discrimination. It also protects people against sexual harassment. Title IX applies to any and all aspects of federally-funded educational programs or activities."

"So? I'm not discriminating against or harassing anybody."

He goes on like I haven't even spoken. "I am the Title IX Coordinator for this University," he says. "As such, I am tasked with identifying instances of sexual harassment on campus, which include the creation of a hostile educational or work environment. Your video definitely creates such an environment."

He's got a point, but I tell him again, "That may be, but I'm not the one who put it up. I'm the one who's being harassed here!"

He gives me an oily smile. "But you don't get to make the determination about who is being harassed, Natalie. I do."

Now he's finally got me speechless.

"Once a Title IX complaint is lodged, I will investigate it," he says. "As the Title IX Coordinator, I can lodge a complaint, as can any member of the University community. If I find that the complaint is valid, I will file it with the Dean of Students and she will process it under the Code of Student Discipline to determine an appropriate sanction. Such sanctions can go all the way up to expulsion from the University."

Expulsion! My bladder begins to ache.

"What can I do about this? Do I get a trial or something?"

"You will be provided an opportunity to meet with the Dean of Students or the Dean's designee after the complaint has been filed." He sounds like he's reciting again. "They will advise you of your rights and responsibilities under the Code of Student Discipline. If the complainant is the Title IX Coordinator, any victims may also attend this administrative meeting."

"What victims? I'm the victim here!"

"As I said, that's not your call. And since this video was widely disseminated on the campus closed-circuit network," he indicates the computer monitor, on which the video is still playing, "it's very likely that others will become co-complainants."

"Turn that off!" I snarl at him. "Right now, you're the one who's creating a hostile environment!"

His condescending smile briefly becomes a frown, then his face reverts to its former expression. But he does turn the screen so I can no longer see it. But he can.

I want to get up and run out of here, but I force myself to remain in the wobbly plastic chair. "What can I do about this?" I ask him again.

Now he's looking smug, like he's got me where he wants me.

"Tell me about your time as Kira Foxxx," he says.

What's that got to do with anything? But since this guy can possibly get me expelled, I decide to comply. "I took that name when I worked undercover to find out who killed a friend of mine and hurt my uncle."

His smug smile broadens. "That's right," he says. "I saw your television interview with Roderigo about that. You fancy yourself a detective."

I don't fancy myself as anything, you asshole, but I don't say it. Instead, "I got a job as a stripper," I tell him. "I broke up a major drug ring."

"And did you discover the identity of your friend's murderer?" The way he says it, it sounds like a slam.

I must be careful here. "Yes. It was the owner of the club." That's a lie, but it's what I told the cops.

"And you had an online stripping business, too," he said. "Tell me about that."

"I did that so I had some street cred when I applied for the job at the strip club." Another lie. I did it to lure my friend's murderer to me. It worked and I killed him! I wonder if this asshole would be acting so arrogantly if he knew that?

"And what services did you provide for your clients?" he asked.

"Interactive exotic dancing…" Oh shit! Now I see where this is going!

"Nothing else?" he asks. "Nothing that could make this Title IX thing go away?"

I don't believe it! The son-of-a-bitch in charge of preventing sexual harassment for the entire University is trying to get me to screw him to make the charges go away!

"No. Nothing else." I don't trust myself to say any more.

His desk phone buzzes and he hits a button.

"Your three o'clock is here early," the witch says.

"I'll be done here shortly. Send her in when McMasters leaves." He turns back to me. "You're sure there's nothing you can think of to do to help yourself here?"

"No. Sorry."

"Pity." He picks up a stack of papers from his desk, bangs them a few times to arrange them and puts them in a folder which he closes. "If you change your mind, make another appointment with Margaret. But you'd best act quickly. It will be much more difficult for you if there are many more co-complainants."

I don't respond.

"You're dismissed." He flips a hand like he's shooing away a fly.

I struggle out of the plastic chair, which is so light it wants to tip over when I do and walk to the door. I push the handle to open it, but the handle doesn't budge. Locked! A bolt of fear lances through my stomach. I turn to look at Simonson. He's watching me intensely and grinning broadly.

"Sorry," he says. "It wouldn't do to let just anyone walk in here anytime they want to." He reaches under his desk and the door lock clicks.

I push the door open. I can't get out of there fast enough!

I see another female student sitting on the sofa where I was. She's a mousy little thing with a blonde butch cut. She looks up at me with a snarl on her face. What's that about? I wonder if she'll give Simonson what he wants?

Chapter 3.

My Z-car is making a second circuit around the beltway that surrounds the city, because I don't know what else to do.

I'm in serious trouble. I don't know who put up that video, or why. I do know that I'm in the power of a man who can end my college career if he wants to. And I know just how to stop him. Submit to rape. Again!

I need advice. I got a voicemail from Rebecca last night asking me to call her, but I can't go back to her unless I'm willing to tell her that I've killed three men. I just can't do that!

There's only one other person I can talk to and I'm pretty sure how he's going to react. Uncle Amos. Maybe he'll at least help me find out who posted the video. I exit the freeway and head for his office.

I love my Uncle, but he's definitely old school. The three things most important to him are his Bible, the United States Marine Corps and his family, in that order. When he found out that I was stripping on stage, he made no bones about telling me exactly what he thought about it. "I don't care why you did it, Nattie," he said. "I thought you were raised better than that. I'm ashamed of you." Those last words really hurt.

So I never did tell him about Lupe and me. To Uncle Amos, homosexuality is an aberration forbidden by scripture. I don't know how he'd react if I came out to him and I really don't want to find out. As far as he knows, Lupe is just my roommate. His partners, Danny Merkel and Leon Kidd, know the truth and so does my Mom, who is Uncle's receptionist. But they'll leave it up to me to tell him or not. They're good people. But I don't see how I can avoid telling him if I'm going to get his help with this.

The 3M office is in Garton, a small town near the capital. It's in an old Victorian house that is also Uncle's home — he lives upstairs and the office is down. I park around back. Uncle's Cadillac is there, as is Mom's bug, Danny's pick-up and the little grey car we use for surveillance.

I enter the back door into the kitchen. The odor of burnt coffee from a percolator on a back burner of the stove assails my nostrils. That coffee is as black as tar and just as tasty. I decide I don't need any to make this harder than it already is.

Uncle Amos and Mom have desks in what used to be the living room. Danny and Kidd use the former dining room as their office.

The afternoon sun is streaming through the three large windows that face Main Street, illuminating Uncle Amos behind his desk. He's not a lot taller than my 5'1" and he seems even shorter in his wheelchair. He's just turning sixty. His face is broad and likeable and topped off with a shock of pure white hair. It's a great face for a PI — it makes people just naturally want to tell him things. He's wearing his usual wrinkled seersucker suit with the collar open and his tie pulled halfway down the front of his shirt - I don't think I've ever seen him dressed any other way.

Mom is at the other desk, busily typing on her computer. She's twenty years older than me, with brown hair (my natural color) and thirty pounds heavier. She's got a cute round face that's nothing like mine.

Both of them look up and greet me as I come in. We do the how is your day thing. Not surprisingly, Mom is the first to notice that something's wrong.

She takes off her glasses and lets them fall on her chest. "What's bothering you, dear?"

I sit in the easy chair facing Uncle's desk. "Actually, I came to talk to you, Uncle. Mom, you can stay if you want to." *You'll probably hear about this soon enough on the news*, I think.

I grit my teeth. This isn't going to be easy. Then I launch into my story. Both Uncle and Mom flinch visibly when the words "sex video" come out of my mouth, but to their credit, neither one interrupts me.

"So I came here to ask your help to find out who did this to me, Uncle," I finish.

"Of course, we'll help you," Mom blurts out.

Uncle Amos is silent. I don't like his expression. Finally he says, "Well now, the first person I would ask is the young man in that video with you. Some guys have been known to do this kind of thing for braggin' rights."

Obviously, I left something out of my story.

"It's not a young man in the video with me, Uncle. It's Lupe, my roommate. And she didn't do this."

Again, I'll give him credit. He doesn't flinch, but his face reddens and his frown deepens.

"How do you know?" he asks.

"Because she loves me and I love her. People who love each other don't do something like that to their partner."

He goes quiet again. I can see him struggling with it. Mom knows him, so she stays quiet too.

Finally he says, "I don't think I can help you."

"Why not?"

His quivering jaw tells me that he's trying not to yell. "Because it was your own damn bad judgement that got you into this," he says. "That's the reason you don't work here anymore. Nobody could have made a sex video with you in it public if you hadn't made one in the first place. I think it's high time you learned that actions have consequences and you start livin' with the consequences of yours. Even if I could bail you out of this, you'd just do some other stupid thing down the road and expect somebody to bail you out again."

"Amos!" Mom exclaims.

"Shut up, Judy," he says. "I done ever'thing I could for this young'un of yours. I even signed on the dotted line to get her a PI trainee's license from the state, which put my reputation on the line. This is how she pays me back! Strippin' on a stage! Makin' sex videos! Livin' in sin!" His voice is getting progressively shriller, like a hellfire preacher in his Sunday pulpit.

"I guess it doesn't matter that I took that stripper's job to find the guy who knifed you!" It was the wrong thing to say and I knew it just as soon as it came out of my mouth.

"Don't you dare put this on me!" Now he's totally yelling. "I didn't ask you to do that! The only part I had in this was hiring your sorry ass back after I fired you last year for breakin' into that house. I should'a known better!"

He reaches down and grabs his wheels, then reverses the chair so violently that I'm afraid it's going to tip over backwards. He pops out from behind the desk and trundles towards the hallway door. In a moment, the grinding sound of the elevator on the stairs to the second floor is audible in the room.

I just sit there in tears, still stunned at his outburst. I knew it was gonna be bad, but not this bad! Mom jumps up and rushes over to embrace me.

"Don't cry, honeybunch. We'll get through this."

"What the hell is going on?" A male voice says.

Danny Merkel comes in from the hallway. "Nattie! What's wrong?"

Danny is an all-American boy, six foot two with a blonde crew cut. He's an ex-Marine and an ex-cop. He dresses the part in olive drab tactical pants and a skin-tight, camo t-shirt that reveals bulging biceps. An eagle, globe and anchor tattoo peeps out beneath his right shirt sleeve.

I start to tell Danny to give us some space, but this is gonna be all over the city on the five o'clock news. He might as well hear it from me.

So after I get my breath, I tell the sordid tale again. Danny is also frowning when I'm done — he's a cis man and pretty straight-laced. We made love once, before I knew I was a lesbian. I told Rebecca that I thought I'd done it to prove that I was straight. Danny told me he didn't do one-night hookups, but I chose not to hear that. But he's really tried to be my friend since I told him about me and Lupe. I wish my Uncle would do the same.

"Wow!" is all that Danny can say when I finish.

Mom says, "I'll talk to Amos. He's just got to help you with this!"

"No, don't. He's right, you know," I say bitterly. "A lot of this is my own doing."

"We all screw up, Nattie," Danny says. "That's what we need friends for. And I'm your friend. I'll help you even if Amos won't. And I'm sure Leon will too."

My mind flashes back to that evening when Danny and me hooked up. I force that vision from my head.

"I don't want to get you guys in trouble with Uncle Amos…" I begin.

"Amos is the senior partner, not the boss around here," says Danny. "He said he wanted it that way because he was tired of running things all the time. Besides, it will be three against one."

"Uncle was a Marine too," I tell Danny unnecessarily. "He won't care if there's an army against him."

"I'll talk to him," Mom repeats. "You gave him a big pill to swallow, Nattie. But he'll choke it down. He does love you, even if he doesn't show it all the time. That's why he's so upset."

I get that Mom believes that, but I'm not sure. Uncle can really dig in his heels, especially when his faith is involved.

Danny says, "Hey Nattie, your Mom tells me you have a birthday coming up."

WTF? Oh, I get it! He's changing the subject to make me feel better. I decide to play along. "Yeah, it's the week after next."

"And it's the big two-one, right?"

"Yep." I appreciate what you're trying to do, Danny-boy, but it's just not working.

Now Mom joins in the fun. "So what do you want for your birthday?" Great.

I answer honestly, which will probably put a stop to this nonsense pretty quick. "I want a pistol. I've decided to apply for my concealed carry permit as a present to myself."

"Nattie! Do you really think you need that?" Mom asks.

I touch the scar on my cheek from a pistol-whipping I got a few months ago and Mom winces. "Yes I do," I tell her. She doesn't argue.

"Have you decided what pistol you want?" Danny asks.

"A Ruger LC-9S," I tell him. He looks surprised that my answer is so specific.

"So you have really thought about this," he says.

"Uncle Amos has a federal firearms license. I was hoping he could find me one on the Internet. Now I'm not sure he will help me."

"Oh, he'll help you all right," Mom says. Her tone intimates that she'll make sure of that.

"Hey Mom. I really don't want to start a war between you and Uncle. Just leave it alone. He'll either help me or he won't and if he doesn't, I'll just have to find another way." I'm not talking about the pistol, now.

Mom starts to protest, but then thinks better of it. "All right. You're an adult, make your own decisions." I can totally tell she doesn't mean it.

I hear the kitchen door slam. Uncle is upstairs, so I figure it must be Kidd. Then a female voice yodels, "Yoo hoo! Danny!"

A thirtyish woman flounces into the office like she owns the place. She's just a little taller than me, but twenty pounds heavier. She's got a cute round face and dirty blonde hair up in a bun. She's dressed in green hospital scrubs with cartoon puppies on them. She runs over to Danny, throws her arms around his neck, pulls his head down and gives him a big smack on the cheek. He looks mortified.

She turns to me and says in a Southern drawl so intense that it just has to be fake, "Y'all must be Nattie. Danny's told me so much about you!"

I'm particular about who calls me Nattie. This babe is not on the list.

She extends a hand and I take it, reluctantly.

Danny says, "Nattie, this is…"

"Oh I'll tell her who I am, shug!" To me. "I'm Diane Beasley. Danny's my beau!"

A hot flash burns my cheeks. Good Lord, where you been hiding this one, Danny-boy? "Nice to meet you, Diane," I say, not meaning it at all. I glance at Danny, who's a fine shade of crimson.

Just to make stupid conversation, I ask her, "And what has Danny told you about me?"

"Oh, lots!" she replies. "That you think you're a detective and you're queer with a Mexican girlfriend and a cat. So I don't need to worry about you!" She's still hanging off Danny, who's mouth is now hanging open like somebody clocked him.

I can't even! If I stay here another thirty seconds, I just know I'm going to kill her.

"Mom, I'll call you," I say over my shoulder as I head out the door.

"What's the matter with her?" Diane says.

Later, I'm driving and crying furiously again. It seems like my whole world has gone topsy-turvy. I'm gonna get expelled from college. My uncle thinks I'm a sinner. And where the hell did Danny dig up that bae? He and I don't have a thing anymore, so I really don't care who he sees. But I thought he had way better taste than that!

Chapter 4.

Next day, I'm jammed into the crowd on the campus shuttle bus again. The weather's turned cold and breezy, so I'm wearing my army jacket and a ball cap. An oversize pair of sunglasses completes my disguise.

I make the news again. They don't show the video on TV but they do mention my name and my major, dredge up an old picture that they ran when I was arrested last year and of course, rehash that old business as well. The land line at the townhouse keeps ringing until we take it off the hook. Thank God it's next to impossible to find somebody's cell number!

Lupe and I discuss laying low for a few days, but dammit, we didn't do anything wrong, so we shouldn't have to act like criminals. We decide that I'll go to class, she'll go to work as usual and send Eduardo to school. But the jacket, the hat and the sunglasses seem like just simple discretion. So far, I don't think that anyone's recognized me.

The bus reaches my stop and I file off with the other students, then head to my International Law class. I spy a box that holds copies of the *State of State* and I see my picture on the front page, a blow-up of the head shot on the video. Shit! I open the box and take one, then get out of the pedestrian traffic to read the article.

College Stripper Broadcasts Sex Tape on Campus CCTV, the headline screams. The byline is Andrea Kiefer. *"State students saw a lot more of Ms. Natalie McMasters than they were expecting or wanted to when a tape of her and her girlfriend engaged in a sex act surfaced on the campus closed circuit station…"* It goes on from there in the same vein.

The article is pretty much factually accurate, except for the underlying implication that I had something to do with the publication of the video to promote the Kira Foxxx website, which no longer exists, by the way. It also details my history as a club and online stripper. I'm grateful that Lupe is not identified as the other person in the video. More troubling however, is that the writer alleges that a Title IX investigation may be in the offing because of the video. Title IX supposedly provides complete confidentiality for both accusers and the accused, but it apparently doesn't control speculation such as this. Moreover, the tone of the article suggests that the writer knows more than she's telling. Did Simonson leak it to the press?

"Hey, Nattie!" A feminine voice calls. Somebody has penetrated my disguise.

It's my former roommate, Fields Jackson. No wonder she knew me. She's a junior poli-sci major with visions of law school and a career in politics. We have some classes together.

"I see you've done it again," Fields says, glaring at me over her horn-rimmed glasses. I was living with Fields and Kwan when I became involved in the media circus that led to the interview with Roderigo.

"I didn't put up that video," I tell her.

"I didn't think that you did. But you're all over Facebook, Twitter, Snapchat, Instagram and I don't know where else!"

There's a cold ball in the pit of my stomach. "I thought those social media sites don't allow porn."

"They don't. They'll take it down as soon as they notice it, or when somebody complains. But in the meantime, that video's been disseminated to a ton of users and they can send it on to others."

The magnitude of what's happened is beginning to sink in. I don't keep up much with social media — I think it's totally stupid and gives other people way too much personal information about you. Even when I stripped on the Internet as Kira Foxxx, I didn't give out my real name or personal details — my troubles began after I went public at the club. But I'd never have realized that the video of me and Lupe had gone viral if someone didn't tell me.

"How did you know that it was me in the video?" I ask her.

"Because it's got your name on it, of course. Somebody is really out to get you, Nattie. And frankly, I didn't think you'd put something like that on line, even if you were working as a stripper."

Et tu, Fields? "I didn't put it online," I tell her.

"Then how did it get there?"

"It's complicated."

"Apparently." There's that tone of disapproval again.

We've arrived at Shipley Hall, where the International Law class is. Fields opens the door and motions for me to go first, but I balk.

"You go ahead. I've got to talk to somebody. Can I get your notes if I don't make it to class?"

She waves her phone at me. "I'm recording it. I'll send you a link."

I wait for her to disappear, then I pull out my phone and hit speed dial.

"This is Dr. Feiner."

"Rebecca, it's Nattie. I need to see you. Now."

"Nattie, I have someone else in the office."

"When can I come in?" I try to keep the desperation out of my voice.

I think she hears it anyway. "Hang on a minute," she replies. I hold my breath as I picture her putting her hand over the receiver to talk to her patient. She comes back on. "Come on over now."

I let my breath out with a whoosh. "I'll be right there.

Twenty minutes later I'm back on the black leather daybed, staring at the hyacinths. They're pink and blue today.

"So I heard about what happened yesterday," Rebecca says. How could you not have? "Want to tell me about it?"

No, but I guess I don't have much choice. "That video was made without our knowledge. The guy who did it swore that it was only for his own enjoyment and that he wouldn't disseminate it."

"Obviously, he did," Rebecca says.

"He may have sent it to other guys, but he's not the one who put it up on campus TV."

"How can you be so sure?"

"Because he's dead."

Rebecca looks surprised. "Why don't you tell me about it?"

I tell her everything. That we were launching a website where Lupe could dance to get her out of the strip club. That we made love after a performance thinking that the webcams were off. We didn't know that we'd been hacked and the cameras had been turned on remotely. I tell her how Lupe was kidnapped and how I went to the club with a gun to save her and how I shot and killed two gangbangers. Later, after Lupe and I were abducted again, I seduced a killer to save our lives, then killed him too.

Rebecca just stares at me after I finish, the horror writ plain on her face. Finally she says, "And you've been carrying all of this around with you for five months? No wonder we can't get you off the prazosin!"

I blurt out what's really been bothering me. "Are you going to have to tell the cops that I killed those people?"

"Has anyone else been arrested or charged with the killings?"

"No. Everyone involved besides Lupe and me is dead."

"Then I think that you're protected by doctor-patient confidentiality as long as you're not a significant threat to the public welfare and it's my determination that you're not."

I let out the breath I've been holding with a whoosh.

"But that doesn't mean we don't have a serious problem, Nattie," she continues. "Even if the killings were justified, the psychological effect of killing another person can be very profound. You originally came to me suffering from PTSD and we made some progress in treating that, but the events you've just told me about have likely undid much of what we were able to accomplish."

"There's something else," I say. She looks alarmed. I tell her about Simonson, the Title IX investigation and how he propositioned me to make it go away. I even tell her about the button under his desk top to lock and unlock his office door."

Now she seems both scared and angry. "I've heard rumors about Simonson," she says. "Many in the university community are afraid of him, so nothing has been done. And he's never done anything that can be proven."

"Can you help me with this, Rebecca? He told me that I could have an advocate. I'd like that to be you."

I expect her to immediately agree, but she doesn't. "Let me think about it," she says.

"What's to think about?"

She's silent for a moment, then she says, "Title IX was instituted with the best of intentions — to protect women against sexual harassment and extortion. But to make it easy to apply, it's been couched in very general terms. Accusers have a lot of power. There have been cases in which advocates have themselves been charged under Title IX."

"You're afraid you'll be charged if you try to help me?"

"Nattie, I don't know even if I can help you. I assume that you don't have any proof that Simonson offered to drop the charges if you'd have sex with him?"

I shake my head.

"So while his actions are reprehensible, all I can see an unsubstantiated accusation accomplishing is to incite further charges."

"You're telling me to just give up?"

"Nooo...," she says hesitatingly. "I'm telling you that the best way to fight this is to find some way to prove that you're the victim here, not the instigator. And I don't know that I'm the best person to help you do that. What about your uncle. He's a detective, right?"

I tell her about Uncle Amos' reaction to the publication of the video.

"Dammit!" she uncharacteristically exclaims after I've finished. "God save us from religion! All right Nattie, I've decided. I'll be your advocate. Above all, don't go to another meeting with Simonson without me. And don't do anything stupid - like agreeing to have sex with him while recording it — it could be seen as entrapment and make it that much worse for you. But you must realize that there may not be much that I can do."

"Then I'll be expelled?"

"That is a real possibility. However, we have something much more serious to deal with. You've killed people, Nattie, and the psychological effects of that can be devastating. We need to address that right away. So I'll want you in here a minimum of three times a week, or more."

"When?"

"How about tomorrow morning at ten? We'll set up a therapy schedule then."

I get up and head for the door. I already feel better that I've told her.

"Thanks for helping me with this, Rebecca." I say over my shoulder as I exit.

My cell phone tells me I've got twenty minutes till my next class. I don't really want to go — there's a much greater chance of being recognized there, given all the publicity that the video has received and I just don't want to deal with the stares.

My cell phone plays *Man's Not Hot*. It's Danny! Thank God! I thumb the button.

"Whatcha doin' at lunchtime," he asks.

"Why?"

"I thought we could go to the range and do some shooting."

"Oh, I don't know…" I haven't shot a gun since I killed those two thugs. Am I serious about getting a permit and carrying? Or is it just paranoia?

"C'mon! It'll be just what you need to clear your head." He says. "It always helps me focus."

I guess I won't find out unless I try to shoot. And I really don't want to go to class. I tell Danny that I'll meet him out on Lee Street so he doesn't have to deal with the campus gates.

"OK, see you there." He hangs up.

It's not long after that I see his pickup. He stops, earning an irate blast from a horn behind him and reaches across the cab to open the door for me. I haul myself up into his jacked-up truck.

Despite the cooler weather, Danny's wearing his usual form-fitting t-shirt, tactical pants and combat boots. He greets me. "Hi, Nattie. How's your day been so far?"

Again, that meddlesome vision of our torrid night rears its head.

"You don't want to know."

He goes silent. He seems decidedly uncomfortable. Then he says, "Look, I want to apologize for Diane. She shouldn't have said what she did yesterday afternoon."

"Not your fault, Danny. She's the one who should apologize." A pause. "Where did you meet her, anyhow?"

"There's a bar over near the hospital. Some of my buddies from the job hang out there. Some nurses from University Hospital like it too."

"You picked her up in a bar?" That's not something I expected from Danny.

"I guess. She and some of her friends joined me and my buddies one night and we started swapping cop and nurse stories. Diane's got some real winners — she had us rolling on the floor. I thought she was giving me the eye, so I asked her to dinner and she said yes."

"She said you were her beau. How long have you been seeing her?"

"About six weeks. And she exaggerates."

"Well, she needs to work some on her social graces."

"She's usually not as bad as she was last night. But you know, cops and nurses aren't all that different. There's a lot of stress in both jobs and sometimes it comes out after work. So cut her a break. I think you'll like her if you get to know her."

I doubt it, but I don't tell him that. "Go out with whoever you want to, Danny. I won't mention her anymore."

The range is on the other side of town, a twenty-minute drive. There's both an indoor pistol and an outdoor rifle range — we'll use the inside one today. The smell of gunpowder and hot metal washes over me as we enter. The range itself is separated from a gun shop by a bulletproof glass window, but I can still hear the muffled crump, crump, crump of pistol fire inside.

We approach a glass display case full of pistols and revolvers. The walls are festooned with rifles and shotguns of all shapes and sizes. A middle-aged bald guy behind the case, packing a chrome automatic on his hip, recognizes Danny and raises a hand in greeting.

"Hey, Ernie," says Danny. "Meet Nattie. She wants to shoot."

Ernie looks at me. "Ever shot before?"

If you only knew! "Yes," I told him.

"But not here, right?"

"Right."

"Then you'll have to read the range rules and take a test on gun safety before you can go on the range."

"Sounds good to me."

He hands me a small booklet and a folded paper. "You can go in there." He indicates a small room containing a table and chairs. "Read the pamphlet, then fill in the test." He smiles at me. "It's open book. We just want to be sure you've seen the information before you shoot."

The rules are simple and common sense — no loaded guns anywhere but on the firing line, always keep the gun pointed down range, yada, yada, yada. I know all of this from shooting with my dad and Uncle.

When I'm done, I hand the test back to Ernie and he scores it. He smiles again. "You got a hundred. Need a gun?"

"She can use mine," Danny says. He raises his shirt so we can see the Sig 1911 he carries on his belt.

"It doesn't make a lot of sense for me to practice with a single action .45 when I'm going to buy a striker-fired nine mil."

That raises Ernie's eyebrows. "She has a point."

I ask Ernie, "What do you have in a nine?"

"I have a Glock and a Ruger. Which one do you want?"

"Which Ruger?"

"The LC-9S. It's striker-fired."

"I know it. That's the one I'm going to get."

He takes a small black pistol from the display case, drops the mag and jacks the action open before handing it to me. I stick my pinkie inside and bring it back out with a black smear on the tip. I look at Ernie disapprovingly.

"Hey, we don't clean the range guns every time they get used," Ernie says. "You need ammo?"

Danny says, "Give us 100 rounds each. This is on me."

I start to complain, but Danny says, "Happy birthday, Nattie."

Ernie asks if we want one or two shooting stations and Danny tells him one before I can get a word in edgewise. I don't doubt that I can learn a lot about shooting from Danny with his Marine and police training, but I wish he'd have asked me.

As I feared, shooting brings me back to that day in the club when I shot those two thugs. It's not a flashback -- it's just that those guys are constantly on my mind as I shoot. It throws me off. Danny comes up behind to steady me — is it my imagination or is his grip a little more intimate than it needs to be? I glance at his face, but it tells me nothing. I fight not to push back against him.

My groups spread out more the longer I shoot.

"Don't worry about it," Danny says when we're back outside. "Shooting's like any other exercise. You get worse when you get tired.

You've got to build muscles you don't normally use. Try to come a coupla times a week for while and you'll see an improvement."

"I don't know if I can afford to shoot that much." The 9mm ammo is relatively cheap, but it's a twenty-dollar range fee each time, plus five bucks to rent a gun.

"Yeah, about that," Danny says. He produces a small blue card from a pocket. "Happy early birthday." He hands it to me.

It's a range membership card with my name on it. He must have gotten it while I went to the bathroom to wash the lead and gunpowder off my hands.

"All it will cost you now is the gun rental and the ammo."

"Danny! I can't take this!" I saw the annual membership rates on a white board behind the counter inside. "It cost you over three hundred dollars!"

"Not quite that much. Ernie owed me a favor. Anyway, I can't get the money back and the memberships are non-transferable. Besides, I look at it as life insurance if you're going to be carrying when you're with me." He pauses then asks, "You want to get lunch?"

"Better not. I have class this afternoon."

"Then I'll carry you back to State."

We're mostly quiet on the drive back to campus. If I didn't know better, I'd think that Danny is trying to hit on me, even though he knows Lupe and me are a couple.

Finally, he pulls up in front of the university library on Lee Street.

"Here's your stop." He pauses then says, "I enjoyed shooting with you, Nattie. Let's do it again."

The devil in me comes out. "How will Diane feel about that?"

His expression darkens. "I won't tell her if you won't."

"Thanks for the early birthday present." I slide out of the truck and close the door. He waves and drives off.

If I didn't know better…

Chapter 5.

I'm pulling into my parking space when my cell phone plays *One Kiss*. It's Lupe. Since I'm going to see her in a minute, I don't answer.

The phone starts playing again. Now I'm a little worried. She usually doesn't call right back like that unless something's up.

I get out of the car and head for our townhouse, then I hear "Nattie! Nattie, come fast!" Lupe is about fifty feet away near a clump of bushes. She's holding Eduardo with her arms around his middle and his feet off the ground. He's crying and kicking furiously.

I run over to them. Lupe cocks her head towards the bushes. "Is *el gato!* She hurt!"

I part the bushes and see Xin Niu, lying on the ground with blood pooled beneath her. She mews piteously when she sees me. I squat and touch her gently, trying to see where she's injured. There's a tan, spongy mass mixed in with the blood. I feel the bile rising in my throat. Is that her insides?

Lupe is halfway back to the condo, still carrying the struggling Eduardo. I hurry to catch up.

"Lupe! What happened?"

"I no know." She's lapsed into the broken English she speaks when she's stressed. "Eduardo say he find her like that."

OMG! That little guy loves that cat almost more than he loves his Mama! For him to see that...

It must have been a car! I run inside and find a sheet to wrap Xin Niu in to carry her to the vet. By the time I've found one, Lupe has gotten Eduardo on the sofa and is still trying to calm him down. I tell her what I'm doing, then run back outside. Xin Niu is still alive when I get to her, but her eyes tell me she's hurting.

I spread out the sheet, then try to lift her on to it with one hand under her head and the other under her hips. As I raise her up, I see that she has a wicked gash that runs from her neck to all the way down! I can literally see all of her internal organs. What the fuck could have done this?

There's a strange smell, which I initially assume is coming from the blood, but then I recognize it. Canned tuna! I glance around and I see an open can under a nearby bush. I have a horrible thought, but I don't want to acknowledge it. Not yet.

I can't get Xin Niu on the sheet without picking up her insides in my hands so they don't drag out behind. I suck it up and do what I have to, then wrap her up in a tight little package. I'd like some help getting to the vet, but I know that I can't ask Lupe — she's got her hands full with Eduardo. So I run to my car and slide into the driver's seat with Xin Niu on my lap. She's not moving much, so maybe I can drive like this.

The vet is only five minutes away and has a 24/7 emergency service, thank Christ. I screech into the parking lot and tear out of the car, leaving it running.

"My cat's been hit by a car!" I shout as I run into the waiting room. The girl behind the desk instantly picks up the phone and in no time a guy in a white lab coat is there to take Xin Niu. "Her belly is open," I tell him. He looks me in the eyes and takes the time to smile.

"We'll take good care of her," he says. Then he's gone.

I take a seat. This vet has separate waiting rooms for cats and dogs. There are four other clients here and they take turns trying to comfort me — they're cat people and they get it. But not really. Xin Niu is the last tangible link I have to a very dear friend who's not here anymore.

I've been waiting about forty-five minutes with no word when the outside door opens. Danny! I spring up and run into his arms, crying so hard that I can scarcely breathe. He gently enfolds me and rocks me back and forth. I bury my face in his jacket and inhale the scent of him.

When I've gotten a semblance of control back, we take a seat in the hard, plastic chairs that seem to be ubiquitous in medical waiting rooms. He's still holding my hand.

"What happened?" he asks. I start to tell him when I hear my name. A vet is standing in the waiting room door holding a clipboard and she doesn't look happy.

Danny and I follow her back into an examining room that's barely big enough for the three of us. She motions us to a seat on a vinyl-covered bench while she stands with her back against the counter. Her lab coat tells me that she's Dr. Grant.

"What do you know about what happened to your cat?" she asks. That's a funny question, I think. It pisses me off that she says "your cat".

"I don't know what happened to Xin Niu," I reply, emphasizing her name. "I assumed she was hit by a car. Is she going to be all right?"

"I don't think so," Dr. Grant says. She offers me the clipboard. There's a medical report on top and a cost estimate for treatment. Holy shit! Is that six thousand dollars?

"What…" Dr Grant holds up her hand and begins speaking.

"What we've got here is massive abdominal trauma. Actually, it's worse than just abdominal. The entire body cavity's been compromised, as have some of the organs, especially the intestines. That figure is just an estimate, because I'm sure we'll have to deal with raging peritonitis after extensive surgery. The odds are good that Xin Niu will not survive." She pauses, then goes on, "The second page is an authorization for euthanasia."

"Euthanasia…" I croak out the word.

She nods grimly. "I suggest you sign it. Xin Niu's chances are poor and she could be in pain the rest of her life even if she does pull through."

I cry silently. Danny takes my shoulders and turns me so I can bury my face in his chest again.

When I finally get hold of myself, I hold my hand out for the clip board. I sign and date by the "X" on the second page.

"Why did you ask me what I know about the accident?" I ask Dr. Grant.

"Because it doesn't look like an accident to me. It looks like someone deliberately cut Xin Niu with a knife." I hear a gasp from Danny.

A chill envelops me. That was the thought that I wouldn't let in and it jars me to hear it coming out of the doctor's mouth.

"Have you heard of any other animal mutilations in your area?" Grant asks.

I shake my head.

"This kind of thing is usually done by adolescent boys," Grant says. "Any gangs of kids or lone teenage boys hanging around?"

"Sure, we have some families in the complex," I tell her, "But there's never been anything like this."

Danny says, "Hey Nattie, can I leave you to finish up here? I'll meet you outside."

I can't imagine Danny being queasy about this — he's a former cop and an ex-Marine. But he doesn't look well.

"Sure."

"It will just be a few more minutes," Dr. Grant says.

After Danny's gone, we go over the cost of the euthanasia and the disposal of the body. Turns out the vet has a contract with a local pet cemetery and you can even get a funeral service if you want to. I won't go that far, but the idea of a plot of ground and a marker sounds fine. Xin Niu was a good friend to me and I don't want her to end up in a landfill. Maybe Lupe and I can take Eduardo out there in a couple of weeks and place some flowers.

Danny's not in the waiting room when I come out. I find him in the parking lot smoking a cigarette.

"When did you take up smoking?"

"In the Corps. I try to stay away from them, but sometimes, I just need one."

"Got another one?"

He raises an eyebrow, then produces a pack and shakes one out for me. "When did you take up smoking?"

"On stakeout for Uncle Amos, to pass the time. He finally threatened to fire me if I didn't quit. So I quit and he fired me anyway."

Danny lights me and I take a long drag into my lungs. I don't cough — it's like riding a bicycle. I feel the nicotine rush and realize that it's been way too long.

"I called Amos," he says. "He wants to see you."

I'm suddenly angry. "Why did you do that?"

"Because you need your family at a time like this."

"I've got Lupe. And she and especially Eduardo will need me now, too."

"He said that they should come along too. He wants to see all of you right now."

WTF? He was just badmouthing Lupe yesterday. "I don't know that Lupe will want to see him. He said we were living in sin."

"That was before Xin Niu was killed."

I'm incredulous. "You told him about that? Why, Danny?"

"Because it means that you may be in great danger. Lupe and Eduardo too. Amos knows that. That's why he wants to see you."

"What do you mean, great danger?"

"Let Amos tell you. Why don't you let me drive you home in my truck. We'll leave your car here and pick it up tomorrow. We'll get Lupe and the kid and I'll drive all of you to 3M."

I start to protest, but he touches my lips with his finger. "Please, Nattie. Let somebody else take care of you for once."

I give up and do as he says.

It takes some coaxing to get Lupe to come along, but she says she will when she realizes how important this is to me. Eduardo has finally stopped howling, but now he's silent and morose, which is worse. He doesn't put up a fight when his Momma dresses him and carries him to Danny's truck.

It's dark by the time we pull into the backyard at 3M. The downstairs is lit up like a church.

We go inside and find Uncle Amos, Mom and Leon Kidd in the main office. Kidd is a genial black man a few years younger than Uncle, who is also an ex-cop and ex-Marine. Uncle made him a partner in the agency after Kidd took a bullet for him when Uncle was in the hospital.

Some comfortable chairs and a sofa have been brought into the office. I direct Lupe to the sofa and sit next to her. I glare at Uncle, daring him to say something mean. He doesn't seem to notice.

Danny and Kidd take the other seats and Mom offers coffee all around. There are no takers.

It's obvious that Uncle Amos is holding court. He looks directly at me.

Dammed if I'm going to spare his sensibilities now. "Uncle, this is my partner Lupe Ibanez," I say, "and her son Eduardo."

Eduardo is now asleep and Lupe is holding him on her lap.

"I'm pleased to meet you, Lupe," he says, but I know he doesn't mean it. A southerner is polite to everybody right until the knife goes in. "Would the boy be more comfortable in a bed? We've got one upstairs."

"Thank you, sir," Lupe says in her best English, "but I will hold him. I do not want him to wake up in a strange place."

Uncle nods to acknowledge her answer, then addresses me. "Nattie, when you asked for my help yesterday, I said no. I thought you would get a good lesson about why you shouldn't do things like strip in a club or make sex videos."

My hackles rise and I start to respond, but he holds up a hand. "Let me say my piece, then I'll listen to you." I don't like it, but I decide to hear him out.

"I won't apologize. My beliefs are mine and I have a right to them. But I didn't realize how serious the situation was when I told you that. Now I do. I want to devote the full resources of 3M to this."

Wow. "What changed?" I ask him.

"Somebody killed your cat and by the way, I'm real sorry about that. Danny tells me that it was downright brutal. That's what's got me takin' this thing serious."

Suddenly I'm afraid. "What do you mean?"

"When you told me about the video, I thought it was just some kind of college prank. It was in bad taste and I'm sure it embarrassed you and your friend, but I didn't think it was dangerous. After what's happened to your cat, I'm not so sure."

"What do you mean?" I ask again.

Kidd speaks up. "Nattie, in law enforcement we refer to something called the homicidal triad. It's three behaviors that can be linked to particularly violent offenders and serial killers. Those behaviors are bedwetting past childhood, fire starting and cruelty to animals."

A shiver runs through me, but I try not to show it.

Uncle takes up the thread. "It's become obvious that somebody is pretty PO'd at you, Nattie. They're trying to hurt you any way they can. This cat killin' makes me worry that it might get physical. I'm also worried that they might try to get at you by hurting Lupe or her son."

I glance at Lupe, whose face is now bone white. "So what's the plan," I say to Uncle.

"Well, for starters, I think the three of you should lay low for a while. Also, I think you should report the cat killin' to the police."

"If you mean stay away from school and work, no way," I tell him. "And the cops will just tell me they have better things to do than find out who killed a cat."

"I don't think so," says Kidd. "I was a member of that department. There are some pretty savvy guys who work homicide and understand the triad."

I give in. "O.K., I'll report it, but I'm not hiding from this asshole."

"Me neither," says Lupe. That's my girl!

I think about telling them about Simonson, but I don't want to complicate matters. Rebecca and I are dealing with it.

"Well, I think you're being stubborn, but I can't force you," Uncle says. "But I'd still like to help find this guy."

"How?" I ask him.

"First thing is you and Lupe think real hard and come up with a list of names of who might have done this. Second, let's investigate that video and the cat killin'."

"I'll take the cat," Kidd says.

I'm pissed again. "Quit calling her 'the cat'. She was a lilac point Siamese and her name was Xin Niu. It means 'pretty girl' in Chinese." I can't help the tears that start to flow down my cheeks.

Lupe sees the tears and leans over to cuddle me. "Oh, *cariño*…"

Uncle Amos, his face beet red, is staring at us in obvious disapproval. Screw you, you old bigot, I think, then I'm ashamed. He doesn't like what he sees, but he's trying to help us anyhow. Because family.

Kidd goes on like nothing happened. That's one reason I like him so much. "How did the, …er, Xin Niu get out of the town house? Do you leave her outside routinely?"

I suck it up and stop crying. "No, but she's learned to follow Eduardo out when he leaves for school. We've been trying to stop her."

"What did the vet say about how this happened?"

I glance at Eduardo to make sure he's asleep. "She said somebody used a knife to cut her."

"Well, it seems to me that would be awful damned hard to do to a live cat," Kidd says.

It hits me. "The tuna! Somebody must have drugged the tuna!" I tell them about the can I saw.

"What did you do with it?"

"Nothing. I left it there. I was more concerned with getting Xin Niu to the vet at that point."

"With luck, it may still be there," Kidd says. He pauses a beat. "It's interesting that the doer could have simply chosen to poison Xin Niu, with antifreeze for example. But he decided to kill her brutally, probably to make a point. That's what's so worrying."

I agree with him. I'm totally worried.

"Do you know if your complex has surveillance cameras on the grounds?" he asks.

I remember the rectangular objects mounted halfway up the light poles in the parking lot. "I'm sure that it does! A lot of the residents are well-off."

"O.K., then," says Amos. "There's your place to start."

Uncle Amos looks at Danny. "I guess that means you get the video." He looks like he's stepped in something when he says "video".

"Do you know where it came from?" Danny asks me.

Now I'm red-faced. "It was taken in our townhouse."

"No, I mean where the broadcast originated from."

"No, but it shouldn't be too hard to find out at the campus closed circuit TV station."

"There you go, start there," says Uncle. He turns to me. "Nattie, I wish you'd reconsider and move in here with me and your Mom for a while." He hesitates, then goes on, "I guess we can find a place for Lupe and her boy, too."

I realize how much that last statement cost him and I'm grateful. "Thanks Uncle, but no way. I'm totally not going to let this creep run us out of our home."

"Well, the offer's open if you change your mind." I swear I detect an expression of relief on his face. He doesn't have to have me and Lupe living in sin under his roof.

"Let me take you guys back home," says Danny. "and if you see anything out of the ordinary, you call me and I'll be right there."

I look at Uncle. "Sure wish I could get that pistol a little early…"

"Nope, can't do it," he says. "You can't legally carry concealed without a permit and you can't get that until you're twenty-one."

"I don't need a permit to own one in this state, though. I could keep it in the house."

Uncle looks at Mom and an unspoken conversation ensues. "O.K.," he says. "You do need to be twenty-one to have a handgun in this state, though. Danny, get her my shotgun."

I start to say I'd rather have a pistol but think better of it. Uncle Amos isn't going to risk his license by giving me an illegal handgun, even for a week, and I guess I don't blame him.

Danny goes to the gun safe in the corner and removes a pump shotgun. "You know how to use it?" he asks.

I nod. I've shot plenty of skeet with my dad and Uncle.

Danny hands me a small box of double-ought buckshot and another of rifled slugs.

"When you get home, load this up. Don't forget to remove the plug from the magazine." He's referring to a wooden plug that restricts the magazine capacity to two shells instead of four to conform to Federal hunting laws. "Load two rounds of buck followed by two slugs. Don't leave it with a round in the chamber with a kid in the house. If you need to use it, all you'll have to do is pump it once and you're ready to rock and roll. You can show Lupe how."

"It won't do me any good when I'm not home," I say, still hoping Uncle will offer me a handgun.

"That's why you should stay there until we catch this guy," says Danny. Uncle nods in agreement.

"I'll get you a case for this, then let's get you three home," says Danny. "I'll look for that tuna can when we get there. And Nattie, I'll call you tomorrow about visiting with the closed-circuit TV office on campus."

I look at Uncle, who's still frowning, trying not to look at Lupe, Eduardo and me. I hate it that he won't accept me for who I am, but he's risen above that to help me, at least for now.

Chapter 6.

It's late when we get home, because Danny took me by the vet to pick up the Z-car. I stay awake just long enough to hear that he found the tuna can and is going to have the contents analyzed. I'm pretty sure I know what' they'll find.

I'd love to sleep late the next morning, but I can't — I've got an early class. I'm sitting on a stool on the dining room side of the pass-through trying to get my eyes open with coffee. The TV is on to the local news, but I'm not paying attention to it. Instead, I'm scrolling through my email on my phone and I see the subject line *Title IX Notice of Concern.* I click the email:

Dear Miss McMasters:

This email is to inform you that a Title IX investigation with you as the subject has been opened by the Office of Student Conduct. You are invited to appear this morning at nine a.m. at the office of the Title IX Coordinator, Mr. Fred Simonson, for consideration of this matter. This will be your only opportunity for discussion before formal procedures commence.

Best regards,

Margaret Sheerer
Administrative Assistant to the Title IX Coordinator

Invited, my ass! I forward it to Rebecca with the note "Can you make this?". It's only a moment before I get the reply. "Yes. Meet you there."

My phone tells me it's seven-thirty. I'll have to hustle if I'm going to be on time.

This time I'm a little more careful about my attire. I've never been much for dressing up, but the friend who left me the townhouse had a lot of nice clothes that fit me. I pick out a skirt that's a little shorter than I like but still respectable and a white blouse with a ruffled front that's also SFW. A pair of sheer stockings and black pumps completes the outfit. After a quick shower, I get dressed and have a look in the mirror. Not bad. Not exactly professional, but several cuts above the torn jeans and tight, battered, metal band t-shirts that I usually wear. I don't do make up, so I brush out my long, straight, blonde hair and tie it back in a pony tail.

It's eight fifty-five when I walk into Dragon Lady Sheerer's office. Rebecca is there waiting for me, uncomfortably perched on the beige sofa.

At nine on the dot, Sheerer says, "Mr. Simonson will see you now."

We enter and find Simonson waiting. He's wearing the same outfit as before, right down to that hideous striped tie in the school colors. He's even managed to secure another of those nasty orange chairs for Rebecca — I didn't tell him she was coming, but Sheerer obviously did. I look at the chairs for a second, then go and sit on the leather sofa. Rebecca looks confused, then her face tells me she gets it and she joins me.

"I prefer that you sit here, ladies," Simonson indicates the orange chairs.

I start to reply, but Rebecca touches my leg to silence me and says, "But it's so much more comfortable here, sir."

Simonson looks pissed. "The purpose of this meeting is not your comfort," he says.

"Are you saying that your purpose is to make us uncomfortable?" Rebecca asks naively.

His answer is obvious, but he doesn't say it. Instead, "The purpose of this meeting is to discuss the Title IX complaint lodged against Miss McMasters."

"Then let's do that." Rebecca withdraws a leather business portfolio from her briefcase, opens it and flips back the pages of the legal pad inside to a fresh page. She cocks her head and looks at him attentively.

I think I've said before that Dr. Rebecca Feiner is one of the most gorgeous women I've ever met, even when she's wearing relatively sedate professional attire as she is now. Simonson can't keep from gawking at her. As a psychiatrist, I'm sure she's aware.

He tears his eyes away from Rebecca to look at me. "Things have changed since we last spoke, Natalie," he says. "As I told you then, it was quite possible that others who were offended by your obscene video might choose to lodge Title IX complaints. Well, someone has."

Maybe it's because some son-of-a-bitch butchered Xin Niu last night. Or maybe it's just because I don't like the motherfucker in the ugly tie sitting in front of me. I say, "I forget, Freddy. Did you say that before or after you told me that screwing you would make those complaints go away?"

Now he's way pissed! And Rebecca is openly gaping at me.

"Are you aware you just slandered me in front of a colleague, Miss McMasters?"

One point for the home team. We've gone from Natalie to Miss McMasters. "Sorry, not sorry. It's only slander if it's a lie, Freddy. And it's not."

He struggles for control. "A student has now accused you of creating a hostile educational environment on campus. Based on your last comment, I think I'll sign on to that complaint as well."

"Go for it, Freddy."

Simonson turns to Rebecca. "You might do well to reconsider your position in this affair as well, Dr. Feiner. It's one thing to be a student advocate in a university process and quite another to suborn slander."

I don't believe it! He's trying to threaten Rebecca with a Title IX inquisition for trying to protect me?

"You're the one who's suborning slander by accusing me of uploading that video for cheap publicity with no proof," I tell him.

"As I told you the other day, Title IX requirements are quite different than those in a court of law. I'm the one who carries out the investigation. If I find that a hostile environment has been created, I'll file a complaint with the Dean and the complaint will be processed under the Code of Student Discipline to determine the appropriate sanction."

"And we already know how you're going to find, so why are we wasting our time here?"

Again, I feel Rebecca's light touch on my leg, signaling me to shut up. "I believe there is an appeal process after your finding is delivered to the Dean, Mr. Simonson?"

"Yes. You can request a hearing before a panel convened by the Dean. But practically, she usually leaves it to me to determine the composition of that panel." Talk about the deck being stacked against me! His investigation, his panel. I don't have a chance!

He goes on, "And moreover, were any accusations like the one uttered here a few minutes ago to arise in that hearing, I feel I'd have no choice but to take legal action for defamation."

Rebecca just stares at him for a moment, then replies, "Well, yes. And in that case, it would only be defamation if you could prove in a court of law that Natalie's statement was untrue."

Did she just say what I think she said? Now he's the one who's gaping!

He's not looking at Rebecca lustfully anymore — he's scowling at her. "I can see that this meeting has become non-productive. If I were you, Dr. Feiner, I'd tread very carefully. You don't have tenure, you know."

"I'm aware of that, Mr. Simonson. But neither do you. And rape is a much more serious offense than creating a hostile environment is. Miss McMasters' uncle is a private detective, you know."

"That sounds like a threat."

"You may take it as you please." Rebecca smooths her lab coat behind her as she rises from the sofa. "Come on, Natalie. We're finished here."

"Yes, you are," says Simonson with an evil smirk.

"If you would please unlock the door with the button under your desk, Mr. Simonson," Rebecca says.

We leave him with a shocked look on his face.

Rebecca maintains a brisk pace on the walk back to her office, to discourage conversation, I think. Her regal posture with her head held high as she strides along implies how truly pissed at Simonson she is. I just hope I haven't put her career in jeopardy by asking her to help me.

She maintains her silence until we're in her office with the door safely closed. She gestures towards the couch, then takes her usual place behind her desk.

"We might as well have our session now, Nattie."

"Listen, before that, I want to tell you I'll understand if you don't want to be my advocate anymore. I don't want you to risk your career over this."

Her back straightens as she sits up in her chair, her chin raises and her black eyes flash. Her voice is low and grating. "Do you think for one second that I'm going to let that… degenerate get away with what he's doing? I told you that there have been rumors about him circulating among some of the women on campus. Now that I've had the displeasure of meeting him, I'm sure that all of them are true. Being able to live with myself is much more important than a career."

I'm seeing a whole new side of Rebecca here. The depth of the anger she's just expressed takes my breath away.

"I'm glad you feel that way. Let's get him!" I tell her.

She smiles grimly, then her features soften again. "But now we must address your issues, Nattie. Make yourself comfortable." When I've done so, she continues. "I've done a little research on you. It seems that the first time you killed someone was not what you told me about in our last session. I'm referring of course, to Randall Leighton. I wonder why you didn't mention him?"

Randall Leighton was a sexual predator who kidnapped a young woman from a distant city. He brought her here and imprisoned her in his basement as a sex slave. I found that out while I was on stakeout for Uncle Amos. I broke into Leighton's house and discovered the captive, but Leighton caught me in the act and nearly killed me. He would have, if the girl hadn't put a machete in his back. But because she was so young and had been abused so much, I told the police that I had killed Leighton to spare her any further grief. The district attorney indicted me for murder, which resulted in my interview with Roderigo on the national news and that in turn resulted in dismissal of the charges after a public outcry. I tell Rebecca all of this.

When I've finished, she shakes her head. "I remember hearing about your court appearance at the time. So you publicly admit to killings you haven't done and cover up those that you have! You're a hot mess, Natalie McMasters. Let's see if we can't straighten you out."

I'm frankly surprised to hear her speak so unprofessionally, but I figure she did it to put me at ease. It works.

We move on to talk about the killings that I have done. The first two are easier to discuss. Both of the men I shot had just murdered somebody and were armed. I was able to shoot first simply because they didn't expect a little girl like me to have a gun. It was a clear case of self-defense.

The last one is much more difficult. The man I stabbed. Another clear case of self-defense, but also premeditated.

"You do know that that man raped you, Nattie, even though you instigated the sex?" Rebecca asks me. I nod. "It was not your fault. He didn't really leave you any choice. But frankly, I'm concerned by the brutality of it."

I open my mouth to defend myself, but she holds up a hand. "Hear me out. You didn't do it to get revenge. He left you no choice. You had to fight with the weapons on hand and it took tremendous courage to do that. But a person can't engage in that kind of violence without paying the emotional cost."

"I am paying it," I tell her. "That's why I can't get off the prazosin without the nightmares coming back."

"That's right. But there's another cost that worries me even more."

"What's that?"

"Will it be easier for you to kill the next time and in such a brutal fashion? Such behavior is learned, Nattie."

I don't like that at all. "I'm not going to become some kind of serial killer!"

"I didn't say that you were. But what we have to work on is that while your behavior might have been justified, it was still highly undesirable and savage. Your challenge is going to be forgiving yourself for it without condoning it. Do you understand?"

"No. First you tell me it was right, then you tell me it was wrong."

"I did not use those terms. Leave the moral judgement out of it. I said your actions were justified but undesirable." She pauses. "This is really about the kind of person you want to be. Do you want to be someone who will justify anything, no matter how reprehensible? Or someone who will always seek an ethical choice?"

"The second one, I guess."

She frowns at the "I guess". "Then we need to work to get at the guilt for what you've done and get your hatred for that man out of you." I start to speak again and she hushes me. "Don't tell me you don't hate him. Of course you do. Hate is another justifiable, undesirable and savage emotion."

She's right about that. I do hate him. I hate him so much that it feels good to hate him.

"That's why this affair with Simonson is so dangerous for you," Rebecca continues. "He is a truly wicked man, but we must not fight him with hate. That could destroy both of us."

"How do you not hate somebody who does things like him?"

"By focusing on stopping him, not hating him," Rebecca says. "The man is fundamentally flawed. That does not justify his actions, nor does it prevent us from using lawful means to stop him. Most importantly, you must recognize that hating him will do much more damage to you than it will to him. Can you do that?"

"I think so, if you'll help me."

She smiles. "I'll help you," she says.

We leave things there for today. As I'm leaving, I realize that there was one other person I hated whom I didn't tell her about. But he couldn't be responsible for my present difficulties because he's dead too.

Chapter 7.

I'm awakened by a sharp pain in my back — Lupe's elbow. Then I notice the murmur of the bedside radio. I've been sleeping way heavily since Rebecca put me on the prazosin for my PTSD, so I don't hear the music when it comes on. Poor Lupe doesn't have to go to her job at the gym until mid-morning, so she really doesn't need to get up with me when I have an early class. That's another reason I'm glad I finally levelled with Rebecca — maybe I can finally get off those freaking meds.

I get even more salty when I come into the living room. A gust of wind outside rattles the raindrops against the windows. This is not weather I want to go out in! But I've only been making about half of my classes since the video incident, so I'd better just suck it up.

I cut on the TV and tune to the local news and weather. The pretty girl tells me that the rain is likely to last all day. Great.

It's Thursday and my first class is International Law again. Fields is there, so I plop down next to her, but we don't have time to start a conversation before the prof starts the lecture.

Halfway through class, I hear the text tone on my phone. Hoping the prof didn't hear it too, I glance at the screen surreptitiously.

Meet me outside Brandone Hall @ 11:30 — D

Brandone Hall? Not sure where that is. Of course, I have to start looking for it, which earns me a glare from Fields. I find it in a section of campus where I seldom go, over near the hospital.

When class is over, I thank Fields for the notes from the other day, then I bounce. I've got just enough time.

I hunker down in my army jacket under two hoods to escape the cold, wind-driven rain as I trudge across campus. Eventually I see Brandone Hall, a cubic concrete building with a sign outside that tells me State CCTV is inside. Through the glass doors, I see Danny waiting in the vestibule.

I've always liked watching people who don't know that I'm watching them. Danny is obviously awaiting my arrival — he's looking out the window and scanning the passers-by. He doesn't recognize me because I'm so bundled up against the weather. I hide behind a stanchion to spy on him. He's dressed much like me, wearing a surplus military jacket over his ever-present camo pants and combat boots. Even in such bulky clothes, he's way hot. A twenty-something secretary enters the vestibule from inside the building and gives him the eye, but he's oblivious. After a moment, he stops surveying the crowd, turns away from the window and studies the framed building directory hanging on the wall. He pats his pockets — probably hunting a smoke — and then realizes that he can't smoke in the building. He's looks annoyed as he turns to stare outside again.

I decide to have some fun. I turn the collar of my jacket up around my face, press my chin to my chest then walk straight to the front door. I pull the door open and go right past him. He's standing off to one side, still peering out the vestibule window into the courtyard. I open the inner door and go into the lobby, where I lower my hoods, turn down my collar and open my coat. Then I tap on the window and wiggle my fingers at Danny when he turns around to look. The where-the-hell-did-you-come-from look on his face is priceless!

"Some detective! I walked right past you and you didn't even see me!"

"Yeah, you got me that time. But just remember what they say about payback."

Danny tells me that the security man for the campus CCTV system is a Mr. Harold Upmann. "I didn't call ahead for an appointment because I was afraid he might not meet with us. We'll have to be careful not to spook him — he might worry that we're gathering material for a lawsuit or something."

Upmann turns out to be a balding guy in his thirties wearing the typical nerd uniform of khaki pants and polo shirt. He's got a round face with a poor complexion and wire-frame glasses that don't do a thing for him. As Danny feared, he's initially way leery about talking to us. "I can't really tell you anything about the incident. Mr. Merkel," he says after Danny's told him why we're here.

"Please, Mr. Upmann," I wheedle with just the right amount of pathos in my voice. "They're threatening to expel me over this! I need to prove that this was done to me and that I didn't do it!"

Upmann doesn't even want to look at me. I'm not sure if it's because he's afraid of being sued or because he saw me naked in that video. He addresses Danny.

"Truth is, I don't know exactly how it was done. I couldn't find a matching video file on our server, so it didn't originate from here."

"Where did it originate from?" I ask.

"I couldn't say," he says to Danny.

I run out of patience. "Can't say or won't say, Mr. Upmann?"

He finally turns to me and his tone is hostile. "It really doesn't matter, now does it, Miss?"

"I guess not." A pause. "You know, Mr. Upmann, I've never even considered suing the university over this. I just want to get the guy responsible. But after talking to you, I'm thinking that a lawsuit is sounding better and better. And I'll be sure and mention your name to my attorney and to any reporters I talk to."

"I don't take kindly to threats," he says.

"And I don't take kindly to people who try to stonewall me. C'mon, Danny, let's get out of here!" I rise to go.

Upmann is now a pale shade of green. He looks to Danny for moral support. "I really don't know how this happened," he says again.

"Maybe a smart guy like you could take an educated guess, Mr. Upmann," Danny says. "Anything you can tell us might turn into a lead to find the person responsible. Then Nattie could sue him instead of the University."

"I guess an attacker could have surreptitiously embedded malicious code into the cable signal to the CCTVs," Upmann says. "All he would have to do is splice into the signal at the headend."

"What's a headend?" Danny asks.

"It's the facility where the signal is received and processed before it's sent to the CCTVs. It's a few hundred meters from here."

"So we need to talk to the people over there?" I ask.

"The headend is fully automated," says Upmann, like he's talking to a child. "There's no staff. The building is fenced and locked, but frankly, we've had a lot of break-ins over there. We think it's either homeless guys looking for a place to sleep, or students playing around."

"Do you have any security cameras there," Danny asks.

"No," says Upmann. I look at him in disbelief. "But we've never had any equipment damage or a signal compromised before this."

"How could somebody compromise the signal?"

"Pretty easily. Someone would just have to splice into the feed and feed the signal he wants into the processor. Could be done from a laptop."

"Would there be any way to trace it?"

"We could look for physical damage to the system, try and find the place where he spliced in. But there'd be no evidence to tell us where the signal came from."

"But anyone who did this would have to be pretty tech," I say.

"He'd have to know what he was doing," Upmann agrees, "but you wouldn't need an engineering degree. A smart person could probably find what he needed on the Internet."

"So even if that's how it was done, it's really no help to us," Danny says.

"Maybe the cops could check for prints, or something," Upmann says hopefully.

Danny rolls his eyes. "That will never happen," he says matter-of-factly. "There's a serious backlog of evidence processing for violent crimes. The department would never expend resources on something like this."

My cheeks flush hot. "Something like this," I repeat. "Just not a serious crime, eh? Even though it might get me expelled."

"Take it easy, Nattie," Danny says. "I didn't say it wasn't serious. I said that the department wouldn't think so."

Now I feel ashamed for snapping at him. "I know you didn't," I say. Danny's handsome features radiate genuine sympathy and concern. He's been nothing but a friend throughout everything I've been through since we met. "I'm sorry, Danny."

We thank Upmann for his help, but I don't really mean it.

Danny and I part in front of Brandone Hall with a promise to meet up later at the 3M office. I feel a little wistful watching him walk away in the rain. If there's one thing that this affair is teaching me, it's that the only important thing in life is your friends and family. I don't know what I'd do if I didn't have Danny, Uncle, Lupe and Rebecca to rely on.

I begin slogging back to the Commons for my next class, but the closer I get, the less I want to go. Screw it! I hop the bus for the parking lot. Next thing I know I'm driving and listening to the rhythmic clicking of the windshield wipers. Where am I going? I know! The range.

I rent the Ruger again. After putting on my ear protectors and safety glasses, I open the glass door that leads into the anteroom. There's a rack of targets on my right. I start to grab a standard silhouette target, then I notice that the one beneath it is a cartoon of a bad guy peering over a revolver that's pointing straight at me. I take that one instead. Then I open the door to the range and go in.

It's lunchtime, so all of the booths but mine are occupied. The mix of men and women shooters is about equal. I hang the target on the trolley and run it out to seven yards. I pop the mag, load it and jam it back into the grip, then aim at the face scowling at me over the revolver. I picture the face as Simonson's. I start squeezing off a round at a time.

The shooting is oddly therapeutic. Fire five deliberate shots. Drop the mag. Reload. Put it back in the gun and close the slide. Fire five more shots. Repeat. The gunsel's head is a smallish target, so not all of my rounds hit, but bit by bit the cartoon face is obliterated by an expanding ragged hole. It gives me a great deal of satisfaction, which I sorely need after the frustrating encounter with Upmann. I need to find another lead to the asswipe who posted that video and right now, I'm not sure where it will come from. I also realize that everyone is assuming that the posting of the video is linked to the murder (yes, it was murder!) of Xin Niu. But was it?

The shooting ritual also allows me to confront something that I've been avoiding until now — my repeated flashbacks to the night Danny and I hooked up. There's no question in my mind that I'm deeply in love with Lupe. Almost from the moment I saw her, I felt a deep connection that I'd never felt before with another person. But I can't reconcile my feelings with the obvious attraction that I have to Danny. I thought I had finally resolved what I am — a lesbian. Then why am I still having fantasies about a man? Even though I haven't betrayed Lupe, I still feel guilty about it. I know that I'll have to bring this up with Rebecca, but I'm reluctant to. Why?

I finally have to stop shooting because my hand is throbbing and the last ten rounds have missed the bad guy entirely. I've gone through two hundred rounds — I'll have to stop shooting that much at a session or go broke. I exit the range and pay Ernie for the target and the ammo.

Once again, I find that the thought of going to class has no attraction for me. I point the Z-car for home.

Chapter 8.

I drive home as fast as the weather allows. I get a bad scare when the Z-car hydroplanes when I'm changing lanes on the highway. I wrestle it back into the right lane and slow down.

Inside the townhouse, Lupe is sitting on the living room sofa. She looks up at me and the skin on her face is icy white and as tight as a painted-on mask. Her eyes are wide and her mouth sags half open. Her normally lustrous dark hair is dull and tangled, probably because she's been repeatedly running her fingers through it.

"Lupe, what's wrong?"

She hands me an official-looking envelope. It's got one of those strips that you tear away to open it and it's addressed to Ms. Maria Ibanez.

The return address is the U.S. Immigration and Naturalization Service.

No!

She hasn't opened it. Our mail comes at mid-morning. Has she been sitting her all that time just staring at it?

I tear the strip and take out a single sheet of paper folded in half.

Notice to Appear

In removal proceedings under Section 240 of the Immigration and Nationality Act.

You are an alien in the United States who has not been admitted or paroled.

You are ordered to appear before an immigration judge of the United States Department of Justice at:

A list of allegations and charges of removability follows. The notice gives the address of the federal courthouse downtown and an appearance date of two weeks from today.

Lupe didn't open it, but she sure as hell knew what was in it.

"What am I gonna do?" She croaks.

"OMG, Lupe! We'll think of something! I'll call Gary…"

"What am I gonna do?"

This is no accident, nor the result of an investigation by a federal agency. Somebody turned her in! Probably the same motherfucker who posted that video and murdered Xin Niu.

What could I have possibly done to have earned this kind of hatred?

My mind leaps back to men I killed. Killing somebody's loved one is certainly a reason for hatred, but nobody other than Lupe and now Rebecca even knows what I did. Hell, I don't even know the name of one of the guys I shot and I know next to nothing about the others, except that they would have killed me if I hadn't killed them. Lupe is the only witness who is still alive.

There was one other man whose death I had a hand in, but he had no family either, or at least, that's what he told me.

So who hates me this much?

I go to the liquor cabinet and pour out two generous slugs of bourbon. I hold the glass to Lupe's lips so she can sip the whiskey. It brings on a fit of coughing, but the color soon comes back into her cheeks.

"I won't let them send you back," I tell her. "You've suffered way too much to get here." I make a lame attempt at a joke. "Besides, I don't want to live in Mexico."

She doesn't get it. "I never ask you to live in Mexico!" She says.

"I know you wouldn't. It was a joke, to make you feel better."

She appears to have regained at least some of her composure, but her broken English belies her fear. "This happen to me before," she says. "That is why I know that envelope. I never go to see judge. I run away instead. Now they find me again!"

Great. I'm sure that will be on record and it will count against her.

Lupe has told me only snippets of her story. I haven't pressed her because I know how painful it is. Eduardo is a child of rape — his father is one of several cartel members who abused the girls in Lupe's village. When we first met, she said Eduardo was her brother because she was ashamed to admit she had a child out of wedlock. She fled her homeland to escape the abuse, only to encounter more of the same in the U.S. Lupe has a phenomenal natural talent as a pole dancer, which she was able to parlay into a living in the strip clubs and she was able to make much more money than she would have doing menial labor. But her undocumented status was obvious, so it was easy for men to sexually exploit her. I was finally able to help her get contracts as a pole dance instructor in several gymnasiums in the city to get her out of the strip joints. She doesn't earn as much as she did in the clubs, but she was able to put the onus of sex work behind her. Or so we thought.

"What am I gonna do?" she cries again.

I take her hands in mine. "What are we going to do, you mean. I'm not letting you deal with this alone. There are plenty of immigrants in the same predicament and there are organizations to help them. We'll start there. We have enough money to get a lawyer. I'm going to do whatever it takes to keep you and Eduardo here!"

She gets a funny look when I mention Eduardo. "They cannot do nothing to Eduardo," she says. "He was born here. He is a U.S. citizen."

OMG! She told me that Eduardo was conceived in Mexico. That means she was pregnant when she made her way here! I can't even!

"I have no birth certificate for him," she says. "He was not born in a hospital."

I know that already — the state doesn't require a birth certificate to enroll a child in school. Lupe just had to provide an affidavit attesting to Eduardo's age. We put some of our household bills in her name as proof of residency for the school district. A troubling thought intrudes — was that how ICE got on to her? Stop it, Nattie! You'll drive yourself crazy with that shit!

The living room wall clock chimes three times. Eduardo's school bus is due in a few minutes. I help Lupe into our bedroom to lie down and tell her not to worry — I'll meet Eduardo at the bus stop. A sudden fear strikes me — surely whoever is doing this wouldn't try to hurt Eduardo to get back at me? I rush to the bus stop and I'm greatly relieved to see him get off.

I get him back to the townhouse and set him up in front of the TV at the Play Station. He knows something's up — Mama Lupe didn't meet him at the bus and he never gets to play video games until his homework's done. I tell him that Mama Lupe doesn't feel well and is taking a nap.

"Okie dokie Mama Nattie! We let her sleep, okay?" Suddenly a tear rolls down his cheek.

"What?"

"*Mi gato*," he sobs. Xin Niu always sat with him when he played his video games.

I take him in my arms and hold him close, trying to kiss the tears away like my Mom did for me when I was his age. I can't let this little guy get banished to a place he's never known! That just ain't gonna happen!

I hug Eduardo even more tightly to me. God help whoever did this to us when I find him!

It's getting late in the afternoon, but I call my attorney Gary McDougall, anyhow.

"I really can't help you with immigration issues, Natalie," Gary says. "That's a specialty unto itself. But some social justice warriors at the State law school have set up a center to help undocumented persons. It's strictly *pro bono* and I hear it's pretty good. Give them a call."

Five minutes later I'm on the phone with the law school. After some back-and-forth with an admin assistant, I am connected with a student named Asunción Cardenas "Call me Chica," she says. "I have class all day tomorrow, but I can meet you at lunch," she says "Bring a brown bag and we'll snag a conference room." I thank her profusely. "No worries," she says. "See you and your roommate *mañana.*"

After I hang up with Chica, I place a quick call to Rebecca. I tell her machine that I can't make our session tomorrow and that I'll explain when I see her on Monday. She won't like it, but I have to sort out this mess with Lupe before I do anything else.

Chica turns out to be a petite, dark-skinned Hispanic girl even shorter than me or Lupe, which takes some doing. Her pretty doll face makes her look so young it's hard to believe she belongs in college, much less law school. But she's all business as she scans the letter from ICE.

"You won't believe me," she says to Lupe after she's read it, "but you're lucky. They could have just broken your door down, arrested you and shipped you off to a detention center. This way, at least you get to live at home before you get to see the judge."

I ask Chica, "What's the judge likely to do?"

"The first hearing is to set bond. The judge will decide whether or not to grant it, taking a number of things into account."

"Such as?"

"Oh, how long Lupe's been in the U.S. and how she got here, whether she has family, or a job. You don't have a criminal record, do you?" She asks Lupe.

"No, unless they find out I run away last time I get a letter like this," Lupe says.

"Then you're really lucky you didn't get arrested," Chica replies. "Since they didn't arrest you outright, the odds are they won't bring that up in court and for Pete's sake, don't tell them."

Lupe looks puzzled "Who is Pete?" she asks innocently and Chica and I burst out laughing. After a moment, she laughs with us, realizing she's goofed again.

"There's no Pete, it's just an expression," I tell Lupe.

One of the things I love about Lupe is her willingness to laugh at herself. I've always been astonished at her mastery of English, given the short time she's been in the U.S., but there's still so much she doesn't know, especially slang and idioms.

"A lawyer from the government will be at the hearing," Chica continues. "If they do know about last time, they'll probably argue that you're a flight risk and ask for a high bond or ask the judge to set no bond at all. That's why you shouldn't tell them if they don't bring it up."

"I guess she should have a lawyer," I say.

"She has a right to one, but in a civil proceeding like this, she doesn't have the right to have one at public expense. She can represent herself, or you can represent her, Nattie."

"Can you do it?" I ask Chica.

"Yes, if you want me to. It will be good experience for me."

"So what happens when this hearing is over," I ask.

"If the judge grants bond and she can pay it, Lupe will be released until her next appearance. If bond is denied or set so high that she can't pay it, she can appeal. In that case, she'll be detained until her hearings run their course or she gets a new bond amount."

"What's the next hearing?"

"It's called a master calendar hearing. It usually takes place right after the bond hearing, but we can request a continuance to prepare, which is usually granted. In that one, Lupe will be informed of the charges against her and she can plead guilty or innocent to each one. She can also request another continuance and the judge decides whether or not to grant it, for how long and what defense against deportation Lupe will be allowed present."

"What defense do I have?" asks Lupe.

"You can ask for asylum, but you have to prove persecution or fear of persecution if you're returned to Mexico. Or you can try to claim a long history in the U.S. without authorization. How long have you been here?"

"About eight years, I think."

Chica frowns. "That probably won't work, then. People who claim history have usually been here ten years or more and have stable family relationships and long-term work."

"She has a son who was born here. That makes him a citizen," I tell Chica.

"Can you prove it?" Chica asks Lupe.

"No. I have no birth certificate."

"Any witnesses?"

"*Si*, but I dunno where they are now."

"Well, you can swear an affidavit, which may help keep your son here, but it probably won't help you."

A thought occurs to me. "What about marriage to a U.S. citizen?"

Lupe looks at me strangely. "But I not married..." I press a finger to my lips.

"It's not an automatic pass to a green card like some people think," Chica says. "But the citizen spouse can file an application to keep the non-citizen spouse in the country, which could delay the issuance of a deportation order." She addresses Lupe. "Your biggest problem is that you came here unlawfully. Even if you left willingly, it could be many years before you were allowed to apply for legal entry, if at all. And if they find out that you have a prior Notice to Appear that you ignored...". Chica just shakes her head.

"You keep saying 'probably', or 'it could'," I point out. "Isn't anything definite?"

Chica shakes her head again. "The prosecutor has discretion, as does the judge. You should bring up everything that might help Lupe stay here. But in the current political climate, I think the chances are excellent that Lupe will be deported."

Lupe breaks down in tears.

Later, we're home. Eduardo has been put to bed. We're sitting on the sofa with our favorite drinks, a beer for Lupe and a shot and a beer for me.

"Why did you ask Chica about marriage?" Lupe asks. "You know I got no husband."

"I wasn't thinking about a husband for you," I tell her. "I was thinking about a wife."

She looks at me with a puzzled expression.

"It just became legal in this state a few months ago for two women to get married."

A light in her eyes comes on. "You want to marry me?"

"Why not? You know I love you."

"And I love you." She hesitates and the light fades. "But the priest would never marry two women."

WTF?

"It is no wedding if the priest does not marry you," Lupe says with a serious face.

I am continually amazed at the depth of the wisdom and the ignorance of this woman!

"Lupe, the state does not care if we're married by a priest or not. We'd still be legally married."

"But to be married without a priest is…" she hesitates, searching for a word, "…*una profanación.*"

I give her a blank look.

She tries again. "*Una blasfemia, una herejía, … un sacrilegio.*"

"A sacrilege!"

"*Si*, that is it!"

"What difference does that make? According to my uncle, we're already living in sin."

"Your uncle is right," she says in a satisfied tone. "But we can be forgiven for that. For *un sacrilegio*, there is no forgiveness."

I was raised Catholic, so I'm very familiar with the diverse varieties of sin that we poor mortals are prone to, as explained every Sunday by my friendly neighborhood priest. I had not heard this particular nonsense before, however.

"Who told you that?"

"The priest."

"A priest told you that getting married to another woman is a sacrilege?"

"No, no! The priest said that marrying somebody outside of the Church is *un sacrilegio.*"

Of course he did. Totally makes sense now. I try again.

"Lupe, if we were to get married, it might help you stay in America."

"But it would mean that you and I would burn in hell forever. Nothing is worth that."

"Well, will you at least think about it?"

"There is nothing to think about, *cariño*," she says with tears running down her cheeks. "We can never be married in the eyes of God."

As before with Uncle Amos, I have run headlong into the unbreakable wall of religion.

Chapter 9.

Saturday morning dawns. It's a struggle to get out of bed. I can see the rivulets streaming down the outside of the bedroom window and the digital thermometer attached to the glass tells me it's fifty degrees out there. Ugh! I'd love to go back to bed, but I know myself well enough to realize that I'd never go back to sleep, as keyed up as I am.

I quietly slip into my robe, so I don't wake Lupe. I watch her sleeping fitfully in the subdued dawn light seeping into our bedroom through the rain-splattered window. Lupe is short, just an inch taller than me, but while I could be described as petite, Lupe has a compact, athletic form. Her skin is the color of coffee with too much cream and just as rich. Her hair cascades over her breasts like braided ebony and mirrors the lustrous sheen of her skin in a darker motif. Her facial features are broad and soft in repose, but when she's awake they generally sparkle with her boundless exuberance. I am always amazed at her cheerfulness because I know about some of her experiences in her short life — multiple rapes, living on scraps both in Mexico and during her early days in the U.S.A., birthing a child in a flophouse and caring for him first as a menial worker, then as a club stripper. To her immense credit, he's now a cheerful eight-year-old tickled to death that he can wear a backpack and go to an American school. It is any wonder that I love her so much? The miracle is that she loves me too.

As I sit and sip bitter coffee with the TV murmuring in the background, I think of how much class I've been missing lately. I need to start doing a lot better or Simonson won't even have to have me expelled. But lately, trying to concentrate on a professorial information dump has been just too much to bear.

My problem is that I don't know how I feel anymore. I'm sad about Xin Niu's horrible death, mad as hell that somebody is doing this to us and baffled as to why. Suddenly, college and law school have become totally unimportant. Goddammit! I need to do something!

But what? Lupe's hearing isn't for two weeks. The CCTV broadcast is a dead end. Danny told me that Kidd delivered the tuna can found near Xin Niu to a local lab for analysis and it's a sure thing that they'll find some kind of drug — you can't just do something like that to a wide-awake cat without taking a lot of damage. But until we know what drug, there's no lead there, either.

I think about the campus TV broadcast again. Like I said, I'm not ashamed about what I did, but I'm way tight that it's out there for everyone to see.

I've just figured out how I'm going to spend my day!

I get dressed and head out to 3M. I want to use the computer there because it has access to specialized databases not available to the general public, as well as an Onion browser that can access the dark net. I don't know that I'll need all that stuff, but it's nice to know it's there if I do.

Because it's Saturday, there's little traffic and it takes less time than usual to get to Garton. The cars in the yard tell me that Mom and Danny are here. Of course, poor Uncle Amos is always here now.

I go in through the kitchen and grab a cup of coffee from the pot — the smell tells me it's freshly made. I go into the hall but avoid the living room and Mom so I don't get dragged into the "how are you doing in school" rag. Uncle set up a small office for me in what was once a laundry room that he never got rid of after he fired me — there's a small table, a file cabinet and a networked PC. All a girl would ever need! I dump my backpack on the floor and pull up a chair.

The first step is to find out what I'm dealing with. A Google search for Natalie McMasters turns up half a dozen porn sites. I try Kira Foxxx and find about ten more! I start checking out the videos. Almost all of the Kira Foxxx videos are performances I did for online clients and some of them involve sex toys and are pretty explicit. I feel like an idiot. Even though I willingly did these performances for money, I didn't stop to think that a client might download one and share it to a porn site. I also find multiple copies of the video of me and Lupe, some tagged Kira and some tagged Natalie. Those I need to get rid of!

I don't know why I do things that are sure to cause me pain. I'm staring at a still picture of me and Lupe, naked and entwined in the heart-shaped bed. In the center of the picture is a black square with a white triangle whose apex points to the right. I click on the triangle and the video that's been seen by most of State campus begins playing.

The heartsickness returns as I watch our lovemaking on the grainy screen. Truly, the two women in the video could be anyone, but I know that it's me and Lupe in our stolen moment. And thanks to whoever did this, so does everyone else.

About that time, Danny walks into the room without knocking, of course. He must've noticed the Z-car in the yard when he went for coffee.

"Hey, Nattie!" I turn just in time to see him look at the screen. He immediately turns his head. Is that disgust I see on his face?

I instantly minimize the video. "Sorry."

Now when he looks at me, he just looks sad.

"I'm trying to see how far this video of me and Lupe has spread on the Internet." I explain. "I'd like to get it taken down if that's possible."

"Believe it or not, I dealt with a case of so-called "revenge porn" when I was on the job," Danny says. "A woman called the police to come to her house to arrest her husband, whom she was in the process of divorcing. He'd put some of their private videos online to pay her back. I was sorry to tell her that what he did was a misdemeanor in this state."

"What happened? Did you arrest the guy?"

"Sure, we had to since there was a complaint lodged. But the D.A. declined to prosecute. Claimed she had too much serious crime to deal with and cut him loose."

"Great. So I'll get no help from her."

"Not likely," Danny agrees. "But I helped the lady look into how she could get the videos off the net. There's this thing called a DMCA takedown that you can do."

"DMCA? What's that?"

"It's a law that says you own the copyright on any video with you in it and that anyone who posts or hosts it without your permission is infringing your copyright."

"I don't want a copyright on that video! Shit, I didn't even know it was being made!"

"That doesn't matter," Danny says. "Since you're in it, you own the copyright unless you sell or transfer it. And that means you have the say so about who has the right to exhibit it, or whether they can even show it at all."

I do another Google search on DMCA. I find out that there are even lawyers who specialize in it! Since the guy who recorded and posted the video is dead, I don't need an attorney for a lawsuit, but one of the lawyer's sites has a pretty comprehensive discussion about how to get the videos taken down. A little more search tells me there's even a software package you can download that automates the process.

"The first thing I have to do is to identify all of the sites where the video is posted," I tell Danny. "Then I can use the software to send their ISP or hosting service a DMCA takedown notice, telling them I want the content removed from the site. But what if they just tell me to screw off?"

"That won't happen as often as you think," Danny says. "These porn sites are businesses. Some of 'em do millions of dollars of revenue a year. If they refuse to remove the content after they've been notified, it's a Federal offense. They're not going to risk that for one lousy video."

I'm not a hundred percent sure he's right, but it's certainly worth a try. "I've found the video on about fifteen or twenty sites," I tell him.

"Make a list," says Danny. "Amos said you can use the resources of the agency on this case, so we can get your Mom to use the software package to notify them. You might want to hire somebody who really knows what they're doing to do a really extensive search for you."

"Got any suggestions?"

"I'll talk to some of my buddies in the department and let you know."

I decide that as long as I'm at it, I might as well get the Kira Foxxx videos taken down too, since I never gave permission for them to be posted. Danny pitches in and helps me make the lists. He seems to have gotten over his problems with the videos. But it seems like he's going out of his way to be around me these days. I hope he's not getting the idea that we can hook up again.

When we're finished, I send everything along to Mom with instructions about what to do next.

Just a few minutes later, a message pops up on my screen. Leon Kidd is back and wants to see me and Danny in his office.

I didn't much like Kidd when I first met him. He was the detective in charge of investigating Becca's murder and he intimated that it might never be solved because she was an online stripper. It's well known that there's a prevailing attitude in law enforcement that such women are getting what's coming to them. Turned out that it wasn't Kidd's attitude though — he was just acknowledging some painful realities of a cop's day-to-day job, but I didn't know that at the time. Later on after I had been arrested, Kidd saved me some jail time when he didn't have to and when no one else would guard Uncle Amos from a killer, Kidd did and took a bullet for his pains. When Uncle got better, Kidd expressed a desire to retire from a police force that he believed was no longer doing its job, so Uncle offered him employment as a pair of legs that Uncle no longer had. Of course, Kidd's ex-Marine status didn't hurt.

"We got the lab report back on the tuna can yesterday," Kidd says. "Xin Niu was poisoned with ketamine, a veterinary tranquilizer."

That makes sense. "So maybe we can start checking vets to see if we can find out where it came from," I say.

"We can, but ketamine is also a party drug that's sold on the street under the name of Special K. So tracing it may be a problem." He hesitates, then continues, "And I talked to the people in the rental office at your complex yesterday, Nattie. We checked the security footage. We were able to find a suspicious-looking guy in a hoodie near the bushes where Xin Niu was hurt, but it could have been anybody. We checked several parking lot cams to see if we could attach him to a car, but he apparently didn't drive into the complex — we caught him walking out towards the public street. Since your complex is in the suburbs, there are no traffic cams on the streets."

"Goddammit!" I explode. "This bastard is either totally lucky or way smart!"

"Nattie," Danny says, "this has all of the indications that it's personal. The best thing you could do is make a list of people who you think might have it in for you."

"I've tried to, but I just can't think of anyone who would hate me that much." I remember that I haven't told Danny and Kidd about Lupe's immigration issues. I do that now.

When I'm finished, Kidd says, "Now there's no doubt in my mind that you know the person who's doing this to you, Nattie. Make that list!"

Kidd goes back to his office, leaving me and Danny alone.

"It's scary," I say. "Given what this guy's already done, I wonder what else he might be capable of." I can't vocalize the next thought, but I know I have to. "Danny, if he ever hurt Lupe or Eduardo…" Dammit! I start crying.

Danny immediately takes me in his arms like he did at the vet's office. He strokes the top of my head. "Hey, don't worry…," he begins.

A shrill female voice shatters the moment. "Well! What's going on in here? I thought we had a lunch date, shug."

Oh no! It's Diane! Today she's traded in the puppy scrubs for a body clinging, long-sleeved red dress with a plunging neckline — if you want a visual, picture a body suit on an egg with boobs hanging everywhere. She's got on full length black gloves, black stockings and black spike heels and the whole ensemble is topped off with a little red pillbox hat. Ugh!

"Daniel, you should be ashamed of yourself! I thought you said she was a dyke!"

Danny grips me harder as I struggle to get out of his grasp. He knows what I'm about to do and he's not going to let me.

"Settle down, Nattie. I'll handle this," he says in a low, no nonsense voice. He does an about face, keeping me behind him.

"Diane. You're way out of line. Apologize to Nattie, now."

"I'll do no such thing, shug…"

"Apologize or get out. Now."

Diane's got a look on her face that says nobody's ever talked to her that way in her life, or at least not for a long, long time. Both she and Danny are looking daggers, each waiting for the other to give in. My money's on the Marine.

"Fine," she says finally. "If that's the way you want it. Don't come cryin' to me when she goes back to her sweet Mexican thang." She wheels to leave the room and Danny grabs me by both wrists as I reach for something to throw.

"Nattie, she's not worth it."

I try to get free, but I might as well be trying to break out of handcuffs. I glare at him, but all I see on his face is concern. I relax and he pulls me close as I start crying again.

"I'm sorry, Danny. I didn't mean to break you guys up…"

"Hey, you did me a favor. I'm well rid of her."

He holds close me for a few more minutes until I settle down. Enclosed in those strong arms, I reflect that I've never had a man for a friend before, but it sure looks like I've got one now.

Chapter 10.

It's lunchtime on Sunday and I'm in a small park across from City Hall. The weather is still a little cool, but the rain is gone so it's not nearly as uncomfortable as it has been the past few days. Many of the park benches are occupied by homeless people. It's a scandal that so many of them congregate here, so near the seat of government. The cops tried to run them off but a local TV station got involved and made the police look like storm troopers, so they let them be. A few unfortunates hit on me for handouts but I ignore them. When they see who I'm here to meet, they'll leave me alone.

I've got a sack with two fried chicken boxes from a local place that has the best fried chicken in the world. It's a shameless bribe. I see my man on the bench in the middle of the park — our usual meeting place. LeBrowne Ellis is the current president of a street gang called the Urban Legends and he looks the part. You'd never mistake him for a homeless dude, not with his matching red leather jacket and pants outfit, his white panama hat and the heavy gold chains gleaming against his black t-shirt.

He studiously ignores me as I sit next to him on the bench. I offer him a box of chicken. He cocks an eyebrow at me when he sees it.

"You think just cause I's a nigga I eat fried chicken all de time?" I know that his ghetto talk is affected, because I've heard him speak as clearly as any executive in a board room. In a way, as the chief of the Legends, that's what he is. He's proud of his distinctive argot, which is a unique mix of gangsta slang, urban rap and prison *patois*. He'll be as deliberately as obtuse as he can to make me ask him what he means. Everything is a competition with him.

"Hey, if you don't want it, I'll keep it for dinner. Hope you don't mind if I eat while we're talking, though."

"Dass alright," he says as he takes the box from me. He pops the lid, extracts a drumstick and attacks it with his strong teeth. It's gone in two bites and he slings the bone out onto the lawn. "Got to leave suthin' for the rats."

The disquieting thought arises that the chicken remnants on that bone won't be eaten by a rat with all the homeless people around, but I squelch it. He probably tossed that bone just to rattle me.

"So I hear you really got dem jumpin' over at State wit' your TV booty show."

I refuse to let him bait me. "That's not what I'm here to talk about. I want to know what you know about ketamine."

"Special K? Dat shit's last year, Mama."

"What do you mean?"

"I mean it's a party drug for wanksters. Nigga ain't gonna get no cream wit' dat shit."

"So where would a girl get some if she wanted it?"

"I dunno, boost some from the doggie doc. Dass where a lot of it comes from."

"You don't know anyone who deals it?"

"Like I said, no lucci there. Oxy, blow or crystal will get a nigga a livin'." He pauses then says, "But if you got scruples and you jonesin', you could mebbe get a nigga to boost some for you. Cost you tho'."

Dammit! LeBrowne owes me, so I really don't think he's lying. I hesitate, then ask, "I don't want you to steal any. What I would like is if you asked around to find out if any has been stolen lately."

"I look like five-oh to you? Ask them."

"They won't talk to me anymore than they'll talk to you."

"No, but they'll talk to your homies who used to be po-po."

LeBrowne doesn't know that neither Danny nor Kidd is on the best of terms with their former employer. But his suggestion still worth a shot. "I'll do that," I tell him. "But I'd like it if you asked around too."

"Watchoo gonna do for me? You could come down to the crib and do some lap dances for the bruthas, Kira," he says with an evil leer.

"I'm not Kira anymore. Besides you owe me!"

"Sheeit, that was yesterday."

"Yeah and you'd still be in Shawshank if I hadn't helped you out." He raises a respectful eyebrow at that one. I hesitate again. I swore I'd never ask, but I can't help myself. "What did you do with him, anyway?"

"You do not want to know," he says in a serious tone.

I believe him, so I drop it. "So will you ask about the ketamine for me or not?"

"Yass'm. But Sweetcheeks, that bill is now paid. A'ite?"

"I guess so."

"A'ite?"

"Dammit, yes. It's paid."

He smiles like he's won, revealing his gold tooth and pulls another piece of chicken from his box. I realize that I haven't touched mine.

Later, me and Danny are at the range. We've got one booth again and we're taking turns, him with his 1911 and me with the LC9. When we're finished, he retrieves the target. This sheet has nine separate bullseyes, so we could each shoot our own. He smiles when he sees how well I've done.

When we're back outside in the parking lot, he says, "Nattie, your practice is paying off. You shot much better today."

"Still haven't beaten you yet, though." You could cover some of Danny's five shot groups with a quarter.

"Hey, I spent a lot of Uncle Sam's money to get an expert rating and it took years. You'll get there."

We get in the cab of his truck. It's late afternoon now and the weather has warmed considerably since I was in the park. I hit the button to bring the window all the way down after I shut the door.

I haven't told Danny about my talk with LeBrowne and I'm not going to. A girl has to have some secrets. But I do ask him about the banger's suggestion.

"Do you think you could talk to some of your buddies on the force to find out if there have been any recent ketamine thefts? And maybe Kidd could too?"

"Leon and I have already discussed that. The answer is yes, but don't hold out hope that it will go anywhere. That kind of theft falls in the category of non-serious crimes, like revenge porn. Meaning that it gets recorded but not investigated."

"Dammit! What the hell do they consider a serious crime?"

"Violent crimes, bank robberies, firearms violations and anything that's high profile. And believe me, there are enough of those here in the state capital to keep everybody hopping."

The conversation stops as the truck reaches the end of the driveway and Danny has to look both ways to avoid an accident before pulling out on the main drag.

When we're going again, Danny asks, "Well, how are things between you and Lupe these days?"

Where the fuck did that come from? I turn to look at him. He's looking straight ahead.

"We talked to a girl at the law school about our options on Friday."

"And those are?"

"Not many. There's a real good chance that Lupe's going to get deported." My voice breaks up on that last word and I'm suddenly in tears again.

Danny jerks the wheel, pulls into a handy parking lot and kills the engine. He unbuckles and reaches across the seat for me, but the gearshift and console are in the way.

"Dammit, Nattie! You do not have to go through all of this alone!" He pauses then continues, "Somebody knows way more about you than they should. That didn't happen overnight."

I get control of myself and gently disengage from him. "There's something else." I take a deep breath. Do I really want to get into this with him? "Danny, I asked Lupe to marry me. I thought it might help her stay in the country."

Now he's looking decidedly uncomfortable.

"Well, it's probably for the best if it will help her stay here," he says. It doesn't sound like he means it.

I get angry and the tears start to flow again. "After I asked her, I realized it was more than that. I really want to share my life with her." I stop. It's so hard to get the last part out. I feel like I'm choking on the words. "But she said no."

Now he looks concerned. "Why?"

I tell him.

His silence tells me that he doesn't know what to say. This is why I don't talk about me and Lupe at 3M. Uncle has made no bones about how he feels, but I really don't think any of them are totally comfortable with same-sex relationships, even Mom.

He says, "I guess that all you can do is wait and hope she changes her mind. Maybe she'll give in as deportation becomes more of a reality to her."

"Goddammit! I don't want her to marry me because she's afraid of being deported! I want her to marry me because she loves me!"

He looks lost. Finally, he says in a plaintive tone, "You don't have control of that Nattie. I guess you'll just have to wait." He reaches for me again and this time I lean over so he can hold me.

Chapter 11.

The hyacinths on Rebecca's desk are pink and blue this Monday morning and just as fragrant as ever. But they don't do anything for my mood.

I've just finished giving her a total data dump of the last few days — Xin Niu's murder, Uncle's reaction and Lupe's immigration issues. However, I don't mention my proposal to Lupe. "I'm so salty I could scream!" I finish.

"I'm sorry about Xin Niu," says Rebecca. "And I think Danny and your uncle were right. Anyone who could do that to an animal is a very dangerous person. You need to watch yourself. Maybe taking a leave of absence from school isn't a bad idea."

"I'm tired of hearing that!" I explode. "I hope I do meet the person who did that to Xin Niu! I'll…" I stop abruptly.

"Kill them?" Rebecca says it for me. "Are you sure that it's just a figure of speech?" I don't say anything, so she goes on, "I'm sorry, Nattie. I say that only to show how easy it can be to make violence a habit."

"I would like to kill someone who could do that to a cat," I say defiantly.

"And what would that get you? Two dead bodies instead of one?"

"That's just one too many."

She looks at me silently as if to say, *Are you done?* When I don't answer, she takes it for a *Yes* and says, "I heard from your teachers that you haven't been coming to class."

"What, you've been checking up on me?"

"Yes, I have. It's my job, remember?" She continues, "So a leave of absence might not be a bad idea if you're not going to class anyway."

"I don't want to give whoever is doing this the satisfaction of thinking that they've scared me away from school."

She surprises me by saying, "I think there's some wisdom in that. But a leave of absence would freeze your grades, so you won't suffer if you can't keep up because of the stress, or because of conflicting priorities."

"What about the Title IX thing? Could it make me look bad for that?"

"I don't see how. Again, it would give you the time to deal with it and with Lupe's problems, too. You really have a lot on your plate right now."

"Tell me about it."

"Would you like me to get the paperwork together? You can sign a blank form and I'll fill it out and send it over to the registrar's office later today."

"Okay, but that doesn't mean I'm gonna bury myself at home. I need to find out who's doing this to me!"

"Fair enough."

"There's something else I'd like to tell you." She looks at me expectantly. "I asked Lupe to marry me and she said no."

"Why? Did she say?"

"She said we'd burn in hell because we weren't married by a priest. And of course, a priest wouldn't marry us because we're both women."

Rebecca is quiet for a moment while she digests this. Then she asks, "I've never asked you this before, Nattie, but are you religious?"

"I was raised Catholic," I tell her. "My dad was an Irish catholic and my Mom converted to marry him. I don't think Uncle Amos has ever forgiven Mom for that."

"But are *you* religious?" she asks again.

"I guess I'm an agnostic." Rebecca makes a face at that last word.

"What?" I ask.

"What do you think that means?" Rebecca asks.

"Agnostic? It means that I don't know if there's a God or not."

"I wrinkled my nose at you because so many people misuse the word *agnostic*. You're only partly correct. It means that you can't use reason or logic to justify whether God exists or not."

"Isn't that what I said?"

"No. You said you don't know if God exists. You didn't say you can't know."

"Isn't it the same thing?"

Rebecca smiles. "Let's take this back to the problem at hand. Lupe and your Uncle are very similar. They both believe, or say that they know, that God exists and that he has some very strict rules they have to follow. Since you don't know whether God exists, you just make up your own rules as you go along in life. Is that a fair statement?"

I think about it for a moment. "Yes," I say, "that's about right."

"But you do think that there are rules at all? In other words, do you think that morality exists?"

"Yes." I think I see what she's getting at. "It's just that my morality is different from theirs."

"And what would you do if I asked you to do something that you didn't believe was moral?"

"I wouldn't do it."

"What if I could show you that your belief was erroneous?"

"Then it would probably be okay if I did it."

"Do you think you could convince your Uncle that his beliefs are in error?"

"I doubt it. He's been reading that Bible of his since he was a kid and he's always tried to live by it, even when it brought him trouble."

"How about Lupe? Same question."

"I don't know. Maybe. Lupe keeps a candle in a painted glass next to her side of our bed. It's got a picture of Our Lady of Guadalupe on it, her namesake. She lights it when she says her rosary. On the other hand, Lupe's a survivor. She's very practical."

"Are you sure you want to marry Lupe?"

I think back to the conversation that I had with Danny yesterday. "Absolutely. When I first had the idea, it was because I thought it would help keep her here. But after I thought about it some more, I realized that I want to marry her because I love her. If she gets deported anyway, I guess I'll just have to go with her."

"Well I think you have your answer then. You'll just have to find a way to convince Lupe that her thinking is in error."

"But how do I do that?"

"I don't know. You know her much better than I do. Maybe something will come to you." She looks at the clock on her desk, then back at me. "Well here we are with only about five minutes left and we haven't really talked about the most important thing. Those men you killed and your feelings about that. We'll have to do that next time."

"You know, I've been thinking about that and I don't think I really have to feel guilty about it. I did what I had to do."

"Yes, you did." It makes me feel good that she agrees with me. "But just because you had to do it doesn't mean that you shouldn't feel sorry that you had to do it. Do you?"

I think about it for a minute, then say, "I'm sorry that Lupe and I got in a situation where it was necessary. But I think that I did a good thing by getting those guys out of this world. They didn't deserve to be here."

Her expression tells me that that's not the answer she wanted to hear. But she says, "If that's so, then you should be able to back off the prazosin without the dreams coming back. If you do and the dreams return, then there's something left unresolved."

I know the procedure for weaning myself off the drug because I've done it before. So I say, "Well, let me try. If I can't I'll let you know." Another thought occurs to me. "The guys at 3M want me to make a list of people that might have it in for me enough to want to do this to me. I've thought about it, but I can't come up with anyone that would hate me that much."

"There are some techniques we can try to help with that," she says. "Let's put it on the agenda for next session."

She prints out the paperwork for the leave of absence and I sign the forms. It's a relief to have my academic concerns vanish. I start to feel like that maybe I can beat this thing after all.

After leaving Rebecca's office, I'm on the porch overlooking the courtyard again. The rain has gone and the sun has returned, but it's still a little bit cool. That hasn't daunted the sun lovers, who are out on the lawn on their beach towels and blankets. My eyes stray to the orange and blue newspaper holder on the periphery of the porch. I see a familiar face looking at me from behind the glass. Mine!

I open the door and see that it's the same picture as last time, but the date tells me it's a new edition. I grab a paper and peruse the article. Andrea Kiefer again. It's an update on the Title IX investigation. It's written in general terms, but it does mention that at least one complainant in addition to the Title IX coordinator has signed on. It alludes to the trauma that many students have suffered because they were exposed to my scandalous video. And there's a quote from Simonson saying that he can't give out any information on an active investigation, nor will he confirm that an investigation is in progress, so he's totally covered his ass. Kiefer's got to be getting her info from somewhere. Maybe I'll just go and ask her from where.

I use my phone to get on the Internet and find out where the newspaper office is — Lacey Hall, straight across the courtyard from where I'm standing. I've had several classes there. Time to pay Ms. Kiefer a visit.

Lacey Hall is a large modern building made of blonde bricks and glass that stands out in stark contrast to the older red brick buildings surrounding it, like so many outbuildings around a manor. It contains classrooms, mostly — on the State campus, the department offices tend to be separate from the areas where students congregate, maybe to give the profs a sense of security. For some reason known only to the architect, you enter Lacey Hall on the second floor after climbing a broad staircase from the courtyard. Definitely handicap unfriendly. I check the directory after I get inside and find out that the newspaper office is on the sixth, or top floor. There's only one tiny elevator for the entire building, to discourage the students from using it, I guess. I let the designer win and take the stairs.

My calves are burning when I hit the sixth floor. The corridors in Lacey Hall run around the perimeter with the rooms in the center, which can be damned inconvenient because there's no quick way to get from one side to the other. I walk around, scanning the room numbers as I go until I reach the newspaper office. I open the blue metal door and go inside.

It's an office containing six steel grey desks with a computer monitor on each one. Only one is occupied. It's the butch blonde chick from Simonson's office! She's typing furiously, so enraptured with what's on her screen that she doesn't even notice I'm there. I approach within five feet of her desk before I say, "Andrea Kiefer?"

She holds up one hand to stop me without looking away from the monitor and finishes her typing with the other hand, banging her keyboard with a flourish worthy of a concert pianist. Then she turns to look at me. A look of anger mingled with fear transforms her face.

"What do *you* want?" she says. She reaches for the phone on her desk. "I'm calling campus security!"

"Hold on!" I tell her. "I'm not here to beat you up. I just have a few questions."

"Well, I don't want to talk to you. Swerve!"

"That's a pretty poor attitude for a journalist." I almost say *so-called journalist* but I stop myself — insulting her is no way to get any information out of her.

"What do you want?" she says again.

"I want to know where you're getting your information about a supposedly confidential investigation. And I want to tell my side of the story."

She folds her arms and stares at me. "I don't reveal my sources," she says. "And I don't need your side of the story. You'll just lie about everything and make yourself out to be the victim here."

Wow. "I thought a journalist was supposed to be disinterested and you know, fair and balanced."

"That's so yesterday. All my profs say that today's journalists are activists, fighting for social justice on the front lines."

I'm beginning to lose it with this biotch. "How does publishing lies about me qualify as fighting for social justice?"

She gives me a look like I'm shit on her shoe. "You should be so ashamed of yourself! I've been fighting for LGBTQIA rights for years, then somebody like you comes along and spreads lesbian porn all over campus to attract men to your porno site just to make fuckin' money. I know about Kira Foxxx and Carmella Picante. I know what you did in that club before it burned down. Pornography is violence against women — it depends for its continued existence on the rape and prostitution of women, just like Dworkin says! And you call yourself a lesbian? Your video just so reinforces everything bad that everybody thinks about us!"

Where the fuck did that come from? Do we even live on the same planet? I try again, "I didn't put that video up…"

She cuts me off. "Suuure, you didn't!"

I'm so mad I can hardly speak. I've got to hold it together! I try again. "Look. That was a private moment between me and my gf. I didn't even know that it was being recorded. Having that video out there is the worst thing that's ever happened to me!" I can feel the tears rolling down my cheeks.

"Boy, you've totally got it down." Her tone would freeze booze. "Tears and all. But you don't fool me. I'm a gold star lesbian and proud of it! And you created a hostile environment for all the women on campus with what you did. Made us nothing more than sex objects for men to leer at. You're so totally going to suffer for that!"

Now my anger has turned cold — I could really hurt her without a thought. But her words *hostile environment* tell me what I came here to find out.

"You signed on as a co-complainant with Simonson, didn't you?" I think about that for a second, then say, "Was that before or after you let him fuck you? Or did you just give him a BJ? Some gold star lesbian you are!" I add that last just to hurt her. It works.

She grabs a chemistry book lying on her desk and throws it at me. It opens as it flies, so it misses.

"Get the fuck out of here!" she screeches. She reaches for the phone. "I'm calling security."

I'd love to stay and slap the shit out of her, but reason wins. I bounce.

"Bye Felicia! Just wait until you see my next article!" I hear as the door closes behind me.

By the time I'm back outside, I'm so mad I'm shaking. A couple of female students approaching me notice and give me a wide berth. *Calm down, Nattie!* I hear Rebecca's voice in my head. If Kiefer did screw Simonson and I'm sure she did, it's likely she was forced to. That means she deserves compassion rather than resentment. What happened to me in that strip club basement rushes back into my head. At least I had the satisfaction of getting revenge. Kiefer, obviously proud of her lesbian identity, just has to suck up Simonson's abuse. I wonder what he's got on her?

On the other hand, her anger level towards me was totally off the charts. She knows a lot about me, too. Too much. Carmella Picante was the name we chose for Lupe to take my place as an online exotic dancer. But Lupe only gave one performance under that name, with me doing my last performance as Kira Foxxx, before the website got shut down. That means that Kiefer knows who Lupe is. Does she also know that Lupe's undocumented? Could she be the one who turned Lupe in and killed Xin Niu? She probably could have bought some Special K right here on campus. A sudden bolt of fear pierces my belly. *I know what you did in that club before it burned down,* she said. Exactly what the hell does she know? What's going to be in that next article?

Chapter 12.

Living in the South means that we have some fine days in autumn and winter but today is not one of them. The rain is back. I know it instantly when I awaken because of my throbbing sinuses. Only one thing will fix that — coffee.

Lupe is up before me this morning to get Eduardo off to school. As I come out into the great room, I smell Lupe's *café de olla*. It's hot, strong and spicy, just like her.

I pick up the remote from the coffee table and turn the TV on. Seconds later it drops from my hand.

"… a raging fire this morning in an old house on the southeast side," the anchor is saying. The screen switches to a shot of the blaze, obviously taken from a helicopter. "Police tell WPQR that it is the headquarters of the notorious street gang known as the Urban Legends. Several fire companies have responded and have been fighting the blaze for nearly an hour. Reports indicate that some alleged gang members escaped from the house and have been taken to University Hospital for treatment. It is unknown at this time how many people remain inside and what their status is. It is also unknown whether the fire was the result of gang warfare."

LeBrowne! Was he caught in the fire? A more disturbing thought enters my mind. Could somebody have followed me and discovered that I had a meeting with him? Am I responsible for this, too? Stop it, Nattie!

I pick up the land line and call University Hospital. When the receptionist answers, I ask if LeBrowne Ellis is a patient there.

"Just a minute, I'll check." I go on hold and strains of elevator music fill my ear. She comes back on. "I'm not finding that name."

"He would have come in with the victims from the fire this morning."

"Oh, those people are still in triage. Those names won't get down here till later this morning, at least."

"Could I find out if I came over there?"

"Are you family?"

I think fast. "Yes," I lie.

"You could check with emergency. But come in, don't call. They'll tell you if they know."

I hang up and tell Lupe where I'm going.

"Nattie," she says, "have some *café* and some breakfast. If your friend is there, they will take care of him. Let me take care of you." I want to protest, but I hold my tongue. She's right — I'm jumping the gun, again.

Her words give me pause. Is LeBrowne my friend? I've never thought of him that way, but there's no denying that I'm concerned for his well-being. Maybe the secret we keep between us has made us closer than I thought, at least from my point of view.

It's midmorning when I finally make it to the hospital. I had to park on the top level of the parking deck open to the sky, so my hoody is uncomfortably damp when I enter the cavernous glass and steel lobby. I have to empty my pockets and pass through a metal detector — the hospital implemented even tighter security after Uncle Amos was shot here a few months ago. I find the sign to Emergency, but then I think again and ask the receptionist for LeBrowne. She checks her computer.

"Yes, he's on the Burn Unit. Sixth floor."

I spent a lot of time in this hospital a few months ago when Uncle Amos was a patient here, so it's no problem to find the correct elevator. I get in with an older lady who's wearing an old-fashioned hat with a veil and a coat with a faux fur collar. She reminds me of somebody's great-grandmother. I turn to face front and press "6".

"Six is where I'm going too," she says. Then, "Are you here for the trial, Miss?"

"What trial?"

"Oh, the painkiller trial." She indicates a small TV screen just above the rows of buttons next to the elevator door. It shows slides about the various events at the hospital. NA meeting, Room 514, 8 p.m. — Seniors Tai Chi class, Hospital gymnasium, 1 p.m. — Oral CL-581 clinical trial, check in on the 6th floor. Normally people who try to start a conversation with a complete stranger in an airplane or an elevator bug the shit out of me, but I stifle a salty retort because I can hear the nervousness in her tone. Walk in the other guy's shoes and all that.

"No ma'am," I say with my best Southern manners. "I'm just here to see a friend."

She smiles at me. "Well, I hope your friend is all right."

Me too. A chime sounds and the elevator doors open. A printed sign outside has an arrow pointing right for the clinical trial and an engraved blue wall sign indicates that the Burn Unit is the other way.

I pass through double glass doors and find myself in a smallish room with a desk where a middle-aged woman in scrubs wearing a long-sleeved shirt underneath is busily typing on her keyboard. There's a metal door on the other side of the room that leads into the Burn Unit proper and three plastic chairs like the ones in Simonson's office next to the door I came in. An older guy, 30 or so, wearing a loud sport coat and a bad tie is sitting in one of them. He looks vaguely familiar, but I can't place him.

The woman looks up. "Can I help you?"

"I'm looking for a patient. LeBrowne Ellis. He came in this morning."

"Just a minute, hon."

I hate it when people who don't know me call me hon, dear, shug or use any other term of endearment. They don't know me and likely don't care about me at all. My mood is not improved by the fact that its freezing in here and my damp hoody is making it worse. But I don't say anything back.

"Ah," she says, then looks up from her monitor. "He's here hon, but you can't see him now."

"Why not?"

"Because he's in debridement and he likely won't be coherent for the rest of the day. Next time y'all call first before you come."

"How is he?"

She purses her lips before answering. "He's listed as serious, hon."

It's like pulling teeth. "Can you tell me anymore."

"Not really, sweetheart. You'd have to talk to the doctor."

"Who is the doctor?

"Dr. Nizamani. He's doing the debridement, so he's not available right now." She indicates the plastic chairs. "If you want to wait, I can let him know you're here."

"How long will it take?"

"I don't know. Debridement can take hours. You can call him, but he may not tell you much. HIPAA, you know."

Shit.

"Call this afternoon and I'll let you know if Mr. Ellis can have visitors. If not then, maybe tomorrow."

One flunky tells me come don't call, another tells me call don't come. What a totally effed-up morning!

"Thanks," I say, not meaning it and she smiles at me sweetly.

I turn to leave and find myself confronted by the guy who was sitting in the plastic chair. "Miss?" he says. "Would you mind answering a few questions? I'll buy you a coffee."

The last thing I need is some guy hitting on me in the hospital. "I don't have time right now," I say, trying to move past him, But he blocks my way.

"Miss McMasters." WTF? He knows my name? "I'm Detective Russell and I need to talk to you now."

Now I remember! "You were wearing a uniform the last time I saw you. You tried to take me downtown then, too."

I found out later that Josh Russell was Danny's former partner and had it in for Danny because he didn't support Russell in an Internal Affairs investigation. Russell apparently has it in for me too, because Danny and I both work for 3M.

"I made detective recently," he said. "And I hope taking you to headquarters won't be necessary this time."

Shit! "Can't we do this here? I'm in a hurry."

"No, let's go to the cafeteria. It will be more comfortable there." He reaches to take my elbow, but I shy away. I notice that the fingers of his hand are bright red, like they've been beet-stained and the rest of his hand and arm is white. A burn? "Ouch." I say. "That must have hurt."

"Not really," he says. "It's just a birthmark. Come on, let's go."

I've got no choice but to do as he says, but I don't have to let him touch me. A flash of anger crosses his face. It occurs to me that he thinks the birthmark repulses me. Too bad.

"Fine. Let's go," I say, heading for the door, letting him trail along behind.

I step in the corridor and head for the elevator, then stop in my tracks. Fuck me if this is not my lucky day! Diane is heading right for us!

"Nattie! Hey, shug!" Today she's wearing the puppy scrubs over a long-sleeved bright orange turtleneck. She sounds delighted to see me and rushes me like she wants to give me a hug. With Russell behind me, I feel like I'm standing on the edge of a snake pit being charged by a bull.

"I want to apologize for t'other day." Seeing my aversion, she reaches for my hand instead of embracing me. Ugh! She's wearing latex gloves. Who knows where they've been? I turn sideways so she can't touch me. "I was so bowed up I didn't know what I was a sayin'!" she says. "Please excuse my bad manners?"

I wouldn't forgive you for living, bitch! But just to get rid of her, I say, "Sure Diane. It's been a rough time for everybody. Don't worry about it."

Now Russell's got my elbow and is steering me around her, toward the stairwell door.

"Well aren't you precious! And tell my Danny I'm sorry too, shug. He won't take my calls."

I wonder why. "I'll do that." Not. And he's not your Danny!

Russell pushes the handle down to open the door and guides me inside.

Silence rushes in as the door closes behind us. "I figured you wanted out of there," Russell says. "The cafeteria is just two floors up."

The cafeteria is getting full because it's close to lunch time. The intermingled smells of grease, coffee and too-cooked vegetables make me feel slightly nauseated. The heat in here doesn't help. Russell is able to circle the crowd and put two coffees on a tray. He grabs two spoons and a handful of cream and sugar packets, then leads me to table in the corner. I want to pull off my damp hoody — it's way hot in here — but I'd feel uncomfortable taking it off in front of him. He quietly watches me, making me even more uncomfortable as I put cream and sugar in the nasty coffee I don't want. Stupid cop trick, I think.

Finally, as I'm stirring, he asks, "So how do you know LeBrowne Ellis?"

There's no way I'm telling a cop the truth about that. I hope I'm maintaining a good poker face as I think of a lie. "The club," I say. "He used to come in when I worked there."

"Funny, I never saw him there," he replies.

"Hey, I never saw you there."

He smiles. "Okay, you got me there. But you two must be pretty good friends for you to come all the way over here to see how he's doing."

In for a dime, in for a dollar. "I used to give him lap dances. He wasn't as handsy as a lot of the guys and he gave good tips. I heard about what happened this morning and since I was on campus anyway, I thought I'd come over and see how he was." His expression is non-committal, so I can't tell if he believes me or not.

He switches gears entirely. "So how's my boy Danny doin' over there at, what is it, 4H?"

"3M. Danny's fine. He talks about you sometimes."

He smiles again. "It's all lies." I swear to God, I think he is hitting on me!

"Look, I totally don't want to be rude, but I do have someplace to be. Is there anything else you want to know from me?"

"Just anything you might know about that fire this morning. Somebody who had it in for Ellis?"

Out of nowhere, the comment Kidd made about the homicidal triad pops into my head. *Fire-starting...!*

I try not to let Russell see fear on my face. "Your gang unit ought to be able to tell you that, I say."

"How did you know that Ellis was in the Legends?" he asks me unexpectedly.

I'm beginning to get his technique now. Small talk punctuated by serious questions. "What do you think? Big black dude wearing leather and bling with a white chick shoving her tits in his face, he's gonna brag."

There's that disarming smile again. "Well, you remember anything, you give me a call." He offers his card.

"Nothing to remember," I tell him. But I take the card anyway.

He offers to walk me downstairs. Can I really say no? But he doesn't ask any more questions on the way. The last time I met him I remember that he was openly hostile. Today, I don't sense that. Maybe his promotion has taken the edge off his bad feelings against Danny.

The rain has slacked off, so I don't get any wetter going to the top of the parking deck. But the dampness from this morning still lingers under my hoodie. God, I can't wait to get home, get out of these clothes and into a warm shower.

I'm greeted by the aromas of Mexico as I enter the townhouse. When Lupe is upset, she cooks. If she's said "*Barriga llena, corazón content*" (full stomach, happy heart) to me once, she's said it a thousand times. The kitchen mess that I see tells me that she's really gone all out this time. I sigh. Because she cooks all the time, I won't let her clean up. Looks like Eduardo and I are going to have a busy evening.

I go to our room to take off my damp clothes and the stench that greets me when I'm naked is truly horrifying. I spend a good twenty minutes in the shower, luxuriating in the cascade until the water is lukewarm. As I come out into the bedroom vigorously toweling my hair, I hear Lupe screeching in Spanish out in the living room. Oh-oh! What did Eduardo do now?

I wrap my hair in a towel, throw on a robe and go see.

She has poor Eduardo sitting on the sofa to harangue him and as soon as I see his face, I know why. He's got a large purple bruise with tinges of green under one eye, a trail of dried blood runs from one nostril down to his upper lip and his shirt is dirty and torn.

Lupe whirls on me as I approach. *"Él ha estado luchando!* Sorry… I mean, he has been fighting!"

No shit, Lupe. "Why? What happened?" I address the question to Eduardo.

"I can't help it, Mama Nattie! Other kids say we ill eagles and they gonna send us back to Mexico!"

I struggle to keep from laughing as a picture of a big bird on crutches flashes in my head. Lupe says, "You fight like this you gonna get thrown outta that school!"

I take Eduardo's hands and pull him off the couch, kiss the top of his head and push him towards the spiral staircase in the center of the great room. "Go upstairs and get cleaned up while I talk to Mama Lupe." He looks at me gratefully and scampers away.

Lupe is giving me the *why did you do that he's my son* look. "I know he shouldn't fight," I say, "but he's been under a lot of stress lately too."

She breaks down in tears. "I am so sorry! It is my fault he hears those things!"

I put my arms around her and press her face to my bosom. "Hey, it's not your fault! You've done only the best for him." I tilt her chin up and kiss her tears.

"What am I gonna do if they send me back?"

"Marry me, Lupe. Maybe they'll let you stay, then."

"I told you, I cannot marry you! And even if I could, what would we do if they send me back anyway?"

I don't even have to think about it. "Then I'd just have to go with you."

She looks horrified. "I could never ask you to do that!"

"You wouldn't have to ask. I love you. What else would I do?" That provokes a fresh round of weeping.

I guide her to the couch and sit down beside her, then take both of her hands. "Eduardo calls me Mama because you told him to. I love that! Whether you agree to marry me or not, you're still my spouse. No religion or law can change that. I will stay with you until you say you don't want me anymore, either here or in Mexico, or wherever else you go. But if you want to stay in the United States, you're going to have to do everything you can to accomplish that. Think about it."

She looks deeply into my eyes. Finally she says, "I will think about it, *cariño*. That is all I can promise you right now."

"That's enough for right now," I tell her and kiss her again.

Chapter 13.

Somebody's got it in for me. This Wednesday morning is my 21st birthday and it's still cold and raining out. Must be all that living in sin.

When I hit campus, I make straight for the nearest newspaper dispenser. Yep, I'm still front-page news. Holy shit! *State Coed Has Gang Ties?*

The article says that I rushed to University Hospital to check on LeBrowne Ellis, president of the Urban Legends street gang (true) and speculates that I have all sorts of connections with the gang including drug distribution and online pornography (fake news). There are no direct libelous accusations, but the text is crawling with snarky innuendoes.

Where the fuck did Kiefer get this shit? I can think of only one answer — Detective Russell. Is this another way for him to get back at Danny, or does he think the bad publicity will drive me into police headquarters to clear myself by providing evidence against the gang?

Since I have a leave of absence, I've got no classes to attend, so I head straight to Rebecca's office for my morning session. As soon as I see her face, I know there's trouble.

She looks like she's about to cry! "Rebecca, what's wrong?"

"Natalie, please sit down."

Natalie? People, this is not good!

After I'm seated on the daybed, she continues, "I'm afraid that I have bad news. Your request for a leave of absence has been turned down."

Shit. "Ok. That just means that I'll have to double down and get working to make up the classes I've missed. I've got friends I can get notes from."

"There's more. The reason that the Registrar's office rejected your request for a leave of absence is that they were informed by the Dean's Office that you're going to be asked to leave the university."

Oh holy shit! "What? Why?"

"Apparently Simonson has made a substantive case that you've created a hostile learning environment on campus, which is something that the University has zero tolerance for."

I open my mouth to go off on a tirade, but she stops me by raising her hand.

"You have a right to a hearing before the decision becomes final," she says. "I will request one right away. And I'll come with you as your advocate."

Screw the doctor-patient relationship! I get up and go around her desk to give her a hug. She hugs me back.

"I want to haul Simonson up on sexual harassment charges," I tell her. "We can't let him get away with this!"

"I agree. But realize that we're asking Simonson to investigate himself. The Dean could require him to recuse himself, but don't count on it, because this looks like retaliation on your part. I'm sure others have tried that tactic before."

"If we only had some evidence to prove what he's doing…," I begin.

She cuts me off. "As I told you the other day, don't do anything foolish. If you're caught trying to get into his office, or you proposition him, it could kill any chances you might have of getting the Dean's decision reversed."

"I don't know why you would think that I would do something like that." She snorts audibly and it's my turn to hold up a hand. "What we need is for someone else that he's victimized to come forward. Preferably several women."

"He's probably done this before," Rebecca agrees. "But Title IX information is confidential. We can't just go and get the names of women he's charged, who have had the charges dropped later."

"I'll bet I know one."

"Who?"

"Andrea Kiefer, the so-called journalist for the *State of State*. I saw her waiting in Simonson's office after my first interview. Problem is, she hates my guts."

"Why do you think so?"

I tell Rebecca about my encounter with Kiefer in her office. "If Kiefer is a committed lesbian, it would be terrible if she were forced into sex with a man," I finish.

She frowns. "Rape is terrible in any form for anyone," she says, shaking her head. Maybe it would help if I talked to Kiefer."

"I probably burned that bridge. But you can try." I have another thought. "Is there any way we can legally force the University to let us look at the Title IX records?"

"The Federal Education Rights and Privacy Act protects the privacy of student records at all public schools and universities. Perhaps we could file a FOIA request seeking all the documents related to an investigation, but I'm sure FERPA will hold unless we have substantive evidence that a particular record is pertinent to our case."

"It's like trying to get a loan from the bank." I say "The only way is to prove you don't need the money."

Rebecca throws up another roadblock. "Another problem is that FOIA requests take forever." Is that apprehension I hear in her voice? Is she afraid of repercussions if she goes after Simonson? A sudden, even more disconcerting thought intrudes. "If I'm expelled, does that mean that I can't see you anymore?"

"It most certainly does not! I'll see you at my home if I have to," she assures me.

I'm totally relieved. "I couldn't handle this without you," I tell her. A pause. "So have we decided what we're going to do about Simonson?"

"Nothing, for right now," she replies. "Let's go to the hearing and plead our case. If we get a reversal, that will remove the pressure on you. Then we can try some of the legal means we discussed."

I'm not happy about it, but I reluctantly accept her plan.

"I'll try to get a hearing scheduled as soon as possible. Why don't you think really hard about any evidence you may have to prove you didn't do this?"

"Whatever happened to innocent until proven guilty?"

"Unfortunately, that doesn't apply to Title IX."

"What do we do if I can't find any evidence?"

"Then we have to rely on character witnesses. I'll be one, of course. Make a list of any others and we'll talk about it next time."

That sounds like an exit line to me. I start to gather my things, then I remember.

"Today is my 21st birthday," I tell her. "They're having a party for me at 3M this afternoon. I'd like it if you came."

"Of course," she smiles. I give her the address and the time.

Late that afternoon, I'm driving down Main Street in Garton. Uncle established the business here instead of in the city because he didn't want to pay the rent for a fancy office there. I've been coming here as long as I can remember — Mom and I used to visit Uncle Amos when I was a little girl. I've always loved the old Victorian house that serves as both the agency's office and Uncle's home. I used to play for hours in the bushes that surround the wraparound porch, then Mom would get all ratchet because she had to pick the ticks off me after I came in. I wouldn't go to sleep at night until they made me a bed on the floor in the circular garret at the top of the house that Uncle used for a storeroom.

The last place I want to be right now is at a party, never mind one where I'm the guest of honor. Mom wanted a surprise party, but Danny, bless his heart, talked her out of that shit. I'm so shook right now that all I want to do is go home and get in my jammies with a twelve pack of Heinie and a fifth of Turkey. I'd probably be sick for two days afterwards, but who cares? I don't have stupid classes to go to any more. But now I have to be in a crowd of people and act like I'm happy. I'm sure as hell not gonna announce that I've been expelled from college to the whole fucking party. That would be a buzz kill to say the least.

When I see the house, I have to fight the urge keep driving right on by. Holy shit! The backyard must be packed because the driveway is totally full of parked cars. The last car is Fields'. I sure didn't expect her to be here.

I park on the street in front. I'm not used to coming in the front door, but it would be way stupid to walk all the way around to the back with a perfectly good entry a few feet away. I go up the wide front stairs and I can see the crowd in the living room office through the porch windows. Shit, Nattie, you can't just go home and pull the covers over your head! I brace myself, open the door and the babble of conversation hits me like a slap in the face. I take two steps down the main hall and turn into the office.

Mom sees me enter and yells, "Surprise!", but nobody else does. They just keep jabbering like I'm not even here. That's fine with me.

The place is totally lit. Everybody's wearing those stupid pointy hats with an elastic band under the chin and there's a banner strung across the middle of the room that says *Happy 21st Nattie!* More of Mom's work, I'm sure.

Uncle Amos is behind his desk in his wheelchair and he's got Eduardo on his lap. Uncle's got his hands under the kid's armpits and is bouncing him up and down on his knee, much to the little boy's delight. Lupe is standing nearby and smiling. Maybe there's some hope that those two will get together after all?

Kwaneshia and Fields, my former roommates, are also here. They couldn't look more different. Kwaneshia is a stout black girl who favors beaded braids and African dress, while Fields looks like she stepped out of the sixties with her long curly hair, black, horn-rimmed glasses, tie-dyed t-shirt and too-tight jeans.

Rebecca is also here, looking radiant as always. Her long black hair tumbles down to her waist now that she's off-duty. Danny is standing next to her chatting her up. Didn't take you long to get over Diane, I think, but Rebecca is miles away a better choice for a companion than that bitch. Danny spots me and goes over to the washtub full of ice water under the banner, plucks out a bottle of Heine and brings it over to me with a hat that he grabbed from the table.

I take the beer and ignore the hat. "Where's my shot?" I ask him.

"Not now," he says. "Wait till after you get home."

Since when are you my nursemaid, Danny boy?

"Hey everybody," he shouts. "It's the birthday girl." His Marine drill sergeant's voice carries much better than Mom's, so everyone stops talking and looks at me. Oh brother, please let's get this over with!

They make me a place at the table with the hats and Mom clears a space for the cake that Danny brings from the kitchen. It's ablaze with twenty-one candles as Danny sets it down in front of me. I take a deep breath and blow them all out, then everybody sings *Happy Birthday* and I tear up in spite of myself. People begin handing me wrapped presents one by one and I dutifully unwrap each one and make polite comments about the contents. When it's Lupe's turn, she hands me a small box wrapped non-ostentatiously in matte silver paper with a blue ribbon. I unwrap it to find a royal blue box with the logo of a local jeweler on top. I pop the box open and find a folded piece of paper. Underneath are two matching rings with two small diamonds embraced by a figure eight on each ring. OMG! Is this what I think? I unfold the paper and find a single word inside. *Si!*

It's a struggle to put the box gently down on the table instead of flinging it away. Then I leap to my feet, put my arms around her and kiss her. I know they're all watching and I don't care!

When I come up for air, I look into her eyes, shining through her tears.

"What changed?" I ask her.

"I think about it like you said. You let me and Eduardo move in with you when we were living in a lousy trailer. You got me away from that strip club and you got me a good job at the gym. You saved my life from those terrible men! I love you and so does Eduardo. So I will go to hell for you." I can feel her trembling in my arms. I kiss her again, like it's the last time I will ever kiss anyone.

I finally turn to look at Uncle and find him studying the wall. He's got a box on his lap wrapped in pink paper with a purple ribbon. I disentangle from Lupe and go over to him.

He looks up at me with a non-committal expression, but I can see the hurt in his eyes. Eat shit old man, I think.

He offers me the box. "Happy birthday, Nattie," he says, but his heart isn't in it.

"Thanks." I open it and find a black plastic gun case. I take it to the table, undo the snaps and open the lid. Inside is a Ruger LC9-S, with the lower done in a pink and black camo pattern. I remove the pistol, drop the mag and put it in the box. Then I try to work the slide. Holy shit, it's tight! I can barely get it to move.

"They're real stiff at first," Uncle says. "You oil it good and put a few hundred rounds through it, it will get better. Now don't you ever make me sorry I got you that."

"I won't, Uncle," I tell him and mean it.

The office has gone dead silent. Guns will do that in mixed company these days. Kwan and Fields give me disapproving looks and Rebecca and Mom both look nervous. Danny and Kidd are wearing great big smiles. So is Lupe. She grew up with violence and no protection, so she knows.

"Don't you carry that concealed without a permit, neither," Uncle says.

"I won't," I lie. "I'll go to the Sheriff's office tomorrow and apply for one."

I put the mag back in the little gun and put it back in the case. I close the lid and redo the snaps.

CRASH! Something smashes through the front window, flies into the room and rolls on the floor. A glowing, orange snake slithers from the bottleneck on to the worn carpet, then a great sheet of flame erupts.

CRASH! A second flaming missile shatters against the wall. The tattered wallpaper instantly goes up.

CRASH! Jesus God, not again! A third bottle dances crazily across the room, spewing flaming liquid everywhere. Kwan screams as some of it splashes on her arm and her blouse immediately ignites. Fields starts beating Kwan's arm with both hands to extinguish the flames.

Except for Kwan and Fields, we've all been standing there like idiots, refusing to believe our eyes. My chest constricts from the hot air and the rising smoke and for a second I'm back in the basement of that strip club in a different conflagration. Something primal courses through me and I whirl and dash madly for the front door. I am not alone.

The only thing that saves me is the proximity of the living room to the front door. By the time I burst out on the porch, I can hardly see through my burning eyes and my breath heaves in great, shuddering gasps. Something hits me from behind and sends me tumbling over the porch railing. I land on the hard ground behind the bushes I used to play in, tearing the shit out of my blouse on the way down. My hand opens when I hit and the gun case I've been clutching leaps out of my grasp. I scramble on my hands and knees to the front lawn and stand up.

I take inventory in the orange twilight. There's Danny and Kidd and Fields and Kwan, who's madly ripping off her still smoldering blouse to stand on the lawn in her black brassiere. Even from here I can see the blisters raising on her ebon skin. Mom is outside too and she's got Eduardo in her arms. Rebecca stumbles through the front door, her hair and clothes smoking. Danny immediately throws her to the ground and begins rolling her in the damp grass as she screams madly. Wait a minute! Where's Lupe? I don't see Lupe! And Uncle!

I start to run back to the front steps when a strong hand grabs my pony tail and yanks me back. The pain in my scalp brings fresh tears to my eyes. Strong arms lock around my chest. I can't see him behind me, but the brown skin tells me who it is - Kidd!

"Lemme go! Lupe! Uncle!"

The arms tighten, pushing the breath out of me so I stop yelling. I may as well be trying to move a boulder. I hear the sound of shattering glass again as the living room windows blow out and a terrible whooshing roar begins to fill the air as the fire bellows its war cry. Black smoke pours out of the front door like an obscene serpent from the pits of hell.

Abruptly an apparition emerges from the snake's head. Uncle in his wheelchair! He's bent nearly double and the only thing that's keeping him from pitching out of it is a hand entangled in his shirt collar. Lupe!

The chair reaches the front steps and he does fall out of it, nose-diving down the stairs, with Lupe and the chair tumbling after. The arm around me goes suddenly slack and I stumble forward as well, because of all of the pressure I was exerting to get free. Kidd is a step ahead of me when we reach them. He grabs Uncle and pulls him away from the burning house while I do the same for Lupe.

She's gasping and vomiting as I help her away from the now nearly unbearable heat. Kidd follows with Uncle in his arms. We have to go clear across the street to get far enough away from the searing inferno before we can stop.

The flames licking out of the living room windows set the porch roof ablaze, then meander up the outside wall to the pointed garret I so loved as a child. The old house is becoming fully involved now — the century-old pine shingles burn like the turpentine that is made from them. The hollow feeling in the pit of my stomach grows until I can't bear it anymore and I fall to the ground in tears.

A fire truck arrives in a blaze of lights with blaring sirens, then another and another. Black-clad men play streams of water over the house and the smoke becomes so intense that we have to move even further back. An ambulance arrives and the paramedics attend to the burn victims — Kwan, Rebecca, Lupe and Uncle. Thank God none of them are burned too severely, although Kwan and Rebecca have second-degree burns that will take painful weeks to heal. The rest of us escaped quickly enough so that we have nothing more serious than a bad sunburn, but the paramedics put all of us on oxygen bottles as a precaution against smoke inhalation. The medics also insist on taking the burned people to the hospital for observation.

Danny comes up as Eduardo and I are getting into the car to go home. He has something in his hand. A gun case.

"Here. I found it on the lawn. At least you'll have something for your birthday."

The tears start flowing again. Danny awkwardly embraces me while he's holding the case.

"We'll find who did this, Nattie."

I push away and look at him.

"Danny, the rings... they're still in the house." I look over there. What house?

He starts to speak, then stops. His face is red and he looks at the ground.

I take the gun from him. I don't say so, but I know I'm going to need it. I totally hope I find the motherfucker before the cops do.

Chapter 14.

It's 9:00 A.M. and Eduardo still isn't up, which is unusual for him. I go to his room and find him asleep under his bed, wrapped up in a blanket like a mummy. I tucked him in when I put him to bed, so he must've gotten up afterwards — I wonder if he slept there all night. He's come and crawled in with me and his Mom before when he's had a bad dream, but I guess he didn't feel comfortable doing that when it was just me there. I feel a totally inappropriate pang of guilt for not checking on him in the middle of the night, but I took some prazosin and slept like the dead.

My phone plays Lupe's song while I'm getting Eduardo his breakfast. She tells me that she's being released from the hospital at noon. The nurse told her that they're keeping Kwan and Rebecca for at least another day. Uncle Amos is another matter entirely. He suffered heart failure from smoke inhalation and is in intensive care. His doctor said that she's guardedly optimistic that he'll be moved to a regular room by the end of the day, but it could be a week or more before he's released.

No sooner do I end the call than the doorbell rings. I look through the peephole and see Danny, looking skyward as people do when waiting at a door.

I open the door.

"Hey Danny. What's up?"

"I was just wondering if you wanted to go to the range this morning, sight in your new Ruger."

And you had to come all the way over here to ask me that? Somebody steal your phone? "Lupe's still in the hospital. I've got to get Eduardo off to school."

"I don't mind waiting."

I think about it. I'm mildly PO'd that Danny chose to pressure me by coming instead of calling, but he's been attentive lately because of all my troubles. But I wanted to go to the jeweler's this morning and replace the rings before Lupe gets home from the hospital. I tell Danny as much.

"Would you mind if I went with you? We could go to the range when you're finished — it shouldn't take all morning to get the rings."

I know which jeweler Lupe used — the business name was on the ring box. So Danny's right — if the rings are in stock, it shouldn't take long at all.

"OK, I guess, as long as you realize that the rings are v important and that I want to be here when Lupe gets home from the hospital."

"That's OK with me."

Eduardo balks at getting ready for school, probably because the kid just knows that Danny and me are gonna be adulting while he's in school and he'll have the JOMO. But Danny gives him a drill sergeant's glare and there's no more trouble.

We walk Eduardo out of the complex to the bus stop and wait until he's safely aboard. Lupe had been letting him walk to the bus by himself, but given recent events, that's just cray. And Eduardo doesn't seem to mind the attention. I think he's taking a liking to Danny.

We hop in Danny's pickup (the guy always has to drive, right?) and we're at the jeweler's when they open. The rings are a stock item, so we're outta there quick. We lock the bag in the toolbox in the back of Danny's truck with my pistol.

The range is not open yet when we get there. There's a bench outside the door, so we park it until the place opens.

The warming trend that began yesterday is continuing and it feels good to just sit and let the morning sun bake me. Danny seems to be making an effort to give me my space on the smallish bench. I swear I can still catch a whiff of wood smoke along with his body odor.

"I hope 3M can recover from this," Danny says.

"What do you mean?"

"We had a rough time when Amos was in the hospital last year. He's the one who knows how to beat the bushes for the insurance jobs that are our lifeblood. Things were finally starting to turn around again and then this happens. I mean, we don't even have an office anymore! All of our computers and records are gone. Clients can still contact us by cell phone, but we don't even have a record of hours spent so we can bill them. Not to mention that your Mom and Amos are now homeless."

"Where is Mom, anyway? I haven't seen or heard from her since last night."

"She stayed with Leon and his wife last night. I imagine she went to hospital to be with Amos this morning."

A pang of guilt stabs me. That's where I should be, not basking in the sun. But I know that I'd be useless hanging around the hospital — besides, they only allow one visitor at a time in ICU and that's Mom.

I push the guilty, negative thoughts away. "So what now, Danny? This asshole showed us that he's not just after me anymore. He's after all of us. We've got to find him!"

"Did you ever make that list Amos asked you for?"

"No, because there totally is no list. I've tried and I can't think of anyone who would hate me enough to do these things."

"Goddammit, somebody sure as fuck does!" His uncharacteristic profanity startles me. "Why don't you talk to that shrink of yours? Maybe she can help you figure it out."

That hits me way wrong. "You sure seemed like you wanted to make her your OTP at the party before the shit came flying through the window." His face tells me that went right over his head. He can be so clueless sometimes.

"OTP?"

"One true pairing. Your bae."

"No! Hey, I was just being nice to her!"

"Doesn't hurt that she's got killer looks, does it? Beats the hell out of Diane."

"That has nothing to do with it!"

He's so damned indignant that I just have to burst out laughing. A vein throbs in his temple and he's on the verge of yelling, then something clicks and he's ROFL right along with me.

We've got our arms on each others' shoulders as the hysteria subsides. I push him back and look at his face. He's totally a big kid - that crew cut makes him look like they let him out of high school last week.

"We really need to be doing more of that," I tell him.

"What, fighting?" he smiles.

"No, laughing, you jerk! If we don't, we're screwed. And I'll talk to Rebecca to see if she can help me come up with a name or two." A pause. "Want me to put in a good word for you with her?"

He gives me a peculiar look, like I said something wrong. "Don't you dare!"

"You could do worse than a beautiful Johns Hopkins Ph.D," I tell him. "Like Diane, for instance."

"Like I said, she used to be fun to be with. I really don't know what's changed with her. She's been just plain nasty lately."

"You guys weren't..." I want to say hooking up, but what comes out is "...really serious?"

"God, no! We went on a few dates is all, to bars mostly. She likes country music, pinball and darts, like I do." He's still got that odd expression, like why do you care? Somehow I don't believe him.

Ernie arrives and lets us into the range. We go thru the first door to the sound lock and grab a target. Danny chooses one with nine separate bullseyes for sighting in — no comic book thugs today. The range is cool and dark when we open the second door and smells strongly of gunpowder. Ernie flips on the overhead lights and we go to our booth.

Since he's the better marksman, Danny sights in the Ruger. He runs the target out to seven yards and fires a five shot group using the iron sights, then reels it back in to check it. You could cover the group with a quarter and I only see three holes, even though I know he fired five times. Looks like Ruger did a damn good job adjusting the sights at the factory.

Danny runs the target back out. With no magazine in the Ruger, he activates the laser using the button on the front of the grip. He sights through the iron sights to check the alignment of the little red dot, then uses the tiny Allen wrench that came with the gun to make an adjustment. He slips in a mag, racks the slide and fires five slow shots with the red dot dead center in the bullseye. He brings the target back and I can see the group is high and left. He uses the Allen wrench again. Back out goes the target, then five more rounds with the laser in the center of the bullseye. He reels it back in and I can see that the group is now dead center.

Since there's nobody else on the range, Danny slips his ear muffs off and lets them dangle around his neck. He motions for me to do the same.

"Go ahead and shoot the rest of the bullseyes," he says. "Just put the red dot in the center and keep both eyes open. Watch the dot to make sure you're not pulling the muzzle off target when you press the trigger."

I do as he says. The Ruger has a short, crisp trigger action and significant recoil because it's such a light gun. The red dot shows me that I'm jerking the muzzle upwards when I shoot, so I concentrate on holding it down and my groups get better. They're still about three inches in diameter, but if that's in the center of the bad guy's chest, I think I'm on fleek.

After I've shot a box of fifty rounds, my stinging hands tell me I'm done.

I clear the Ruger, pack it up in its case and we bounce. In the parking lot, Danny opens the tool box in the back of his truck and I drop the Ruger in and lock it inside.

As we turn to get into the truck, a car pulls up behind it so close it almost touches the bumper, making it impossible to back out. The driver's door opens and Detective Russell gets out. WTF is he doing here? I feel Danny stiffen beside me.

"Hey partner," Russell addresses Danny. I note his sarcastic tone.

"What's up, Josh?" Danny can't keep the coldness out of his voice either.

"You'll be happy to hear that the governor's office has tabbed me to investigate the firebombing of your office. And don't bother introducing me to your girlfriend. We've already met." He turns to me. "Funny how you keep turning up in arson investigations, Natalie." He returns to Danny. "Given our present location, I assume you're carrying. So keep your hands in sight and assume the position." He points to his car. "You too, Natalie."

"She's not carrying." Danny says.

"Right!" says Russell. "On the car, Natalie."

We have no choice but to do as we're told. Russell frisks Danny first, removing the 1911 and the .357 that Danny keeps in an ankle holster as a backup. He unloads both weapons and stows them in the trunk of his car.

"You can show me your CCW when we get downtown, Merkel. Right now, you stay on that car."

Russell then moves on to me. I can smell him as he steps up behind me — the sourness of sweat masked by that cologne old guys wear — Old Spice. His search is embarrassingly thorough — he roughly kneads both of my breasts and spends way too much time feeling my crotch — given the tight jeans I'm wearing, it should be evident that I have no weapon there. That red hand of his creeps me out. I want to turn and slap the shit out of him, but I know that will just land me in jail and probably Danny too. I know he'll come to my defense if I let on that Russell is groping me.

When he's finished enjoying himself, Russell backs off and says, "All right, you two. Time for a ride downtown."

"Can't we do this here, Josh?" Danny asks with an exasperated tone.

"Nope." Russell moves behind Danny with a pair of cuffs and grabs his wrist, pulling it off the top of the car. Danny nearly goes down but manages to straighten up as Russell brings his other hand behind him, then clicks the cuffs tight. He produces a second pair of cuffs, then it's my turn. He cinches them way tighter than necessary, then puts both of us in the back seat of his car.

We ride downtown in silence. My cuffs are cutting off the circulation in my hands, as evidenced by a painful tingling and a spot between my shoulder blades begins throbbing incessantly. But I stay quiet - I won't give that bully the satisfaction that he's got me shook AF.

When we get to the cop shop, Russell parks out front, then his motives become clear. He takes us right through the front door! I know he's getting a huge rush from perp walking his hated ex-partner past his former coworkers in handcuffs. The dude is so zero chill.

He puts us in a small, cinder block room that smells like it started life as a rest room, locking our cuffs to rings in the top of the table in front of us. He goes out and leaves us alone.

"What's going on here?" I ask Danny.

"You know they can hear us, right?" he says. I nod and repeat the question.

"Apparently Josh has held a grudge," Danny says. "I'm just sorry you got dragged into our feud, Nattie."

"How did he find us at the range?"

"Tracked one of our cell phones, likely."

"But what's he even doing on this case? The firebombing happened outside the city and he's a city cop."

"This state has a Highway Patrol for traffic enforcement, but it isn't charged with investigating crimes that cross city or county lines. So the Governor's office has decided that the most efficient way to investigate such crimes is to give statewide jurisdiction to the appropriate local law enforcement agency on a case-by-case basis. That way, they don't have to maintain yet another police force. Since Josh had already caught the Legends firebombing, it made sense to give him this one too, because the two attacks seem to be related."

I realize that I never told Danny about encountering Russell in the hospital. I do so now.

"Well that explains why he's interested in you," Danny says. "How do you know this LeBrowne character, anyway?"

Well aware that the cops could be listening to our conversation, I tell Danny the same lie I told Russell earlier.

"I thought you'd left all that stripper stuff behind you," was Danny's response. It just hits me wrong.

"Hey, like it or not, that club was part of my life for a while. I made some friends there. I don't have to apologize for that!"

"I don't…" His reply gets cut off as the door opens and Russel comes in. He was obviously eavesdropping and when he heard a consistent story, he decided to come in.

"Leave her out of this, Josh," says Danny. "She's got nothing to do with the problem between you and me."

"It's just strange that she's connected to two separate firebombings less than forty-eight hours apart," Russell says.

"I want my lawyer!" I say. That shuts up both of them.

"Why do you need a lawyer if you didn't do anything wrong, Natalie?" Russell says.

"Because it's my right, Josh." I make it a point to use his first name if he's going to use mine. "I'll let him know you've been asking me questions without a Miranda warning."

"I don't have to mirandize you if I haven't arrested you. Should I?"

"Bullshit, Josh," says Danny. "You put us in cuffs and dragged us in here. That's an arrest if I ever saw one. Where's your probable cause?"

"I just told you. She's connected to two firebombings and she went to the hospital to check up on a gang leader."

"Shut up, Danny! Lawyer!" I shout as loud as I can.

"Fine. You want to do this the hard way, that's what we'll do." Russell leaves the room again.

"Now you've done it." Danny says.

"What do you mean?"

"Get ready for a long wait. He can hold us for forty-eight hours without putting us in front of a judge. His probable cause is bullshit and he knows it, so he'll probably hold us as long as he can before cutting us loose, just to be a dick."

"What about a lawyer?"

"You don't have the right to one if you're not being questioned or going before a judge."

"But we get one phone call!"

"That's a Hollywood myth." Danny says. As a former cop, he should know.

It doesn't make sense to me that Russell is doing this. Danny has made it pretty clear that his former partner hates him, but I've never done anything to him. A disquieting thought occurs. Throughout this whole thing, I've been assuming that someone has been doing these terrible things to me for revenge and I totally can't think of anyone who would hate me that much. But what if it's not me that's the target?

What if it's Russell that's doing this? Danny is his former partner and Russell thinks Danny betrayed him to IA. Leon Kidd also used to be a cop in this department. He made enemies when he agreed to guard Uncle Amos in the hospital when the department refused to do so and even moreso when he busted a drug dealer that the department was protecting. So that's one more reason for Russell to hate 3M. A cop would know how to hack surveillance equipment and a closed-circuit TV system isn't too different from that. A cop would know how to use laws and regulations against someone, for instance, Title IX and immigration laws. A cop would certainly know how to make and use a Molotov cocktail. Could Josh Russell and other cops be persecuting me to get revenge on Danny and Kidd?

I notice that my hands locked in front of me on the table have become blue and numb because the cuffs have cut off the circulation. The pain in my shoulders and back is rapidly becoming intolerable and I have to pee.

"Hey! Let us out of here! I have to use the bathroom! You can't do this to us!"

"The room is soundproof unless they have the intercom turned on," Danny says. "They're doing this on purpose to punish us. Screaming only makes it worse. Try to stick it out."

I know Danny's right, but that doesn't make it any easier. I suffer silently, because I don't want to make it any worse for him. Finally, hydraulic pressure wins and my bladder lets go, soaking my underwear and my jeans. Now I know why the room smells like it does.

"I am so sorry that happened to you, Nattie," Danny says. "Don't worry. I'll get Josh for this."

Cold fear almost makes me pee some more. "Don't give them a reason to arrest you, Danny. Let's just get through this."

He doesn't reply.

It seems like forever before Russel enters and unlocks my cuffs. He indicates the mess under my chair. "Some people just have no self-control," he says. "That's why they end up here. Come on, we have a nice holding cell for you."

"What about my clothes? I need to change."

"If you were under arrest, we'd have a jumpsuit for you. But you're not. I've got no probable cause. We're just detaining you pending investigation. So you're out of luck," he smirks.

He takes me to an alcove with a barred window and tells me to empty my pockets. I give my wallet, change and phone to the policewoman inside, who puts them in a brown envelope and seals it. She writes her name across the flap and pushes it out to me.

"Sign it like I did," she says.

I comply and she tosses the envelope into an open plastic container on the floor full of similar manila envelopes. I wonder if I'll ever see my stuff again. I'm so glad my pistol and our wedding rings are still locked in Danny's truck.

Russell then escorts me to an elevator that takes us upstairs and we go into a large room that has a single big cell with half a dozen women inside. Body odor mixed with perfume makes me want to gag, but I stifle it — show no weakness, Nattie! The women's' clothes suggest that all but one are hookers — the last one is an older lady in a dress like my meemaw would wear and she's apparently asleep on a bench against the wall. Russell signals a cop in a room with a window looking out on the cell and the door unlocks with a buzz. He pushes me inside and closes the door.

If Russell put me in here to intimidate me, it's an epic fail. A large black lady in a tight gauzy top, black stockings and high boots takes one look at the front of my jeans and says, "Oh no, honey! What did those pigs do to you?" Apparently, these ladies of the night are routinely mistreated by the cops, so they're treating me like a sister under the skin.

Meemaw eventually wakes up and I find out she's in here for shoplifting. From a grocery store! She tells me she won't go on food stamps because she doesn't want charity. So she steals instead. Go figure.

There's not much more to say about my incarceration. I don't get a phone call. Trays of food and water arrive periodically and we're taken out to the bathroom every few hours. The old lady is eventually removed by our jailers and we never see her again. Gradually, the hookers are released and more come in to replace them. Apparently, the cops don't even bother charging them — they just keep them here as long as is legal, then put 'em back on the street until the next time. What a system!

My life becomes sleeping, eating and using the bathroom. I remove my sodden panties the first time I'm allowed to go and flush them — I hope they jam up their pipes! My jeans dry eventually and the smell fades into the background. I can't tell how much time has passed because there's no clock or window. I ask a woman who's just been locked up what day it is and she's says it's Friday night. Danny and I were taken on Thursday morning. So they've got to let me go soon!

Finally, I hear my name. A police lady unlocks the door, takes me out and escorts me downstairs to the same window. I give my name to the clerk and she finds my envelope in a file cabinet.

"Open it in front of me and verify that everything's there."

I briefly consider saying that something was taken just to cause trouble, but by now I totally want out of here! So I sign the paper she gives me.

"Where's Danny Merkel?" I ask my guard.

"I don't know," she says. She escorts me to the front door of the police station and says, "You're free to go."

It's daytime, warmish and raining lightly. I look for a place to get out of the weather. There are shops and a coffee shop nearby, but I know that I'm stinky AF and don't want to be told to leave. So I put my back to the precinct building and pull out my phone. I've got to call Lupe. I'm not looking forward to it because I know she'll be frantic — she hasn't heard from me in days and I'd rather she didn't drive in that condition. I could call Mom, but she's probably busy with Uncle. I wonder if he's even out of the hospital. I know Fields was discharged, but Kwan was still there as of Thursday. God! Why am I so confused?

A car pulls up to the curb and the door opens.

"Nattie!"

Danny's getting out?

"Come on, Nattie, get in."

I totally can't help myself. I run over and throw my arms around his neck, pee-smell and all!

After we unhook, we get in the car. A woman I don't know is driving. I roll the window all the way down before she catches the smell and orders us out of the car.

"Nattie, this is Melanie." Melanie? Who the hell is Melanie? "She drives for Uber." Oh! Danny gives her the address of the gun range where we left his pickup.

It's another hour before Danny drops me off at the townhouse. "I'm going home to sleep," he says. "I'll call you later."

I've got my pistol case in one hand and the bag with the rings in the other. I see Lupe's car in her spot, so I ring the bell rather than mess with the keys.

She opens the door. Her face hardens when she sees me. "Where have you been?" she says angrily.

Chapter 15.

Lupe is on a total rant. "I was so worried about you! I get home from hospital, see Eduardo sitting on walk in front of door because nobody meet him at bus to let him in!" Her broken English tells me she's way triggered.

"Chill, Bae! I wasn't here because I couldn't be. I got busted!" She looks puzzled now. "Arrested! Thrown in jail!"

"What for?"

I tell her the whole, sad story. Now she's crying and apologizing. I can tell she's not herself. I know that her upcoming hearing is a total mind-fuck.

"If you were in jail, then you don't know," she says.

"Don't know what?"

"We are on TV. The news. The video!"

WTF? "What do you mean?"

"We were on channel 5 last night. It was a story about the fire at the detective agency and about you getting expelled from college even though you saved that girl last year."

This makes no sense! "What do you mean?" I ask her again.

She picks up the remote and clicks on the TV. "Here, you see. I recorded it."

She uses the DVR to play back a news segment from last night. A national news segment! The story begins with the bombing at 3M, then segues into the Title IX investigation, which includes a brief clip of the sex video that's SFW. They interview Simonson, who says "No comment" with a snarky smirk. They even dredge up that business about the girl in the box from last year.

"Ms. McMasters' was unavailable for comment. But I'm sure America is interested in getting her side of the story," the reporter says.

I can't even! This is the last thing I need!

"I unplugged the phone again," Lupe said. "It will not stop ringing and it is all for you."

I pull out my cell and thumb the button, but the screen stays black. It must've gotten drained while the cops had it. I wonder if Russell was snooping on it. I guess he must have been and forgot to turn it off. I plug it into the charger on the dining bar, then I turn on the house phone. The answering machine begins blinking, indicating unheard messages.

I cycle through them, listening to each one just long enough to confirm it's a reporter before I delete it. Then comes a familiar voice with just a hint of a Spanish accent.

"Nattie, it's Roderigo."

Roderigo!

Roderigo Hernandez is a nationally known TV personality, famous for his interviews — he's interviewed people from heads of state to the likes of me. No shit, he actually did do me last year when I was indicted for murder after saving that girl from Randall Leighton. The interview was broadcast nationally and the ensuing public outrage resulted in the rescindment of the indictment by the D.A. because she wanted to punish me for saving a life.

Roderigo called again after the business at the strip club, but I dissed him because I totally wanted to put all the drama behind me. I just can't seem to do that, now can I? The thought occurs to me that an interview might just help with the Title IX bullshit, but I totally do not want to be discussing my sex life on national TV!

The other messages are from the media as well. But then I hear another familiar voice.

"Hi Nattie. It's Rebecca. I'm afraid I have some rather bad news. Please call me at home when you get this."

At home? I hope that doesn't mean what I think it does.

I clap her back and she picks right up. Bad sign.

"This is Rebecca."

"Rebecca, it's Nattie. How are you?"

"I've been better, Nattie." A ball of ice begins growing in my stomach.

"What?"

"I'm no longer able to see you in my office on campus."

"They fired you!"

"Not exactly. I got a call from my department head. She told me it would be much better for all concerned if I withdrew my offer to act as your advocate for the Title IX hearing. I told her that I couldn't do that."

This is all my fault! "Rebecca, you didn't have to…"

"Yes, I did. I can't let you go into that hearing without an advocate. Simonson would eat you alive."

"So what happened when you said that?"

"She told me to take the weekend to think it over. She knows that firing me would create a stink, but I've got a tenure review coming up in a few months. If I'm denied tenure, my career at State is effectively over anyway. And leaving under a cloud would make getting a non-tenured job at another university very difficult."

"Well, if you're not fired, why can't we meet in your office?"

"Because I handed in my resignation."

"What? Why? You should totally fight!"

I can see her smile over the phone. "That's my Nattie!" A pause. "This whole affair has made me revaluate what I'm accomplishing as a University professor. The fact is that I get much more satisfaction from helping you students with your challenges than I do from teaching, writing papers and dealing with university bullshit."

Did she just say bullshit? "I've never heard you talk like that before, Rebecca."

"You must be rubbing off on me. Anyway, I've been thinking about going into private practice for a while now. This gives me the opportunity. And I can still be your advocate. I don't have to hold a university position to do that. And Simonson can't threaten my career anymore."

The tears well up and I can't speak.

"Nattie? Are you there?"

"I'm here. I want to thank you for what you're doing for me."

"It's not all for you. I really do think this will be better for me, too."

"I need to see you soon. We need to talk about who might be persecuting me."

"They've scheduled your hearing for Wednesday evening. We need to talk about what you can expect and formulate a strategy to keep you in school."

"OMG! Lupe's immigration hearing is Thursday morning. Can't we reschedule?"

"I doubt it. Remember, Simonson is in charge of this."

"Right." After hearing that, I know what I have to do. "Rebecca, I don't want you to be my advocate at the hearing anymore," I tell her.

"Nattie, it's all right. It's what I want to do."

"But it isn't what I want to do. I have someone else in mind."

Dead silence on the phone. Finally, "May I ask who?"

"I'd rather not say right now."

More silence. I'm crying inside, but I won't show it! "All right, Natalie, it's your decision," she says.

"Yes it is. I'm sorry you left your job over it. And I still want to meet with you. I totally need your help to figure out who's doing this to me."

Her voice is cold. "We can certainly do that. Monday?"

"Sounds good. I'll call you."

I give Lupe the gist of the conversation.

"Don't you worry about me!" she says. "You do what you gotta so you can stay in school. I talked to Chica and she says the judge will probably continue the matter."

That reminds me. I pick up the bag with the rings from the couch where I dropped it and get out the package. It's wrapped in silver paper with a blue ribbon, just like the one Lupe gave me at my birthday party. She recognizes it and begins to cry. She takes the package and nearly drops it as she tries to unwrap it. I take it back and do it for her, then hand her the blue box.

Her hands tremble as she opens it. She removes a ring and offers it to me. I extend my left hand with my fore- and middle fingers bent so she can slip it on my ring finger.

"Say, 'with this ring, I thee wed'," I tell her and she complies. I take the box back from her and place the other ring on her finger, saying "With this ring I thee wed!" My voice is stronger, more assured. I know that this is the right thing!

Now my voice trembles a little. "That's it, Lupe. We're married. We'll have to go to City Hall on Monday to get a paper from a judge for your hearing, but that won't change anything between us. We're married because we say so, not because a church or a government does. That we love each other is all that matters!"

I take her in my arms and kiss her.

Chapter 16.

I spend the rest of the weekend at home with my fam. My new wife and I make tender love on our wedding night and sleep in late Sunday morning. We are awakened in the morning by our son climbing into bed with us. The old me is a little shook because Lupe and I are both naked, but Eduardo doesn't even notice — he just snuggles between us and goes right to sleep.

Later we get up and Lupe makes one of her fab Mexican breakfasts. We spend the rest of the day watching TV and playing games and the rain outside makes it all totally rad. Later I get online and check out the requirements for a civil wedding. We need $20 for the license and two witnesses. I call up Kwan and Fields and ask if they'll do the honors. Fields says yes but Kwan is still feeling gnarly from her burns and passes. I wrack my brain for somebody else and decide to try Rebecca, because I need to go over there afterwards anyway. Rebecca says she'd be honored, so she's not too mad that I dissed her for the hearing.

Monday morning, we get Eduardo off to school and then get dressed for our second nuptials. I find a tight, knee-length silver party dress among Becca's things and Lupe wears a pleated, multicolored, traditional Mexican dress that falls to her ankles. It's still raining as we go out to our respective cars and warm enough to make me uncomfortable in my finery. Screw it! I won't let shitty weather ruin the most important day in my life.

An old blue-haired lady at City Hall looks at us strangely when Lupe and I ask for a marriage license, but she doesn't throw me any shade so I let her look like she wants. She takes my $20, our names and address and prints out the license.

"Take that down the Hall to Courtroom 1C."

Fields and Rebecca show up while I'm dealing with Meemaw. Fields is in her typical man's shirt and torn blue jeans, but Rebecca is radiant in a deep maroon strapless gown that winds all the way to the floor. She's got her long, ebon hair in a braid that hangs nearly to her waist in front.

A sign directs us to the courtroom where we get in line behind two other couples — an older man and woman who look like they're dressed for church and two guys in matching powder blue tuxedos.

Holding civil weddings in a courtroom makes sense — there's plenty of room for any guests in the gallery. Only we don't have any. The service is short, a simple exchange of rings. After I give our marriage license to the magistrate, we read our canned vows simultaneously from a laminated card:

"Before these witnesses, I take you to be my lawfully wedded wife for better or worse, for richer or poorer, to love and honor and cherish as long as we both shall live." My card said "husband", but I changed that. The magistrate didn't seem to notice.

Both of us tear up as we place the rings on each other's fingers as we did yesterday in the townhouse. The magistrate doesn't tell me to kiss the bride, but I do it anyway. He makes a note on our marriage license and gives it back to me. "Take this to Miss Strickland outside. Bring your witnesses. She'll get you your marriage certificate."

So it's back to Meemaw who still looks like she has a case of hemorrhoids and she gives us the paper that says we're married in the eyes of The Law. We both sign it, as do Rebecca and Fields, then Meemaw notarizes it. Hopefully this will keep Lupe in the U.S.A.

Lupe and I drove separate cars, so we part with a kiss in front of the courthouse, her to go work and me to follow Rebecca to her place.

Turns out that Rebecca's place it not far from our townhouse. I follow her SUV down a long gravel driveway flanked by oak trees into a spacious clearing in which her sprawling home is nestled. It's a modern design, with a glass-walled A-frame overlooking a landscaped circular driveway and two single-story red brick annexes extending from either side, with a riot of small blue flowers blooming along their length. The windows are mirrored so you can't see in from outside. Seems a little ritzy for a college professor, but she did go to Hopkins.

She parks in a matching garage off to one side and I pull the Z-car in front of the other door.

Inside, the house smells of flowers. It's well-lit because of all the windows and airy because of the high ceilings, but the rooms seem somewhat dim and muted by the rain outside. The place is sparsely furnished in leather and stainless steel much like Rebecca's campus office. She leads me to a circular staircase that goes to the second floor of the A-frame. Next to it is a four-sided box with a door, made of black metal and glass, that extends to the second floor. My first impression is that it's some kind of sculpture, then I get it.

"You have an elevator?"

"Some of my patients are physically challenged," she says.

A corridor leads to upstairs bedrooms in the annexes and a spacious office in front has a floor-to ceiling window overlooking the driveway. I follow her into the office. I know we're not far from the state capitol, but the scene outside that window could be miles from civilization. She waves me to a leather chaise from which I can see outside and takes a seat in an easy chair alongside.

"So we're here to help you think of someone who could be responsible for tormenting you these last weeks," she says. "Before we go there, do want to talk about the Title IX hearing on Wednesday evening?"

"No," I say. "I think I've got that under control."

Her brow puckers — that was obviously not what she wanted to hear. "You do realize that this hearing could spell the end of your time at State," she says.

"Of course I do! But I also know that it's stacked against me. That's why I'm going to do what I'm going to do."

"And what is that, Natalie?"

So I'm Natalie again. "I said I don't want to talk about it." I hope she's not going to kick me out again, but my mind is made up.

"Fine. You're a big girl," she says. "Now let's see if we can figure out who's out to get you."

"I'm at a loss," I say. "Before the incidents at the strip club, I didn't really have any enemies."

"You have an ex-fiancé," she points out.

"True. Michael's a loser, but he's the one who broke it off when I started pushing him for a wedding date. He just wanted to screw me and he thought that being engaged was the best way. He's probably out there now doing the same thing to some other girl."

"Any other boyfriends that might have an axe to grind?" A name leaps into my head and she sees it on my face. "Who is it?" she presses.

"Nobody. He's dead."

"Did you kill him?" It says a lot about our relationship that she would even ask me that. I want to say no, but what comes out is "Well, sorta…"

"What does that mean, Natalie?"

I sigh. I see that I'm going to have to tell her the story…

She's dead!

The words echoed in my head as I gazed at the small, crumpled photograph in my hand.

I get premonitions sometimes. It's happened ever since I was a little girl. They're rarely wrong. And mostly, they're totally dismal.

Freshman year, I was living on a quiet side street near the university in an older three-bedroom house with Kwan and Fields. For some reason, we were always finding trash in our driveway — McDonald's bags, beer bottles, even hubcaps and other car parts. We all developed what we called trash radar and when we saw any, we'd pick it up and put it in the garbage can. Some folks in the neighborhood had let it be known that they were not totally happy about college students renting houses there and we didn't want to give them any more reason to be that way. That's why I noticed the crumpled piece of paper lying on the ground where the driveway met the street.

The girl in the picture looked fifteen or sixteen. Cute, with shoulder-length dark hair, large doe-like eyes and a hesitant smile. The photo was black-and-white and blurry, like it had been crumpled into a tight ball before he tossed it, but I could see that she was wearing a double-stranded pearl necklace and a dress that left her shoulders bare — a prom gown maybe. She was holding three white roses against her chest.

There was writing in pencil on the back of the photo. I could make out at least some of it:

CB —

It's been a totally great year! I never knew I could be so much in love! I can't wait to see what happens next...

I couldn't make out the rest of the sentence, nor the signature, which looked like it began with an "A". There was a heart drawn after it. A date from a year ago was written sideways along the border, like an afterthought.

I knew in my heart that this demure, pretty young girl was dead and I wonder if CB, who savagely crumpled her picture and flung it in our driveway, was responsible for that or if he was totally devastated and willing to give anything not to have destroyed her love token. I needed to find out. But where to start?

I had a contact at the police department. Danny. I met him when he was on campus to lecture us women about how to stay safe at a big city university. He handed out his card to all of us at the end of his talk in case we had questions that we didn't want to ask in front of the others.

Or maybe he was just looking for a coed to date. But I thought maybe he could help me find out who this mystery girl was.

It didn't go well at first. Sure enough, Danny assumed that I was calling to ask him out. I tried to let him down gently. Finally, we got to the point.

"You expect me to believe some girl's been murdered just because you found her picture in your driveway? I go to the lieutenant with something like that, he'll give me some days off!"

"I don't want you go to the lieutenant. Can't you just see whether a fifteen or sixteen-year-old girl has gone missing in the last few days?"

"I guess I can. I'll call you back in a little while."

Danny called back to tell me that no girl had been reported missing in the city. But three days later he found out along with everybody else that I was right.

I was up as usual about six, getting my coffee before heading to campus. The morning news was on in the living room, turned up so I could hear it in the kitchen. Kwan was in the shower and Fields was still asleep. The news theme music was approaching a climax and the anchor's voiceover began.

"Our top story this Thursday morning is a terrible quadruple murder in the affluent University Heights neighborhood. Dr. Harlan Robinette, his wife Amy, his daughter Alicia and son Harlan Jr. were found knifed to death in their home…" I ran into the living room in time to see pictures of the family flashing across the screen. The father and mother I did not know, but a sharp pain lanced through my stomach when I saw Alicia's picture. It was her! I knew it!

A little later, Danny called.

"Have you heard the news?" he asked.

"Yeah." I resisted the impulse to say I told you so. "It's her. I saw her picture on the news."

"Have you still got the picture you were telling me about?"

"Yeah. You want it?"

"Yeah. Can you bring it in? Somebody will need to take a deposition from you, about where and when you found it."

"I'll come in this morning. Should I ask for you?"

"No," he says. "Ask for Detective Allen. I'll tell him you're coming."

"Do they have any idea who did this?" I ask.

The line went silent for a moment, then he said, "Yes, but don't say anything. Just keep an eye on the evening news tonight."

I totally felt like I needed to be with somebody to talk about this. "Danny…" I began. "…thanks for calling me and telling me,"

"Sure," he replied. "No problem."

Yeah. No problem.

I wound up missing my classes because I had to stay at police headquarters until early afternoon. Not that they gave me a bad time — it was just hurry up and wait. I totally didn't want to give Alicia's picture to Detective Allen. It was like losing a part of myself. Silly, really. I didn't even know her.

So it was just about dinner time when I got back home. I remembered what Danny said and cut on the evening news.

They got them! A long shot showed five young men, dressed in typical, baggy gangbanger style, hoodies over their heads, being led into police headquarters through a side door.

"The accused are Denny Mayfield, 22, Wesley Harrison, 18, LeBrowne Ellis, 25, a sixteen-year-old and a fifteen-year-old whose names are currently being withheld from the media," the anchor droned. "All are allegedly members of the Urban Legends, a South Side gang. Ellis is the gang's leader. Police say that several items taken from the Robinette household, including an iPad and a cell phone, were found in the gang members' possession."

I sank down on the sofa. The anchor droned on, but I didn't hear her. A sixteen and a fifteen-year-old! An entire family murdered for an iPad and a cell phone! I began to cry.

When I'd composed myself, the urge to call Danny came over me again. I didn't care if he hung up on me.

"What is it now?" he said when he came on the line.

"I watched the news like you said," I said. "I think it's totally awesome that you got them! How did you do it so fast?"

He hesitated and I could tell he really didn't want to answer. Then he said, "Well, it will be in the papers anyway. We got an anonymous tip. Gangbangers are really stupid. They do something like this, first thing they do is brag about it. Somebody who heard them thought we ought to know. So we got a warrant and raided their headquarters and we found stuff that we could prove came from the Robinette house."

"Well," I said, "it's sad that they're so young. I'm older than most of them. But it's great that you got them."

"Yeah," he said. A long pause, then, "Please don't call me anymore, Nattie." My phone went silent.

The next day, I tried to get back to life, but thoughts of Alicia kept intruding. I couldn't figure out why it bothered me so much. I didn't even know the Robinettes and shit like this happens everywhere, all the time.

Yeah, but it doesn't usually end up in your driveway.

I left Constitutional History, remembering little of the lecture. I picked up a city paper at the Student Union to see if there was any more information. A front-page article didn't tell me much I didn't already know, except that the funeral was going to be held the day after tomorrow. Abruptly, I decided to go.

The funeral was at the big Baptist church downtown. I arrived half an hour early but the place was already packed. Several local news trucks were parked outside. The buzz in the crowd informed me that quite a few people attending had no connection with the Robinettes but like me, they were appalled that a thing like this could happen so close to home and they felt a need to join in the mourning.

I elbowed my way inside and ended up standing behind the last row of pews. The organ swelled and ushers pushed the crowd back towards the sides of the nave. I was near the center aisle and I fought for my space — I'm short, so it was the only place where I could see what was happening. Sunlight streamed through the open doors as the procession began — four caskets, each carried by six men in black suits, made their way to the sanctuary. The coffins were closed, of course and I had a feeling that they weren't going to be opened.

The service was mercifully short. It was hot and the air was filled with perfume mixed with sweat. The Reverend said nice words about each of the Robinettes, dwelling on their kindness, their community service and the terrible void that their tragic demise left for all of us. I knew what he meant. He finished by reminding us that our existence in this world was temporary and our time best spent in preparing for our life in the next world. I'm not Catholic anymore and really don't believe there's a God who watches over us. If he was watching, he epically fucked up with the Robinettes.

The organ began again. Suddenly a hot flash and a wave of nausea overwhelmed me. I pushed past the usher who was attempting to keep the center aisle clear for the funeral procession to exit. He gave me a snarky look but I didn't care--I had to get out of there right away! The sunlight blinded me and I stumbled. OMG, I was going to take a header down the stairs! Suddenly, I felt pressure on both shoulders and I was yanked backwards. I managed to get my feet under me again.

The young man who saved me kept a hand on my shoulder and placed the other on my upper arm, accompanied me to the sidewalk, then drew me away from where the caskets and the crowd would exit the church.

He was older than me but still twenty-something, not too tall, with shaggy dark hair, a thin mustache and a pointy little beard. He wore black jeans, a dark sport coat over a checkered shirt and one of those pencil-thin ties that they used to wear in the dark ages. I guessed that those were probably the only dress-up clothes he had.

"Are you OK?" he asks. "You were looking pretty rough up there."

"I think so. Thanks for not letting me fall."

"Fuhgeddaboudit." He hesitates, then, "I'm Nicky."

"Natalie. My friends call me Nattie."

"So how do you know the Robinettes, Nattie?"

I began to tell him the story, but the next thing I knew, my face was buried in his chest and I was crying so hard I couldn't even speak. He did exactly the right thing - just held me until it passed. He took me by the shoulders again when I was finished and looked in my eyes. His were a deep, deep brown.

"I think you shouldn't be alone right now," he said. "How 'bout some coffee and maybe a little lunch? You'll feel better if you eat something."

The trite phrase made me laugh. That started to get out of control too, so I stifled it with difficulty. "I think what I need right now is a drink," I told him.

"We can do that," he said.

A few minutes later I was sitting across from him in a nearby Irish pub. The beer and food scents made me queasy, so I ordered a mug of the house porter with a shot of Jameson's. He didn't bat an eye. When the drinks came, I downed the shot and took a long pull at the dark, sweet beer. I was glad I was sitting down 'cause I'd have fallen down from the soothing alcohol rush if I wasn't.

We ordered and he told me about himself over the Shepherd's pie. His full name was Nicodemus Osman, but he went by Nicky. He was a former student of Mrs. Robinette's (she taught high school) and was currently at State.

"They were like a second family to me," he told me. "I could come and go at their house just like it was mine. I thought of Alicia and Ronny as my sister and brother."

"Well, at least they got the scumbags who did it," I said.

"So what? They'll probably have a better life in jail than they would on the street. It's a shame they won't get what they deserve."

"My feelings exactly!"

Things got a little awkward after the waitress cleared the dishes.

"Let me get this," Nicky said.

"No way! If it wasn't for you, I'd probably be in the hospital with a busted face! The least I can do is buy you lunch."

"Hey, I couldn't let a pretty face like that get busted up!" I could feel the blush rising.

"If you won't let me pay for your lunch, then you'll just have to go to dinner with me!" he said.

It must have been the alcohol - I ordered a second pint after I finished the boilermaker. "Sure. When?"

"How 'bout tonight?"

"OK!"

So we went out that night to my favorite place (he asked!) and Nicky was a perfect gentleman all evening. I found out he was an orphan — his folks were killed in a house fire — so the Robinette tragedy was almost like losing them all over again. He invited me to his place after dinner, but I declined. I had a feeling he wanted to hook up and I had school tomorrow. He gave me a kiss that made me tingle all over when he dropped me off at home. I promised to see him again real soon.

I saw him half a dozen times over the next couple of weeks and we talked on the phone nearly every day. Nicky had this eerie quality about him — when I was with him, it was almost like he could mesmerize me. I had told myself a couple of times that I was going to break it off because I knew where this was going and I was a little scared. I was a good little Catholic girl in high school and had never hooked up with a guy, though several had asked me. I knew that Nicky wanted sex, but for some reason, I didn't. It wasn't because I didn't like him and surely not because I thought some God would send me to hell if I did — I just didn't want to be with a guy that way. Or maybe I just didn't want to be with Nicky that way. I wasn't sure. But Nicky would call and ask me out and I'd say yes without thinking. All the while I was with him, he'd make it obvious that he was bending over backwards to let me decide in my own time whether to have sex and that made me feel way guilty.

It was a Friday afternoon. I had just gotten home from school. Kwaneshia was gone for a long weekend and Fields was not home either. I hadn't heard from Nicky in a couple of days, the longest time he'd ever not called me. I wondered if he'd finally gotten tired of my putting him off. I could have called him, but so far in our relationship, I hadn't done so. Hadn't had to — he always called me.

I was contemplating whether or not I wanted to spend a quiet evening at home when the doorbell rang. I nearly jumped out of my skin! I pulled the curtain aside before opening the door.

Chapter 17.

I t was Nicky of course, in his only dress clothes, with a bouquet of roses and a bottle of wine!

All I could think of to say was "Hi!" I took the flowers, blushing furiously.

"Thought you needed some TLC," he said, "so I made reservations at *St. Tropez* for eight. That gives us time to sample this before we go. It's *Beaujolais Nouveau*."

I'd known Nicky long enough to know that he was not wealthy. Restaurant *St. Tropez* was pure fire and pricey! And that wine and the flowers must've set him back nearly a hundred, easy.

I was roiling with conflicting emotions as I was getting the roses in water. I was flattered that he'd go to all this trouble, vaguely angry that he didn't call and ask first and scared to death because I was pretty sure that knew what he wanted and but not sure at all whether I wanted to give it to him. By the time I was finished with the roses, he'd scouted up a couple of wine glasses, gotten the bottle uncorked and was pouring.

He handed me a glass with a flourish. *"Voila, mademoiselle!"* he said.

We sat on the sofa and sipped. I hardly tasted the wine.

Finally, I said, "Nicky…, you shouldn't have. The flowers, the wine, St. Trope's…, you don't have the money…"

He took the glass out of my hand, then gave me a long, lingering kiss. He sat back and looked at me with his bittersweet chocolate eyes. I felt myself melting into them.

"Some things are way more important than lousy money," he said.

OMG! I was totally owned!

Later at his place, I was a little buzzed — Nicky had insisted on ordering wine with every course at St. Trope's. He led me to the sofa, then put on some soft music. I smiled. Always the gentleman, Nicky.

He returned with a small wooden box. As he put it down on the low table in front of the sofa, I could see that the top was heavily inlaid and polished to a high shine. He flipped it open and removed a metal straw, a mirror and a packet of coarse white powder. The hairs on the back of my neck rose and a hollow feeling swelled in my stomach.

He dumped a pile on the mirror. He reached into his pocket and took out a folding knife, which he opened with a complex hand motion. He laid out a line.

"Is it coke?" I asked him

"No, it's crystal. Cheaper and better."

"Nicky…," I began. He cut me off.

"You don't want to, right?" I shook my head. "It's just that we've both had quite a bit of wine," he said. "Alcohol tends to kill the libido. One hit of this stuff and you'll never know you had a drink. I want our first time to be special, Nattie."

"Nicky, it's just that I've promised myself that I won't do drugs. I want a career as a lawyer someday and a lot of firms require blood screens and lie detector tests before they'll hire you. They'll ask you if you've ever done drugs in your life."

"That's stupid!" he snapped petulantly. "You're not even in law school yet! It will make everything better! Try it, you'll see!"

OMG! I think I really want to! But I've told him the truth — many law schools and firms have a zero-tolerance policy about drug use. And I totally want to go to law school.

"No, Nicky, I really can't. I won't. Please respect my choice."

He looked pissed. "Well, I won't force you. But I hope you don't go to sleep on me after all that wine." He hesitated a moment, then said, "You gonna get all bent out of shape if I do?"

I wish he wouldn't. "I guess not," I lied. I was feeling guilty AF again. Damn him!

He finished laying out the line, then used the flat of the knife to get the residual back into the bag. He carefully snorted the powder, then put everything back in the box and closed it. He leaned back on the sofa and shut his eyes. I could see his body stiffen as the drug kicked in.

He opened his eyes and stared at me, letting his gaze flow hungrily over my body. His eyes were no longer meek. He leaned forward and reached for me and I reluctantly moved to meet him.

Afterwards, he was laying on top of me on the couch, nuzzling. Instead of an afterglow, I felt let down. While his performance was enthusiastic and athletic, it was like I wasn't even there. Reflexively, I rumpled his curly brown hair and he looked up into my face.

"That was awesome, Nattie," he said. "Better than I even thought it would be."

What does a girl say to that?

"I'm glad you let me be your cuddly bear," he said.

He started kissing my neck. He was becoming aroused again. I braced myself.

Eventually he ran out of energy and fell asleep, but I lay wide awake. The only remaining effect of the wine was a lingering headache.

I wiggled out from under him as gently as I could and headed for the john. His place was several miles from mine and we came in his car but that was fine. I needed to walk and think.

I was more than halfway home before I got to what was really bothering me. I stopped dead in my tracks. Bile rose in my throat. I started walking again at a quicker pace. I totally wanted to get home!

What was on the back of that picture?

CB —

It's been a totally great year! I never knew I could be so much in love as I am with you. I can't wait to see what happens next…

It couldn't be! CB? Cuddly bear?

They got the guys that did it! It was the gangbangers!

I was really glad to see Fields' car in the driveway. I locked the door behind me.

Needless to say, I got no sleep the rest of that night. As the sun peeped through the curtains, I decided that I did not want to spend Saturday here. I knew that Nicky would come hunting me after he woke up and he wouldn't be happy that I'd left him.

Later, I was at the main library on campus, so far back in the stacks that nobody could find me without a bloodhound. My laptop flickered on the desk in front of me. My phone sang once, about nine o'clock. The ringtone told me it was him. I didn't answer it. Shortly thereafter, Fields called.

"Nattie, what in the world did you get into last night? Your BF is going crazy!"

I told her I didn't want to go into details right then. "I'll tell you all about it later. And hey, he might come over there looking for me."

"Oh, he's been here already," she said. "Pushed right past me when I opened the door and went all through the house looking for you! Wouldn't believe me when I told him I didn't know where you were. He finally left when I threatened to call the cops! What did you do to this guy?"

"It's complicated, Fields. Do me a favor and go visit your Mom for a day or so."

"You gonna be OK, Nattie?"

"I think so. I can always call the cops if I need to."

After hanging up, I mulled over my relationship with Nicky. Was I nuts to think that this sweet, considerate guy killed a whole family? Why would he do that? Sure, he was different last night, but that was the meth, right? I wished he hadn't taken it — I wanted to be with him, not with whatever the drug turned him into. But nobody's perfect. Maybe if I just told him how his behavior affected me…

When you stopped to think about it, how much did I really know about Nicky? I knew he was twenty-something, that he grew up here in town and he went to State. That was it.

I typed his name in the Find People form on State's website. Nothing! I typed my own name in. Yep, it worked! So why was Nicky not listed?

Google told me that Nicodemus Osman was not that uncommon a name after all. I found several on Facebook, LinkedIn, Twitter and other social networking sites. However, when I added the name of the city to the search string, an obituary popped up.

It was for Nicky's dad and it was dated seven years ago. It had all the usual stuff about his life history, family, etc., but didn't mention a house fire. That wasn't uncommon — obits often don't contain gory details about the manner of death. I found out that Nicky had a younger brother and a sister. Did they die in the fire, too?

A little more digging unearthed a local news story. Apparently, the fire happened in the middle of the night. Nicky's family didn't have a chance — their rooms were on an upper floor. The article mentioned that one son was not home when the fire occurred. It also said that the fire was suspicious and was being investigated.

A second article a few days later confirmed that it was arson — the investigator found evidence of an accelerant. A third article a week after that reported that a man was arrested — a transient — and some articles taken from the home and an empty gas can were found hidden near his campsite.

I can't even!

The son-of-a-bitch had done it before! He killed his fam, then he framed some poor bastard who he knew would have no credibility! And I made love with this guy?

I called Danny and told him what I'd found.

After a long silence, he asked me, "Nattie, do you have any evidence to back up this charge?"

"Just what I've told you. He lied to me about everything!"

"The D.A. has gotten an indictment against the Legends. She thinks that her evidence is really solid — she has the items from the Robinette home with the bangers' prints all over them! She'd throw me out of her office if I went to her with these unsubstantiated allegations!"

I knew he was right! But I had to try once more. "Did any of the bangers cop to it?"

"Not yet, but they will. The DA is going to offer no death penalty to anyone that does. Once it gets through their heads that they're screwed, they'll fall all over each other to confess."

We hung up.

I didn't know what I was going to do, but I just couldn't let him get away with this!

It wasn't ten minutes after I got back to the house that there was a knock on the door. Of course, it was Nicky. Had he been watching the place?

Against my better judgment, I let him in. I was afraid not to!

He had another bottle of wine in his hand as a peace offering. I ignored it and went into the living room. He followed. I sat in an easy chair so he couldn't sit next to me.

"Nattie, what happened?" he asked. I heard what sounded like genuine plaintiveness in his voice. "Was it the crystal?"

"You lied to me!"

"About what?"

"You're not a State student. I checked"

I saw a flash of anger flit across his features, then the melancholy look returned.

"You're right," he said. He hesitated, then, "I thought if I told you what I really did, you wouldn't want me."

I was pretty sure I knew, but I asked anyway, "And what is that?"

"I deal, Nattie."

"And you thought if you could get me to use that I'd accept what you do? Is that it?"

"Something like that"

I had to be really careful heading down the path I'd chosen, but I had to be a hundred percent sure.

"And let me guess. The Urban Legends are your supplier."

The fear that sprang into his eyes told me all I needed to know! Now I had to give him an out.

"You were living with the Robinettes and you brought those low-lifes into their home. And they saw the Robinettes' stuff and decided to rob them. You got a whole family killed, Nicky!"

I saw the brief flash of relief in his eyes because I was looking for it, then the sorrow returned. Oh, he was good, Nicky was!

"You can't know how bad I feel about that! And I knew if you found out, you'd want nothing more to do with me!"

"You're right about that, Nicky."

Now the anger came back again and he didn't bother to disguise it. Did he really think I was going let him off the hook?

"You can't just cut me off!" he says.

Cut you off from what? "I told you, Nicky, I'm working towards a career as an attorney. Unfortunately, there's no place for someone like you in that life. So I won't be seeing you anymore!"

"Just like that?" he snarled.

"I'm afraid so."

He jumped up and drew back his arm, still holding the bottle of wine. OMG! I curled up in a ball, protecting my head. At the last second, he regained control and let the bottle fly across the room instead. It hit Kwaneshia's grandmother's mirror, which exploded like a bullet had struck it.

Oh yeah, this guy could kill!

I said in a low voice, "Nicky. Please go. Don't make me call the cops."

He stalked toward the front door, then turned back to me.

"I fucked Alicia, you know. She was only fifteen and she was better than you!"

He slammed the door so hard that I could feel it a room away.

He just had to hurt me one more time and when he did, he confirmed what I already knew. He'd killed them because Alicia's parents had found out he'd molested their daughter! He was facing prison, life on the sex offenders registry and maybe his drug dealing would've come to light as well. So he killed the Robinettes and framed the Legends, just like he framed that tramp when he killed his own family.

I knew that I was in a totally bad way. When Nicky cooled down, he was going to realize that I might question that the Legends did it. I had no proof, but I could at least direct unwanted attention his way. If he'd already killed his own family and a second one, how long would it take him to decide what he needed to do with me?

No way I was staying alone in that house that night! My roomies weren't due back until evening the next day. I looked outside — no sign of him. I got a roll of duct tape and my sharpest paring knife. I put the handle of the knife in my right palm and wrapped my hand round and round with the tape. Then I could leave the house.

I didn't think he followed me to the motel. I stuck to main, well lighted streets to get there. I undid my knife before I went inside to check in.

I had a really bad night, getting almost no sleep. But by morning, I knew what I had to do!

I was back at my place by Sunday afternoon. I'd emailed my roomies that I was having guy trouble and could they please stay away till tomorrow. I picked up the phone and punched in his number.

"Nicky," I said when he answered. "I know what you did to the Robinettes. If you want me to stay quiet about it, you'll bring me some money. A couple thousand, at least. You're a dealer, so I know you've got it."

Dead silence, then, "Give me a couple of hours."

It was more like thirty minutes when there was a knock at the door. "It's open!" I called from the living room.

He came in with murder in his eyes.

"You've got it?" I ask.

"Yes," he says. "Two large, like you asked. But that's not going to be all, is it?"

"Well, I was wondering how I was gonna pay for law school if I don't get a scholarship...."

He reached in his pocket and took out a roll of bills.

"Put it on the table. Don't come near me."

He took a step towards the table, then, quick as a wildcat, he pounced! I went down under him, fighting to keep his knife from my throat! I heard the bedroom door slam into the wall and his weight was abruptly removed from my chest! I looked up to see him struggling in the grasp of two large, very angry gangbangers!

I push myself up on my elbows and addressed them.

"LeBrowne, you promised you wouldn't do it here and get blood all over."

Nicky was the color of a piece of tripe, so shocked he couldn't even scream.

LeBrowne picked the roll of duct tape and wound it around Nicky's head, covering his mouth. Nicky then stupidly tried to scream and

LeBrowne crammed the tape inside of his mouth. What came out was just a croak.

"The Legends owe you," LeBrowne said to me.

They pulled Nicky's arms behind him and wound half a roll of the duct tape around his wrists. Then they dragged him out, kicking futilely.

After they were gone, I wondered briefly if I'd be able to live with myself. Then I thought about Alicia and the rest of the Robinette family and I decided that I'd be just fine.

When my story is finished, Rebecca just stares at me. Finally, she asks, "Did you ever find out what happened to Nicky?"

"Nope. LeBrowne never told me. I finally did ask him last week and he told me that I didn't want to know."

"Do you think it's possible that Nicky's alive?"

"I doubt it. One of LeBrowne's homies copped to killing the Robinettes on his own. That got the death penalty off the table and it got LeBrowne off the hook, which was the point. The Legends are nothing if not loyal. But LeBrowne wouldn't let it stand that one of his boys got life because of Nicky. So I'm pretty sure they killed him."

"And how do you feel about that?" She says in her dispassionate therapist's voice. It makes me mad!

"You don't want to hear this, but it makes me feel good! That lowlife killed two whole families and one of them was his own. And he was gonna get away with it! That didn't happen and I had a hand in it. That makes me feel just fine!"

She's got a strange look on her face, almost like she's alarmed. "You seem to be awfully fond of revenge, Natalie."

What does that mean? "It wasn't revenge, it was retribution. I've never hurt anyone who was innocent, or whom the Law would call to account for their crimes. Those guys I killed, it was in self-defense. Nicky was self-defense too, because he surely would have killed me if LeBrowne and his homie weren't there. And remember, I did tell the cops before I told LeBrowne."

"That's true, you did. But every time you participate in a vengeful act, it seems to fill some inner need. That's what troubles me."

"Don't you want to see people who hurt others punished?" I challenge her.

"Not necessarily. I want to see them prevented from doing more harm. And even that makes me sad that it's necessary. You don't seem sad."

"The only thing I'm sad about is that innocent people got hurt. The bad guys got what they deserved."

"Are you off the prazosin?" she asks out of left field.

I suddenly realize that I haven't taken any of the drug in a while. "Yes!" I say. "And the dreams haven't come back, either."

She looks like maybe she didn't want to hear that. She writes something in her notebook, possibly to figure out what she's going to say next. Then "Well, from what you've told me, it seems like Nicky would have ample reason to do the things you've been experiencing. So maybe you should ask LeBrowne what happened to him. If he's truly dead, we'll have to look elsewhere to find your nemesis."

"That may have to wait. LeBrowne is on the Burn Unit at University Hospital. There was a fire at the gang's headquarters."

Now she does look alarmed.

"I think you should talk to LeBrowne as soon as you can." She snaps the notebook closed. "Unless you have anything else you want to talk about today, I think we're done. Why don't you come back Thursday and we can talk about your Title IX hearing."

"Thursday is Lupe's immigration hearing. How about Friday?" A thought occurs to me. "Since you're not working for the University anymore, shouldn't I be paying you for these sessions?"

"Yes, but we can arrange that through your insurance later. Let's get you through next week first. And Friday's fine. I'll put you down for ten o'clock."

It's just about noon, so I decide to bounce over to the hospital. I go to the main desk and ask if LeBrowne can have visitors.

"Yes," the nurse says. "He's still on the Burn Unit, but he can have visitors." Another thought occurs to me. "How about Amos Murdoch?"

She moves her mouse and peers at her monitor. "Mr. Murdoch is due to be discharged later today. But he's still in his room. You'd better hurry if you want to see him."

I ask for the room number and she gives it to me, then I go to another desk to get a photo badge made that will allow me to go upstairs. Uncle Amos is in a private room in the red section on the third floor. When I enter the room, he's sitting up in bed with Mom in a chair alongside.

"Hey, Nattie," they both chime as one as I enter.

"Hi, Mom. How are you, Uncle?"

"Ready to get outta this damn place," he says in a husky voice. His hoarseness notwithstanding, I'm pleased to hear him sounding like his old, feisty self.

I've decided that now is not the time to tell either of them that Lupe and I are married. I'm also not sure if Uncle knows that his home is now uninhabitable, but Mom removes that as a concern.

"Amos and I are going to Fayetteville when we leave here," she says. "I still have the old house." She means the house I grew up in. "We can live there while we decide what to do."

"It will be sad that you're not around," I say, but I only partly mean it. I'm kinda glad that two people I care about will be safe from whomever is out to get me.

Uncle Amos clears his throat. "Nattie, it's likely we won't see each other for a spell, so I've got something I need to get off my chest before I go." Oh, God! Not another living in sin lecture, please! He hesitates like he doesn't want to say what he's got to, then, "I owe you and Miss Lupe an apology. You see her, you tell her I'm grateful to her for saving my life." Are those tears I see on his cheeks?

"I had no right to say the things I did to you," he goes on. "I forgot one of the most important lessons that Jesus taught us. In Matthew chapter seven, verse two at the Sermon on the Mount, He says, 'For with what judgment ye judge, ye shall be judged, and with what measure ye mete, it shall be measured to you again.' It means that only the Lord has the right to judge a person and He'll forgive you your sins only if you don't judge your fellow man. I was wrong when I criticized you and Lupe for your lifestyle. It wasn't my place to do it and I'm sorry for it. Can you forgive me?"

Now I'm crying and so is Mom. This is the Uncle Amos I've come to love! I run to the bed and throw my arms around his neck.

After we get unentangled, he says, "I'm sorry too that I won't be here to help find the S.O.B. who's doing all these bad things to you. You stick real close to Danny and Leon and carry that Ruger ever'where you go. Look after Miss Lupe and her little boy. You got any idee yet who might have it in for you?"

"Maybe," I tell him. "I've got to talk to someone first, then I'll let you know."

The nurse comes in to help Mom get Uncle ready to travel, so that's my cue to leave.

I'm sorry to say that I've spent so much damned time in this hospital lately that I can go straight to the Burn Unit without missing a turn. As I get out of the elevator, the sign informs me that the Oral CL-581 trial is still going on. There's a different nurse at the desk in the Burn Unit than the first time I was here. I ask her for LeBrowne and she gives me a room number.

All the rooms on the Burn Unit are private, probably so the patients, many of whom are in considerable pain, are disturbed as little as possible. I close the door of LeBrowne's room after I enter — I don't want anyone overhearing the conversation we're about to have. LeBrowne seems smaller and less imposing lying in bed, his head and hands swathed in bandages with his face exposed like he's wearing a *hijab*. There's an IV next to his bed with four hanging bags and a large syringe clamped into a holder. All of the tubes run down into a pump with red glowing numbers on the front counting down like a timer in a bad spy movie. A single tube comes out of the pump and goes into an IV in the back of his hand. Looks like it hurts. Wires run from beneath his hospital gown to a heart monitor next to the bed where he can't see it and a blood pressure cuff on his arm runs to a second display stacked on top of the heart monitor. His heartbeat looks strong and his BP is 100/70.

He jerks a little as the door shuts, which tells me he heard it, but he can't turn his head because his neck is clamped in a vise that holds it straight and upright. How the hell can he sleep like that? I move so he can see me.

"S'up, girl? No flowers?" He could use some. The room is cold and sterile and stinks of iodine.

"Didn't think a big man like you would want any. How you feeling?"

"Watchoo think? Like shit."

I'm sure he does, given the absence of his usual palaver.

"What do the docs say?"

"I'll be outta here in a few days, just as soon as they're sure the burns won't get infected."

"So what happened?"

"Watchoo think?" he says again. "Some Judas torched our crib."

"How?"

"Threw some bottles full of gas through our window. Old place went up like a freebase pipe. I damn near didn't get out and a couple of the homies didn't make it."

That was disturbingly familiar. "Any idea who did it?"

"Coulda been a lotta niggas. The Legends got enemies." There was a touch of pride in his voice as he said that. "But we'll find 'em. They be hell to pay in the hood when I'm outta here."

"I don't think it was one of your enemies. I think it was one of our enemies."

"Watchoo mean?"

I tell him about the attack on my birthday party. I finish with, "I can think of only one person who would hate both of us enough to do something like that."

"Ain't him," LeBrowne says. "Muthafucka's history."

"Are you sure? What did you do with him?"

"I tole you, you don't want to know."

"I'm going to have to know."

"All right, but remember, you axed for it." Gimme some of that water there and I'll tell you."

There's a container next to the bed that has a snap-on top with a straw in the center. I hold it for him so he can sip. He spits out the straw with a grimace when he's done. I can see the pain in his eyes.

"One of the homies got a uncle who's got a farm," he begins. "Uncle's old now and caint farm no more so he lives in town, but he caint let the old place go neither because family. But it's quiet out there and ain't nobody close by to hear the screams. That's where we carried him."

The IV timer beeps and he stops to look at it. There's a whirring sound and I see that a mechanism is pressing the plunger on the syringe on the IV stand, adding the contents into the stream of drugs flowing into LeBrowne's veins. I swear I can see the pain retreat from his eyes as the stuff takes hold.

"We stripped him and hung 'im on a hook in the barn by the duck tape on his wrists. We took the tape off'n his mouth so he could scream all he wanted and the niggas went to work on him with a sledgehammer and a pitch fork. Then somebody found a blow torch that still worked. He passed out while we was workin 'im over with that. We woke him up with a bucket of water and had at him with the torch some more until he passed out again. The water wouldn't wake him up no more, so we took some pix on our cells to show the folks in the hood what happens to you when you fuck with the Legends. You wanna see 'em?"

I shake my head as Uncle Amos' words come unbidden into my thoughts, "...*and with what measure ye mete, it shall be measured to you again.*" Something like that should never happen to anybody! Then I remember, *he murdered two families.*

LeBrowne is speaking more and more slowly and slurring his words a little. Must be the shot of pain meds he just got. I need to hurry him up.

"Was he dead?"

"Nope, not yet. We took him down and put him in the trunk of the car, then carried him over to the Sirvale quarry and dumped 'im in."

"Was he dead then? Maybe he could have survived?"

"Word, we didn't check. But we carried him round the back of the quarry and threw him off the cliff. It had to be fiddy feet down to the water. So yeah, he dead all right."

His eyes close in spite of himself. I'm not gonna get any more out of him today, but I don't think I need to. How could Nicky not be dead after all of that? I shudder inwardly. *But he murdered two families!* Still, I wish I could have just turned him over to the cops.

I turn to go, then a high-pitched squeal fills the room and I look back at LeBrowne. His sepia skin has an unhealthy greyish cast and his chest isn't moving. The heart monitor is flat-lined and his BP monitor reads ERROR. Shit! I grab the call button on the side of his bed, mash it and hold it in. Nothing happens! I throw it on the bed, rush to the door, thrust it open and scream, "Somebody get in here! He's dying!"

The door slams open as the emergency team barrels into the room with a crash cart. An intern takes one look at the heart monitor, then she rips off LeBrowne's hospital gown shouting, "Let's shock him, stat!"

The paddles are greased and they hit him once, twice. "He's still coding! Hit him again!" She grabs a large syringe from the cart and begins filling it.

"I think he's overdosed," I holler. "He got a shot from his IV just before he passed out!"

The intern gives me a who the fuck are you look, then reconsiders and yells, "Get ten milligrams of Narcan, stat!" A nurse bolts from the room and returns in a minute. He hands the intern a syringe and she injects it into the IV stream. "Hit him again!" she barks.

They shock him and this time there's a blip on the heart monitor that wavers, then struggles into a line of irregular peaks. The intern says to nobody in particular, "He's not responding to the Narcan like he should. Let's get him intubated." The nurse dashes out of the room again. The intern takes an oxygen mask from the tank near the bed and places it over LeBrowne's nose and mouth. She glances at me and says "Get the fuck out of here, now!" I don't want to be in the way, so I bounce.

Standing outside LeBrowne's room in the hallway, I realize that I'm totally shook. Part of me wants to stay here until I'm sure he's all right, but the rest of me wants to be sure that Lupe is OK. I can't use my cell in the hospital, so I take the elevator down and go outside where I can call. I ring her and it goes to voicemail -she's probably with a client at the gym. Abruptly I decide to drive over there. I just have to see her and know she's OK.

As I'm driving, my thoughts are whirling like images in a kaleidoscope. It's obvious to me that what happened to LeBrowne was no accident. Somebody was able to get to him in the hospital and mess with his IV And that somebody is very likely the same person that killed Xin Niu, reported Lupe to INS and firebombed 3M. It has to be Nicky! Nobody else would hate me that much! Somehow, that fucker managed to survive everything the Legends did to him and is getting even with me and them. But how in the hell did he survive all that?

How he survived is really not the important thing. What's important is how do I find him?

I'm in front of Lupe's work on Lee Street. The gym is on the second floor with a parking deck underneath. I pull in and punch the button for a ticket, then drive through the gate. I see Lupe's car a few spaces away so I park next to it and cut off my engine.

I'm way stupid. I know she's upstairs working with a client on pole dancing. If I go up, I'll just interrupt her at work. Her car is here, so she's OK. I start the car again and head back out to Lee Street — I stick the ticket in the slot and waste two bucks to open the gate to let me back out.

Goddammit! I'm struggling to hold back the tears as I drive home and I'm not sure if they're from fear, anger, frustration or all of the above. I cannot let this bastard get to me this way! Tracking him down has become life goals for me. But I need to clean up some of the mess he's made of my life first.

Chapter 18.

I t's Wednesday evening. I'm at home with Lupe, Danny and Kidd. Lupe and I are on the couch, Kidd's in the easy chair and Danny's on the futon. Eduardo has school tomorrow, so he's been in bed for hours. I asked Rebecca to be here too, but she refused to come. She's totally unhappy with me.

On the big screen TV hanging on the great room wall, the eleven o'clock news is just ending. The screen goes black, then unmelodic single notes from a bass guitar reverberate through the room, gradually coalescing into a rhythmic thrumming. The abrupt, unexpected wailing of a lead guitar precedes the eruption of a single word on the screen, which flickers and scintillates with red, white and blue bands:

Roderigo!

The name dissolves into images that whiz across the screen almost too rapidly for the eye to discern details, accompanied by cascading chromatic guitar riffs — a battle in the Middle East, the smiling face of Queen Elizabeth, a rocket launch, a flaming crash at an auto race and the President's inauguration fly by. All of these events have one thing in common — they were covered by the show's quintessential host. His name gradually re-emerges from the iconographic cacophony, obliterating the scrolling chronicle of newsworthy events and fluttering emblematically on a dead black screen:

Roderigo!

His well-known face materializes from the blackness - the trademark slick, steel grey hair, black pencil mustache, well-coiffed goatee and garish bow tie.

"Good evening, America! This is your host, Roderigo Hernandez, bringing you yet another shameful incident from a famous American university, supposedly a bastion of free-thinking and diversity, but in reality a kangaroo court, persecuting one of its own. Many of you will remember Natalie McMasters, the brave college coed we introduced you to last year, who risked her career and even her very life to save a young woman from the clutches of a vicious sexual predator. Because of your efforts, America, Natalie was spared a prison term and the ruination of her career and her life, as her reward for that good deed. Well, guess what? Her enemies have apparently regrouped and she needs your help again!"

A clip of the video of Lupe and I appears on the screen, with very little left to the imagination. Roderigo's voiceover explains how the video was made without our knowledge, how it maliciously surfaced on campus and how it resulted in the Title IX investigation that threatened my tenure at State.

The inside of an auditorium fades in, with Roderigo and I sitting at classroom desks in front of a panel comprising two women and two men, who sit behind a long table on a stage in front of us. Another camera pans the gallery, showing about a dozen people, including Rebecca, seated there. One of the men on the stage is Fred Simonson, who is speaking.

"Naturally, Mr. Hernandez, everyone here knows who you are and is familiar with your brand of shock journalism. However, I question your appropriateness as Ms. McMasters advocate at this hearing."

"It's not your place to question it, Mr. Simonson. The rules for a Title IX hearing clearly state that Ms. McMasters may choose anyone she wants as her advocate."

Naturally, Roderigo was not permitted to bring a camera crew and microphones into the Title IX hearing room. But it's amazing what can be done with miniaturization these days. Roderigo and I are both equipped with concealed cameras and mikes, as are several of the onlookers in the gallery.

"Fine," says Simonson. "But if you try to run this hearing like one of your media spectacles, Mr. Hernandez, I'll terminate the proceedings and have you evicted."

Simonson begins by showing the offending video, then asks me to state for the record that it's of me. Since there's no point in denying it, I do so.

He then calls Andrea Kiefer to speak to how the video made her feel uncomfortable on campus and how seeing it interfered with her ability to concentrate on her studies.

"Why did it have such an impact on you, Ms. Kiefer?"

"Because I am a self-respecting lesbian who has fought for mainstream acceptance for many years." Bullshit! She isn't old enough to have fought for anything for many years! "A video like this shown strictly for prurient interest and to generate publicity for an online pornography business is offensive to me and would serve to negate much of the social image that I and other LGBTQIA persons on campus have worked so hard to create for ourselves."

"Where is your proof that Ms. McMasters posted the video to promote a pornography business?" Roderigo asks.

"Mr. Hernandez, you don't get to question witnesses at this hearing. This is not a court of law," Simonson says.

"Obviously not, Mr. Simonson. The accused has the right to confront the witnesses against her in a court of law!"

"Mr. Hernandez, if you do not stop interrupting, I'll terminate this hearing at once and Ms. McMasters' expulsion will stand."

Roderigo ignores him. "Ms. Kiefer, have you been engaging in sexual activity with Mr. Simonson? Has he coerced you to say these things about Ms. McMasters?"

Kiefer is speechless. The camera zooms right in on her face and the answer to Roderigo's question is obvious to everyone.

"That's all, Mr. Hernandez!" Simonson shouts "This hearing is over!"

"Is it true, Mr. Simonson, that you sexually assaulted Ms. McMasters in your office and you only brought these charges after she repulsed your scurrilous advances?"

"What! Did she say that? No, I did no such thing! That's libelous!"

Roderigo turns to me. The camera in his bow tie zooms in on my face. "Natalie, is that what happened? Did Mr. Simonson sexually assault you?"

My mind snaps back to the pre-interview. I had just finished telling Roderigo about that first session in Simonson's office. His burnt umber eyes bored deep into mine — it seemed like he was looking straight into my soul — and he asked me that same question. His fervent expression told me what he wanted to hear.

"Yes, he did." I lie with a straight face.

Simonson's face is crimson and the camera shows the spittle flying from his lips as he screams, "If you repeat that canard outside of this room, I'll sue you for libel in addition to terminating your enrollment!"

"Oh, it's already out there, Freddy," I tell him.

Wait for it… Bam! He gets it! "You're recording this? Security! Search McMasters and Hernandez, then put them out! Confiscate any recording apparatus you find! No, arrest them…" He stops abruptly, like a mechanical toy whose battery has run down.

Of course, Simonson doesn't know who else in the room has recording equipment and he also doesn't realize that everything's being live-streamed to a van outside, so nothing would be lost even if he did confiscate all of the tech.

The cameras that Roderigo and I are wearing zoom in on the two campus cops who are rushing us in response to Simonson's commands.

"Don't you lay a hand on me, you Nazi! This the United States of America!" Roderigo shouts. The camera zooms out to show me and Roderigo being cuffed and led out of the room.

By the time we exit the Octagon on to the New Commons, a traditional camera crew has arrived to record the proceedings, making any confiscation superfluous. Roderigo is maintaining a continuous stream of patter, reading the cops' names off their name tags, describing in detail the indignities to which we're being subjected and threatening lawsuits and other mayhem to be visited on the unfortunate officers. The cameras are the last straw — the cops unhook us with orders to leave campus forthwith and never return.

The scene on the TV shifts to an interview with me and Roderigo in the great room of my townhouse, in which I tell my side of the story. And yes, I again repeat the lie that I was sexually assaulted by Simonson that first day in his office. Why not? That son-of-a-bitch has been lying on me since day one. I never had a chance in that hearing and I knew it. Fight fire with fire!

The show's closing music comes up large and I snap off the TV. For a moment, everyone just looks at me, the pity evident on their faces. It makes me mad. I explode, "C'mon people! Let's quit draking and talk about how we're gonna get the motherfucker who's responsible for all of this!"

"You're right, Nattie," Danny says. "But since the video and ketamine leads have petered out, we have no place to start."

I've been keeping secrets about my life from everyone but Rebecca and I get it that it has to change. I tell them the story of me and Nicky and about what LeBrowne told me in the hospital on Monday afternoon. When I've finished, I'm confronted by a circle of shocked faces.

Finally, Danny says, "I remember that. I thought at the time that the Legends had killed the Robinettes. So did the D.A. Are you sure this LeBrowne character was telling you the truth?"

"I'm sure Danny. Nicky as much as admitted he'd done it when I confronted him. And he probably would have killed me but for LeBrowne."

Danny shakes his head. "You take way too many chances, Nattie."

That hits me wrong. "It's not my fault that a serial killer decided he wanted to hook up with me, Danny. And knowing what I did, I couldn't let him get away with it if the justice system wouldn't step up."

Kidd speaks up. "All right guys, there's no use arguing over ancient history. The point here is to figure out where we go next." Thanks, Kidd! He continues, "Nattie, I think your idea of looking for reports about an injured man found in the vicinity of the Sirvale quarry about that time is a good one. I've still got some contacts in the department who owe me favors, so I can start there."

Danny says, "Then I'll take the hospital and see if a burned man was admitted that night and find out about what happened to LeBrowne. It's not the easiest thing to spike someone's IV"

"What's that leave for me?" I ask.

"With Amos and your Mom gone, we'll need someone to report in to and to synthesize the information that we gather." Kidd says. "That can be your role, Nattie."

Hmmph. Just trying to keep me safe and sound, away from the action, are we?

"And you can concentrate on Lupe's bond hearing tomorrow," Danny says. "See if you can work with the people at State to come up with a strategy to keep her here."

I realize there's another thing I haven't told the guys. I put one arm around Lupe and take her hand with my other one. "We have a strategy," I tell them. "We got married Monday morning."

There's a moment of surprised silence, then Kidd gets up and comes over to the sofa with his arms spread for a hug. I jump up and pull Lupe up with me and Kidd embraces us both at once. When he lets us go, Danny is behind him. He offers me a hand and I take it.

"Congratulations, Nattie." The smile on his face seems forced. He releases my hand and turns to Lupe, but instead of taking his hand, she pulls him into a warm hug.

"Thank you, Danny," she says. "You had much to do with this."

Danny doesn't look too thrilled about that.

The wall clock tells me it's pushing 2 a.m. "OMG! Lupe and I have to be in court tomorrow at nine, so I'm gonna kick you guys out of here. Danny, I'll call you when we're done and tell you how it went."

Lupe goes upstairs to check on Eduardo before going to bed and Danny and Kidd gather up their things in preparation for leaving. Kidd says goodnight and goes, but Danny lingers. He's still got that glum look on his face.

"What's up?" I ask him.

"Nothing."

"Come on, Danny, I know you well enough to know when something's wrong."

For a minute I don't think he's going to tell me, but then he says, "I guess I'm just disappointed that you got married without telling me."

"I did tell you. Just a few minutes ago."

"You know what I mean." No, I don't. "I would have liked to have been there, is all. It was a big event in your life and I would have liked to have been a part of it."

"We wanted to keep it low key. The only reason we had the civil ceremony at all is because we needed a piece of paper for the judge. It was just Lupe, me and the witnesses."

"Okay. It was your wedding. I guess you can do it how you want." Gee, thanks, Danny! That's big of you. "I'll get over it," he finishes.

Guys are always worse than girls for hurt feelings. I walk him to the door and give him a hug. "Maybe when all this is over, Lupe and I will have a party to celebrate our marriage. You can come to that."

"Thanks," he says, but it doesn't sound like he means it. I close the door behind him.

Chapter 19.

Thursday morning we're in a courtroom again, but not the same one we were married in on Monday. This is the federal courthouse and the room is packed. There's a strange silence given the size of the crowd and a pervasive sour, goaty smell accentuates the undercurrent of fear in the room. A uniformed bailiff calls the cases one by one and the parties involved make their way from the gallery through the wooden gate in the center aisle to sit at a long table to the left of the judge, who reigns from her podium. An identical table on the right is reserved for the government prosecutor and I.C.E. agents. The thought enters my mind that a courtroom is not much different than a church.

I'm dressed in the most conservative outfit I could find — a tight, black dress that comes to just above my knees. I can't even remember the last time I wore a dress. I look like I'm sixteen — my hair is tied back in a pony tail and I'm wearing no make-up. Lupe chose to wear a pair of black slacks and a black blouse. She's got her long, dark hair up in a bun and is wearing no jewelry or perfume. Belatedly, I realize that we look like we're going to a funeral. I hope that doesn't bode evil.

There's a tap on my shoulder and I turn to see Chica in a tan business suit. OMG, she looks even younger than I do! Her smile puts me at ease, though. I called her the other day to tell her Lupe and I were married and she told me to be sure and bring the marriage certificate as well as some other documents to court today. She says to Lupe, "Remember that you don't have to respond to anyone besides the judge. Stand when she addresses you and answer all of her questions politely — say 'Your honor' when you address her. But don't volunteer anything — answer only the questions she asks you. Don't respond to anything that anyone else says, especially the prosecutor. Let me do the talking when you can." Lupe smiles uneasily.

"Here are the things you asked me to bring." I hand Chica a manila envelope containing copies of our marriage certificate, the lease for the townhouse with Lupe's name added to mine, a few household bills also in her name, affidavits of her employment at local gyms and IRS vouchers for payment of the estimated taxes that must be filed by an independent contractor.

Chica nods toward the judge. "We're in luck," she says.

"What do you mean?"

"You'll see."

We wait while the inexorable machinery of justice grinds on. The unfortunates in the gallery are summoned to the dock one-by-one. Some stride proudly to meet their fate while others timidly slink forward. The judge is a silver-haired grandmotherly type in her sixties. It's obvious she considers her activities a holy mission because she deals with the defendants who stand before her with alacrity and dispatch, brooking no foolishness. Tears are ignored and pleas fall on deaf ears or are rewarded with jail time if they don't cease at her command.

Finally, the bailiff calls, "Maria Ibanez."

We rise and proceed to the gate, which the bailiff holds open, and take seats at the defendant's table. After we're seated, the judge directly addresses Lupe.

"You are Maria Ibanez?"

Lupe stands. "Yes, your honor." She says nothing else. She remembers her lessons well.

The judge picks up a sheet of paper from the bench, pushes her glasses up on her nose with her middle finger and reads, "You are not a U.S. citizen or national of the United States of America. You are a native and citizen of the United Mexican States. There is no record of your entry into the U.S.A., so your entry was unauthorized because you did not present a valid visa to enter the U.S.A." She looks up from the paper and addresses Lupe again. "Is all of this accurate?"

Lupe opens her mouth to speak, but Chica shushes her with a hand on her wrist. "Your honor, I am representing Ms. Ibanez."

"I reckoned as much, Ms. Cardenas." The judge knows Chica! One point for our side.

"We are not prepared to respond to any allegations at this time, your honor," Chica says. "Ms. Ibanez entered the country over eight years ago and is unsure of her exact point of entry. We would like more time to investigate the existence and location of any documentation that will show that her entry was not illegal."

I know for a fact that Lupe was snuck across the border by a coyote, because she's told me so. I marvel at the way Chica deflected that issue without telling a direct lie. This is why I wanted to go to law school. But that's over now.

The government attorney, a twenty-something with a short haircut and a pot belly, is wearing a tie that's too short. He rises and says, "Your honor, you cannot grant Ms. Ibanez bond if her entry was illegal."

"Mr. Fletcher, y'all should know by now that I don't cotton to anyone telling me what I can and can't do in my courtroom." Fletcher sits back down, looking like a whipped puppy.

"Your honor, the burden of proof that Ms. Ibanez's entry was not legal is the government's, not ours," Chica says. This little lady is way lit!

"Why is everybody telling me what I already know?" the judge asks rhetorically. "Mr. Fletcher. Can the government prove that Ms. Ibanez's entry was illegal?"

"We have no documentation of her entry at all," Fletcher says.

The judge cuts him off. "Then that would be no."

"However," Fletcher goes on, "the government argues that Ms. Ibanez is a flight risk and should be remanded."

"On what basis?"

"A Notice to Appear was issued to Ms. Ibanez four years ago. She failed to respond to said Notice and an Order of Removal *in absentia* was granted at that time." Oh shit! So much for them not knowing about that. I look at Lupe. Her face is as pale as a fish's belly.

"Well, that does make the illegal entry issue a moot point, now doesn't it?" says the judge.

Fletcher is redeemed. He puffs up like a rooster and says, "Yes, your honor."

"In that case," says Chica, "we would like to request relief from removal."

"Your grounds, Ms. Cardenas?"

"Ms. Ibanez's spouse is an American citizen and would like to petition for an adjustment of status."

"Has the petition been entered?"

"No, your honor."

"Why not?"

"They just got married on Monday," Chica says. "There hasn't been time to file the paperwork."

I swear I can see the judge roll her eyes. People, this is not good!

"That's convenient," says the judge. "I think there has been time. They just chose not to bother." Shit! "Is Ms. Ibanez's spouse present in the courtroom?"

I stand. "Yes, your honor. I am Ms. Ibanez's spouse."

The judge stares at me for a moment, then breaks into a broad grin. "And you are, Miss?"

"Mrs. Natalie Ibanez-McMasters," I say proudly. I had it changed after the wedding.

"And I suppose you brought me a marriage certificate?"

"Yes, your honor."

The judge grins even more broadly. "Okay. Mr. Fletcher. Since you have no proof that Ms. Ibanez is here illegally, I guess I can grant bond. Ms. Cardenas. Since Ms. Ibanez has already skedaddled on one hearing, I'm going to make the bond significant to ensure that she shows up to the next one." The gavel cracks, making me jump. "Bond is set at fifty thousand dollars." Holy shit! Chica told us earlier that a normal bond for this kind of thing was fifteen hundred dollars. "Pay the clerk or go directly to jail, do not pass Go and do not collect two hundred dollars." She turns some pages in a large book in front of her on the bench. "Ms. Cardenas. You will get that petition for relief filed by COB a week from today. This MCH is continued until two weeks from today. Bailiff. Call the next case."

As we're going back into the gallery, I say to Chica, "I thought we were dead when they brought up that first hearing."

Chica turns and smiles at me. "The judge is a lesbian. She's got a wife, too."

We go to the back of the courtroom to see the clerk. Lupe and Chica have to remain here while I run to the bail bondsman and get a cashier's check for five thousand dollars. I put the townhouse up as collateral. I take Lupe's hand as we walk to her car to go home.

Later, I'm watching mindless music videos on the TV in the great room with the volume low because Lupe is exhausted from the stresses of the day and is taking a nap. Post Malone's *Psycho* begins playing on my cell phone. Oh shit! This is a conversation I do not want to have.

"Hey, Rebecca."

"How did it go this morning, Natalie?" I'm still Natalie. It figures.

"Good. The judge gave Lupe bond. We have a hearing in two weeks and Chica thinks we have a better than even chance of getting Lupe a green card."

"That's good to hear." Silence on the line. "Natalie, we need to talk."

"Isn't that what we're doing?"

"You know what I mean."

I'm suddenly angry. "Yes, I do know. And no, we don't have to talk. From now on, I'm handling this."

"Not very well."

"That's your opinion."

More silence, then, "In that case, I think we need to terminate our relationship. You are protected by doctor-patient confidentiality, but I have no wish to be complicit in any more lies."

"Fine," I tell her. "You know where to send the bill." I mash the button with my thumb to end the call.

Appropriately, the strains of Drake's *No Lie* waft throughout the air. I grab the remote and cut the TV off, then draw back my arm to fling the remote across the room. Sanity strikes at the last second and I throw it onto the futon instead.

There's a hollowness inside me. The adage, *Revenge is a dish best served cold*, arises unbidden into my mind. Maybe a nice cold supper is what I need to fill me up again.

Chapter 20.

Next morning, Lupe has made a pan of her totally awesome breakfast *enchiladas*. I'm having one with a fried egg on top and a cup of steaming *café de olla*. As I cut into the egg and watch the bright yellow yolk mingle with the vivid red *enchilada* sauce, the doorbell rings. Shit! Who could be here at this hour? I slip Ruger into the pocket of my robe, then peer through the peephole in the front door. A twenty-something guy I've never seen, who's wearing a white dress shirt with no tie over a pair of jeans, rings the bell again and makes me jump. I open the door with my left hand. My right hand is on the Ruger.

"Ms. Natalie McMasters?" he asks.

"Yes," I answer automatically.

He produces an envelope from behind his back and says, "You've been served."

I take the envelope and he touches his eyebrow in a salute before walking away.

Too late I think about what would have happened if he'd brought out a gun instead of an envelope.

I open the envelope. Inside is a piece of white paper folded in thirds. I take it out, unfold it and read:

Frederick Richard Simonson, plaintiff,

vs

Natalie Simone Ibanez-McMasters, defendant.

SUBPOENA

WTF! It says that I have to appear at the law offices of Willy, Talbott and Hightower Monday morning at ten to be deposed in a libel suit filed against me by Simonson. Shit! Can he do that?

The egg yolk is now cooled and congealed in the sauce. Suddenly, I'm not hungry.

There's nothing for it but to call Gary McDougall.

"Yes, he can do that," says Gary, "And given your interview with Roderigo, I'm not surprised that he has. You really ought to talk to me before you give an interview to a sensational journalist, Natalie."

Here's somebody else that wants to run my life. He should call Rebecca. They could start a club.

"He sent the subpoena to make this look like it's mandatory. You don't have to go unless you want to. But I think you should."

"OK, I'll go."

My cell phone vibrates in my hand and Fields' face pops up in place of Gary's. I tell Gary, "I've got another call. I'm putting you on hold."

"No, you're not," he replies. "I or one of my associates will meet you at WT&H on Monday at 9:45. By the way, turn on your TV. You're on the news."

He hangs up. I punch the button to bring in Fields.

"S'up, Fields?"

"I know you're not a social media queen like I am, but I thought you'd like to know you're all over Facebook, Twitter and Instagram again."

OM fucking G! This is not the first time I've been at the center of a viral media firestorm — it happened after my interview with Roderigo last year. See a pattern there, Nattie? I'd told a lie that time, too, claiming credit for a killing that I didn't do. But the subject of that lie wasn't going to sue me for defamation.

Fields got me a Facebook account when we lived together, though I don't hardly use it. I log in and find I've got 1000+ friend requests! Many people have posted messages of support on my timeline and a few contain stories about similar incidents that have happened to them.

I check my email and find a similar situation — my inbox is overflowing! Obviously, I can't look at each one, but a quick scan of the headers indicates that most support me. One header prompts me to click on it though — *Request for Interview*. Holy shit! It's from a well-known daytime TV show. They'll fly me to New York and put me up in a hotel if I'll chat with the hosts about my situation.

A hollow feeling grows in my gut. It occurs to me that I would have likely gotten a similar public response if I'd told Roderigo the truth about what really happened in Simonson's office. It was sexual harassment and extortion for sure, but Simonson never laid a hand on me (I'd have hit him if he had!), so it wasn't sexual assault. And he sure as hell did sexually assault other women!

"But you can't prove that, Nattie," says that nasty little voice in my head.

It's probably way too late to come clean because not only did I lie, I lied on a nationwide TV show in front of millions of viewers. I'd like to blame Roderigo because he pushed me to tell him what he wanted to hear, but he surely didn't hold a gun to my head. This is on me.

But I was mad, goddammit! Simonson had no right to do what he did to me!

Lupe gets Eduardo off to school and herself to work, leaving me alone. Now that I've been expelled, I have no place to be during the day and it feels strange. And lonely! I don't even have Xin Niu to keep me company anymore…

Uncle Amos' voice echoes in my head. "Nuthin' ain't more worthless than feelin' sorry for yourself. Do it for long enough and all you'll be is sorry. Where's the good in that?"

My cell phone plays *Rockstar*, momentarily relieving me of the responsibility of determining my own fate.

"Nattie, we've caught a break," Kidd says. "I talked to a friend in the department and she searched the calls for those dates you gave me. It turns out that an injured man was picked up near the Sirvale quarry. There wasn't much info about his condition except that he was in a bad way and was taken to University Hospital as a John Doe."

"I'll tell Danny. He's checking out the hospital."

"Ten-four," says Kidd. "I'll keep digging here."

So Nicky may have survived the Legends torture session! He was never too tightly wrapped to begin with, so I could totally see him doing these things to me after that happened to him. And I also can totally see him killing me, or someone I love, when he gets tired of tormenting me. Fear for Lupe and my other friends arises again.

Chill girl! You don't have any proof yet that it is him, or where he might be.

I call Danny and tell him what Kidd said.

"That's great news!" he says. "I've been trying to find a source here in the hospital for details about what happened to your friend LeBrowne, but they've got all the PII locked down because of HIPAA. Give me those dates again and I'll see if I can find out anything about the admissions at that time."

I feel better after talking to the boys. We really haven't accomplished much yet, but because we're actually investigating, I'm beginning to have some hope that we'll find this guy.

A while later there's a knock on the door. I check the peephole and see a woman in a business suit and a guy with a camera. Reporters! I decide to belatedly take Gary's advice and let her get a sore finger from ringing the bell. She actually has the nerve to bang on the door!

"Ms. McMasters, we know you're in there! I'm Ally McAdams from WNCQ news. We just want to get some more information from you about what Fred Simonson did to you!"

I briefly wonder how she'd react to a couple of nine-millimeter rounds coming through the door. FOH, bitch!

Eventually she goes away, but the knocks resume a little later. I go upstairs and surreptitiously peer out of a window that overlooks the parking lot. I see three of those TV vans with the giant antennas taking up multiple parking spaces, so I report them to management. A little later, they're gone. Oh, the perks of living in the high rent district!

There's more good news at noon. I cut on the TV. The male and female anchors are discussing my interview with Roderigo and the aftermath.

"And we're getting reports, Jill, that several women at State besides Ms. McMasters have reported being sexually abused by Frederick Simonson. So far, the University will neither confirm or deny those reports because of privacy concerns."

"You said 'several women', Tim. Does that mean that there's more than one? Any idea how many women have come forward?"

"Well, Jill, these reports are coming in from unofficial channels, so those details are not clear quite yet."

"And what about Natalie McMasters, Tim? Has anyone talked to her about this?"

"We've tried, Jill, but Ms. McMasters evidently wants to remain incommunicado."

"Well, that's understandable, Tim. These types of situations are very stressful for the victims."

"Right you are, Jill. Now, in other news…"

So now I'm a victim. Damn right!

Danny calls me back mid-afternoon with even more good news.

"I was able to confirm the admission of a badly burned man to the hospital as a John Doe on the night in question two years ago," he says. "I'm sure it's the same guy Leon found. Unfortunately, that's all I've gotten so far. The medical info around here is locked up tighter than a drill sergeant's ass. But I've got an idea how I might be able to get what we need."

"You've got to do it, Danny! If we can confirm that the patient was Nicky, we're totally on to something."

"I'll see what I can do." He kills the call.

I hate sitting here on the sidelines while the boys do all the field work!

I go outside to meet Eduardo at the bus stop at three thirty — it's only a couple of blocks from the townhouse but I'm totally not comfortable with him walking home alone with that psycho out there. Lupe gets home about an hour later. I sit at the pass-through while she cooks dinner and tells me about her day. I'm not really listening — I'm just enjoying the intimacy of watching her, sharing the joy she takes in her cooking and her habitual gossip.

Eduardo and I clear the table and clean the kitchen (I absolutely will not let Lupe do that!) after another of her fab Mexican meals and settle in for an evening of mindless TV, but the doorbell rings. With my Ruger in my pocket, I go to the door and check the peephole. Danny! Why did he come instead of calling?

I let him in. "What's up?"

He glances at Lupe and Eduardo on the couch — I can tell he's unwilling to speak in front of them.

"C'mon upstairs," I tell him.

We ascend the spiral staircase in the center of the great room and go down the corridor. I open a door and the room light comes on automatically. I motion Danny inside, then. I press a wall switch to keep the light on as I follow him in.

The room used to be the site of my online stripping business when I was Kira Foxxx. We've removed and sold most of the stripping accouterments including the cameras and the heart-shaped bed so prominent in the video released on campus. We still haven't repainted the ostentatious red walls, but we've kept our rad computer system and turned the room into an office.

I wave Danny to a love seat and take a seat in the swivel chair at the desk.

"What's up?" I ask him again.

He makes a face as he sits down and says, "Excuse me a sec." He hitches up his pants leg to reveal an ankle holster that holds a revolver, which he removes and sets on the seat beside him. "I really have to replace that holster," he says. "It chafes."

"Why do you carry that thing, anyway?" I ask him. "Isn't one gun enough?"

"It's a habit I picked up when I was on the job," he says. "A lot of the guys carry a backup. You'd be surprised how easy it is to lose your weapon in a firefight."

"I guess." A pause. "So what's so important that you had to come over instead of calling?"

He makes me wait for it, then says "I got into the medical records for patient X."

"What! How?"

He ignores the question. "If patient X was your Nicky, your gangbanger buddies really did a number on him."

"He didn't die?"

"Not that I could find out. He was on the Burn Unit for weeks, though, undergoing multiple skin grafts and surgeries."

"What happened to him after that?"

"They shipped him over to Tubman Sanitarium for long-term convalescence."

"Is he still there?"

"I called them and they said they currently have no patient that fits that description. It was getting late by that time, so I decided to follow up over there tomorrow."

"Wow. You really are a good detective to get all this." He looks at the floor and his face reddens. Now I'm way sus. "How'd you do it, Danny?"

"A good detective never reveals his sources," he says.

Suddenly, I know. "It was Diane! She helped you, didn't she?" Now he's really red!

He puts his hands on his knees and leans toward me. "What if it was? A good detective uses the sources he has."

"And just what did you have to promise her to get her to help you?"

"That I'd give her another chance. She really is sorry about the things she said to you, Nattie. Her job on the Burn Unit is really stressful. She gets invested in a lot of the patients who don't make it and that takes a toll."

I can't picture Diane getting invested in anyone but Diane, but I don't want to fight with him so I don't say so. But I know Danny pretty well by now. There's something going on between him and Diane that he's not telling me. They've gotta be doing the Netflix and chill thing — so much for Mr. I-don't-believe-in-one-night-stands. But shit, it doesn't matter to me what he does with who. I change the subject.

"Was Diane able to find out anything about what happened to LeBrowne?"

"She said that there didn't appear to be anything wrong with his IV meds. She thinks the fact that he had heart failure after the timed injection went off was a coincidence and so does the hospital's investigation board."

I can't believe it! "I'm sure they do! Why would they find otherwise and open the hospital to a lawsuit?"

"If they are suppressing something, I'm sure they've got those records buried so deep that no one will find them," Danny says. "So that's a dead end."

I think for a second. "Dammit! Patient X has *got* to be Nicky! Who else would have a grudge against both me and the Legends? If he's not in that sanitarium, we have to find out where he's gotten to."

"That's going to be tricky. It was nearly two years ago…" His voice trails off and he stares at me with a peculiar look on his face.

"What?"

"I read patient X's file pretty thoroughly and what was done to him was horrifying."

"What do you mean?"

Now he's a little green instead of red.

"Worse than the stuff you saw when you were in the Marines?" I ask him.

"Way worse. I saw some pretty bad things in combat, but it was… well, it was combat. You did what you had to do to stay alive. What was done to this guy was deliberate, cruel and unnecessary."

I don't say anything, just wait for him to go on.

"His arms were broken in multiple places and so were his legs. So were his teeth! He had third and fourth degree burns over most of his body. They even burned off his…" He couldn't say it. "Now we're not a hundred percent certain that patient X was your Nicky, but it sure looks that way." He hesitates again. "Nattie, don't take this the wrong way, but there's something I need to ask you."

"What?"

"When you turned Nicky over to the Legends, did you know what they we're going to do to him?"

"I knew that they were probably going to kill him, if that's what you mean."

He just looks at me.

"I thought a lot about it before I called LeBrowne," I continue. "Danny, Nicky murdered two families. I told you that on the phone before I called LeBrowne and you told me that nothing could be done about him. I couldn't let Nicky get away it! Besides, it was just a matter of time before he came after me."

"But did you know how the Legends were going to kill him?"

"I totally didn't even think about that. All I thought was that Nicky had to pay for what he'd done. And I sure as shit wasn't going to let him kill me."

He can't just leave it alone. "If you had known what they were going to do, would you still have called LeBrowne to come and get him?"

Suddenly I'm furious. "What do you want me to say, Danny? You know, maybe I would have called LeBrowne anyway. What part of *Nicky murdered two families* don't you get? I just couldn't let him get away with that!"

Now he's looking at me like he's seeing me for the first time. And he doesn't like what he sees. He looks at his watch. "It's getting late. I'd better go."

"Yes, you'd better."

"I'll call you tomorrow and we'll figure out what to do next."

"Whatever."

He straps his holster back on his ankle and leaves. I don't walk him out.

A few minutes later, the office door opens.

"*Cariño*? Is something wrong?"

I start to tell her to go away, then the tears begin. I throw myself into her waiting arms.

After I've settled down, we cuddle together on the love seat and I tell her about what just happened between me and Danny.

"Danny probably thinks I'm some kind of monster," I finish. "I didn't know how the Legends were going to kill him. But Lupe, I couldn't let Nicky get away with it!"

"No, you could not," Lupe says. "That is not who you are. It is too bad that Danny does not understand that." She kisses me on top of my head as I burrow my face into her bosom, inhaling her scent.

She's right. Lupe is the only one who understands me. What would I do without her?

Chapter 21.

Monday morning dawns cool and clear — it looks like the rain over the last several days is gone at last. I dress conservatively — jeans and a not-too-tight t-shirt — and go to the kitchen for breakfast. Today Lupe's made *chilaquiles* with leftover *enchilada* sauce, poached eggs on top and beans on the side.

I worry about eating such a heavy breakfast given the stressful morning that I expect, but when I say as much to Lupe, she replies, "*Lo que mal empieza, mal termina.*"

I wait for it...

"A bad start makes for a bad ending. If nothing else goes like you want all day, at least you will not be hungry."

I can't argue with that.

I cut on the morning news and it's not long before my picture pops up on TV. It's a still taken from the footage of the Title IX hearing with Roderigo, so I've got a wild look in my eyes. What did you expect, Nattie — that they'd use your high school yearbook pic?

The story is heartening, however. Apparently six women, all State students, have now publicly stated that Simonson extorted sexual favors from them by threatening them with Title IX proceedings. But Freddy's fighting back. He's suing every one of them for defamation. It's nice to have company, though. The struggle is real!

I so wish I hadn't lied to Roderigo, but this news stiffens my resolve not to recant. If I admit to the lie, I'll weaken everyone's case, not only mine. And the fact is that Freddy can't prove I'm lying — it's my word against his. The only two people who know that I lied are Rebecca and Lupe. Rebecca can't spill the tea because of doctor-patient confidentiality and Lupe won't because she loves me. So it looks like I'm on solid ground.

I drive downtown and park in a deck not far from the law office. The sidewalks teem with the Monday morning crowd scurrying like ants to a grease spot. I'm grateful for the anonymity they provide me. I flip my hoodie up and keep my eyes on the pavement as I head for the law office.

Their building, the tallest in the city, is an easy find — it's right across the street from the courthouse where Lupe and I were married. Somebody must have leaked this morning's meeting to the press!

There's a camera crew filming a little coterie of women that circle in front of the building, carrying signs. Me too! Just say no to sexual harassment on campus! I see my name and picture on one of them. Car horns blare at a broadcast van blocking traffic and the smell of engine exhaust is dizzying.

I can't rely on my hoodie to keep me anonymous if I approach that crowd, so I go a block further and around the corner to see I can find another entrance to the building. I find an alley that might lead to the back of it, so I pass by the overflowing garbage cans and a sleeping drunk. The sweet trashy banana smell mixed with urine makes me wish I hadn't eaten so much of the chilaquiles, no matter what Lupe thinks.

The alley does a ninety and I see the back of the building I'm looking halfway down. Holy shit! The first floor looks like a prison with all the windows barred and there's a single, solid metal door in the center of the wall A skeletal fire escape clings to the side of the building like a poison ivy vine, but the bottom of the ladder is a good fifteen feet above street level. Not getting in that way either! Even though I know it's hopeless, I approach the door and pound on it with a doubled fist. Nothing. I pound again — I so totally don't want to run that gauntlet out front. One more time and now my hand and my wrist are throbbing. Shit! I turn away and head back for the street. Then I hear "Hola!" from behind me.

When I turn, the door is open. An older woman with coffee-colored skin like Lupe's, wearing a black polo shirt and a white skirt, holds the door wide and beckons. I run back and scoot inside.

"*Gracias, señora.*"

"*De nada,*" she says, then pushes her cleaning cart down the corridor.

I really don't want to go into the lobby either, so I ask her, "*¿Qué señora?* Do you know what floor Hightower, Talbot and Willy are on?"

Her look of befuddlement is replaced by comprehension when she hears the name of the law firm. "*Si. Nueve.*"

Nine floors of stairs. Shit.

By the time I reach the ninth floor, my thighs are burning and the sweat is rolling down my chest and back underneath my hoodie. Great! I'm gonna smell like a goat again! I strip the hoodie off and tie it around my waist, then go down the corridor while scanning the frosted glass doors until I find the law office. I go inside and there's Gary McDougall sitting on a sofa in the foyer reading a copy of Capital! the city's promotional magazine, like he doesn't have a care in the world. He lays the magazine on the low table in front of him when he sees me, rises and extends his hand.

He leads me to the receptionist's desk. "This is Ms. McMasters, here for a ten o'clock deposition. Do you have a room we can use for a few minutes so I can prepare her?"

The receptionist looks at his computer screen. "Sorry," he says. "All the conference rooms are in use. You'll have to go out in the corridor." He glances at the clock on the wall. "And they're expecting you in five minutes."

So that's the way it going to be, is it?

"They can wait," says Gary. He takes my hand and leads me out in the hall.

We go clear to the end of the hall next to a window and Gary rests his butt on the sill. "The first thing you need to understand," he says, "is that this is not a hearing. It's a deposition. You don't need to answer a single question they ask you if you don't want to."

"Then what am I doing here? They sent a subpoena!"

"They did that just to scare you into showing up. Lawyers usually take depositions so we can agree to a lot of stuff before a hearing. One side or the other submits the deposition into evidence prior to calling their witnesses — saves time. The other likely reason they're doing this is that they're afraid that their case is weak, so they're hoping to trap you into saying something that you shouldn't, which you are not going to do."

I'm confused. It sounds like I didn't have to be here at all. "Then what am I doing here?" I ask again.

"This will give us a chance to hear the kinds of questions that they'll ask in the hearing," he says. "We can find out if they've got any evidence that your accusation against Simonson may not hold water, or if they're just blowing hot air. They may even offer a settlement or drop the suit entirely."

I'm beginning to feel a lot better.

"No matter what you're asked, look at me before you respond. I'll nod if I want you to answer. When you do answer, truthfully respond only to the question asked and don't embellish. Can you do that?"

The truthfully part bothers me, but I'm not telling Gary that. I nod.

"Good," he says. "Let's go in there and get this over with."

After we re-enter the offices, the receptionist directs us to a conference room. An older gentleman who reminds me of Uncle Amos, wearing a retro three-piece suit, is sitting at the head of a long conference table. Simonson sits on his right like an acolyte. Gary extends his hand to the old gentleman, saying, "Good to see you, Jedidiah. It's been a while." He turns to me. "Natalie McMasters, this is Jedidiah Hightower."

"Pleased t'meetcha, Miss McMasters," Hightower says, but his eyes belie his words. "Of course, you know Mr. Simonson."

I nod to Simonson, but I won't take his hand. He looks at me with a smirk on his face. Just what are you planning, Freddy-boy?

Hightower motions us to two seats on his left. Gary takes the seat next to him, leaving the next one for me. I see what he's done. I can't respond to Hightower or Simonson without seeing Gary's face first. Smart!

They've got a large TV screen on legs set up at the far end of the table, with a small box in front of it. I hope they're not going to show the video of me and Lupe again. I make up my mind that I'm walking out if they do that.

Hightower consults a legal pad in front of him, then addresses me. "I trust Mr. McDougall explained what we're tryin' to do here today, Natalie. May I call you Natalie?"

"No," I tell him. Gary smiles.

"Very well, Miss McMasters. Or is it Mrs?" There's a hint of a smile in his lizard eyes.

"Ms. will do."

"Well as I say, Miss McMasters, what we're tryin' to do is to get some facts on record so we can hit the ground runnin' when we get to the libel hearin'. None of us wants to be in that courtroom any longer than we've got to be. So I'm just gonna ask you a few questions about that meetin' you had with my client here, in which you allege that he assaulted you…"

"Oh he assaulted me, all right," I say and mean it.

"Well, as you say. I just want to get a few specifics about what happened, is all." I look at Gary. He frowns, then nods briefly.

"So let's see, you were sittin' in a chair in front of his desk about what, ten feet away from him?" He looks at Simonson for confirmation. Simonson nods.

"Then y'all had a talk about that pornographic movie that you, 'scuse me, that was shown on campus. That right?"

I nod.

"Please speak up, Miss McMasters. We are recordin' this."

"You know you were required to tell us that before you started, Jedidiah," says Gary.

"I thought you knowed it, Gary." There's that evil glint in his eyes again. "Miss McMasters?"

"What?"

"You and my client had a talk about the movie. That right?"

Gary nods almost imperceptibly. "Yes," I answer.

"Then Mr. Simonson advised you about the specifics of Title IX and told you he had to investigate whether you'd created a hostile environment on campus with your dirty movie. Right again?"

"It's not my dirty movie," I say before Gary does anything.

"But it was you in it," Hightower says. "You and your..." he hesitates, then says, "...wife." Believe me, I heard what he didn't say.

Gary speaks up. "C'mon, Jedidiah. It's pretty obvious that you're trying to rattle her. Quit, or we're out of here."

"Is that what I'm doin' here, Gary? I didn't think so. Anyway, Natalie, you and Mr. Simonson talked about the movie and he said it was his job to investigate you. Right?"

Gary nods. "Yes," I say.

"And when in all of that did Mr. Simonson sexually assault you?" Hightower asks. Gary nods.

"After he brought up my former job and asked me if I could think of anything that could make his investigation go away."

"Your former job?" The condescension drips from his tone. "What job was that?"

I open my mouth to answer, but Gary gets there first. "We're willing to stipulate that Miss McMasters worked at a strip club for a time. But that doesn't prove she was responsible for that video."

"Maybe not," says Hightower. He puts one hand in his jacket pocket. "But she was responsible for this one." The TV at the end of the table wakes up and I'm suddenly on the screen on my back on a heart-shaped bed, legs splayed wide, pleasuring myself with a large pink dong. The sound comes up. "Yes! Oh yes! Give it to me, baby! Fuck Kira! Fuck Kira hard!"

I leap to my feet to stomp out of the room and Hightower says, "You can go if you want to, Natalie, but you won't find it as easy to leave when I show this in court."

Gary grabs my wrist and pulls me back into the chair. "You won't be showing that in court, counselor," Gary says.

"Sure we will. That is you, Natalie, isn't it?"

Gary shakes his head. "It's immaterial who it is. It has nothing to do with who showed that video on campus."

"But it has everything to do with the credibility of Natalie's assertion that my client sexually assaulted her."

"How's that, counselor? She made a dirty movie, so it's impossible to subject her to sexual contact against her wishes?"

Hightower smiles. "That's how a jury might see it. Especially a God-fearin' Southern jury."

"And that's why a judge won't allow them to see that video."

"Well then, maybe he'll 'low this one."

Hightower's hand comes out of his pocket, holding a remote. The TV screen comes on again, then I see myself sitting in the wobbly chair in front of Simonson's desk.

"I am the Title IX Coordinator for this University," Simonson is saying. "As such, I am tasked with identifying instances of sexual harassment on campus, which include the creation of a hostile educational or work environment. Your video definitely creates such an environment."

Simonson, you son-of-a-bitch! You recorded our interview?

"Once a Title IX complaint is lodged, I will investigate it," he goes on. "As the Title IX Coordinator, I can lodge a complaint, as can any member of the University community. If I find that the complaint is valid, I will file it with the Dean of Students and she will process it under the Code of Student Discipline to determine an appropriate sanction. Such sanctions can go all the way up to expulsion from the University."

"What can I do about this?" I sound like I'm pleading with him. "Do I get a trial or something?"

"You will be provided an opportunity to meet with the Dean or the Dean's designee after the complaint has been filed. They will advise you of your rights and responsibilities under the Code of Student Discipline. If the complainant is the Title IX Coordinator, any victims may also attend this administrative meeting. And since this video was widely disseminated on the campus closed-circuit network," he indicates the computer monitor, on which the video is still playing, "it's very likely that others will choose to become co-complainants."

Wait! That's not how that went down!

"What can I do about this?" I say on the screen.

"Tell me about your time as Kira Foxxx," he says.

"I took that name when I worked undercover to find out who killed a friend of mine and hurt my uncle."

His smug smile broadens. "That's right," he says. "I saw your television interview with Roderigo. You fancy yourself a detective."

"I got a job as a stripper. I broke up a major drug ring."

"And did you discover the identity of your friend's murderer?"

"Yes. It was the owner of the club."

Simonson's desk phone buzzes. "Your three o'clock is here early."

"I'll be done here shortly. Send her in when McMasters leaves. You're sure there's nothing you can think of to do to help yourself here?" he says to me.

"No. Sorry."

"Pity." He picks up a stack of papers from his desk, bangs them a few times to arrange them and puts them in a folder which he closes. "If you change your mind, make another appointment with Margaret. But you'd best act quickly. It will be much more difficult for you if there are many more co-complainants. You're dismissed."

I struggle out of the plastic chair and walk out of the camera's field of view. The screen goes dark.

"Did you see a sexual assault in that, Natalie. I sure didn't." Hightower thumbs the button on the remote again and the screen flashes to life.

I'm in a spotlight, sitting on a stool in a bare room. Roderigo is sitting next to me, leaning towards me, asking, "Natalie, is that what happened? Did Mr. Simonson sexually assault you?"

"Yes, he did." I say.

"I know this is painful, Natalie, but can you tell America exactly what Mr. Simonson did to you?"

"He came up behind me," I tell Roderigo. "He pulled up my t-shirt and put his hands on my breasts."

"What about your brassiere?"

"He pushed that up so he could touch my nipples. He took them between his fingers."

"And what did you do?"

"I fought him! I tried to get his hands off me!"

"And what happened?"

"He turned me around to face him and he kissed me! Put his tongue in my mouth and pushed his penis up against me!"

"And what did you do then?"

"I bit him and he let me go. Threw me on the floor. Called me a bitch and told me I'd be sorry and to get out of his office!"

The TV goes dark again. "Did you have another interview with Mr. Simonson that we don't know about, Natalie? Cause I sure didn't see any of that in this one." He calls up the video of me in Simonson's office again.

The motherfucker doctored the video of me in his office?

"Simonson! You shit! You fucked with that video!" I yell. Simonson's smirk is broader.

"Which video?" says Hightower. "The one of you and Roderigo? Most of America saw that one."

"The one in his office! He cut stuff out..." Simonson is openly leering now.

Simonson speaks for the first time in the meeting. "I've never been anything but honest," he says. "Unlike you, Natalie. You've even convinced all of those other women that there's fame and money to be had if they support your trumped-up charges."

"You mother fucker!" I erupt from my chair and lunge across the table at him, claws extended. Gary grabs me by the shirt collar and hauls me back, while Simonson goes over backwards in his chair to get away from me. I hope he broke his fucking neck!

Gary is standing behind me with his hands on my shoulders, pressing down so I can't get up. When he feels me go limp, he slides his hands to my arms and pulls me up out of the chair.

"We're leaving, gentlemen," Gary says.

"Go ahead and leave," Hightower says. "But you're going to have to respond to this in court. We'll even give you copies of the videos so you can test them for authenticity. But there is an alternative."

"And that is?" asks Gary.

"Mr. Simonson has generously agreed to drop his defamation suit if Ms. McMasters will appear with him on Roderigo Hernandez's show and confess that she lied about what happened in his office that day."

Fuck no!

"And what about Ms. McMasters expulsion from State?" Gary asks before I can get a word in edgewise.

"Mr. Simonson has no control over that, but he can certainly talk to the Dean to see if something can't be worked out. Ms. McMasters obviously has severe emotional problems and perhaps expulsion is too harsh a penalty for someone with such an affliction. Perhaps the Dean will agree to readmission after a treatment program has been completed."

I can't even! I see the insidious ingenuity in Simonson's plan. A public apology from me on national TV will cast aspersions on the claims of all of the other accusers. If I admit I lied, how many of them also lied? And if Simonson had the foresight to record his interview with me and edit it, maybe he's got doctored footage of the other women too...

"I'll never..." I begin. Gary claps his beefy hand over my mouth.

"She'll never make a decision like that without talking it over with her attorney first," he says. "Come on, Natalie. We're out of here."

"Lookin' forward to your call, counselor," drawls Hightower as we exit.

Chapter 22.

I try to talk to Gary as we're walking to the elevator but he shushes me. "Wait till we're in my office," he says.

We ride down to the lobby and Gary marches me straight out the glass doors into the street and the maw of the lurking mob. Holy shit, the crowd has at least doubled in size! My name is commingled with the boisterous blasts of car horns. "Natalie! We love you!" People's fingers nip at my clothes like the teeth of a pack of hounds. A reporter begins, "Ms. McMasters, can you tell us..." "No comment," Gary snaps. A woman carrying a sign grabs my hand and pushes something into it — a folded piece of paper. We elbow our way out of the crowd and Gary hustles me into a waiting limo as cameras record our every move. The liveried driver shuts the door, locking me into cool, sweet leathery silence.

I unfold the paper. There's a name — Emmaleigh Calhoun — and a phone number. Underneath is scrawled *Call me*.

The street door opens and Gary slides in next to me.

"A limo?" I ask him incredulously. "Who's paying for this?"

"You are. That crowd would have had you stripped naked by the time we got to my office."

"Who leaked this meeting?"

"Likely Jedidiah did. They want to keep the pressure on you."

Gary tells me to hold any more discussion until we're at his office, which is only a few blocks away. There's a small group of onlookers gathered outside his building, but nothing like the crowd we just left.

Gary's office building couldn't be more unlike Hightower's. It dates from the early 1900's and there's a city museum on the first floor. A skylight four stories up floods the lobby with sunlight and the warm wood and paper aroma of the museum has a calming effect. We ride the elevator to Gary's offices on the second floor and exit onto a terrace that overlooks the lobby. Gary leads me to his office, waves me to a sofa and shuts the door.

"Lie down," he tells me. "You've had a rough morning." I do as he asks and he pulls up a chair to sit next to me. "How you holding up?" he asks.

"I'm all Gucci." He lowers his eyebrows. "Okay, so I'm not. I'm shook."

"I don't blame you Nattie. That's what they wanted."

"Gary, Simonson doctored that vid of us in his office. It didn't go down like that!"

"How did it go down? Like you told Roderigo?"

I start to say yes, then I think about it. Shit is getting real, people. Simonson's a liar, but so am I. I don't know if I can keep this up, especially in court where it's called perjury.

"Not exactly," I say to Gary, then I start crying.

I come clean about what happened in Simonson's office, or at least as best as I can remember it. "The fucker's got me so confused with his phony video that I don't know if I can remember exactly," I finish.

"But you lied to Roderigo," Gary says. "Simonson never touched you?"

"No, he never did."

Gary puts his hands on top of his head, closes his eyes and tilts his head back, sighing audibly. Sorry, not sorry I made trouble for you, too! Finally, he looks at me and says, "In that case, I really think you should take Simonson's offer."

"But if I do that, he'll get away with everything!"

"Maybe. Maybe not. There are other accusers out there now, you know."

"But if I say I lied, it'll make it look like they're lying too."

"What it looks like matters less than what people can prove," says Gary. "At least I hope that's still the case."

"Maybe we can prove he faked that video."

"Maybe. Maybe not. I'm sorry to tell you that kind of fakery has become much more sophisticated in the last couple of years. Scam artists are using CGI techniques and passing the doctored files through multiple algorithms to mask the alterations. And Simonson has the resources of a major university behind him. You were worried about the cost of a limo. You should see what digital forensics analysts charge."

"Maybe I can find out who doctored it for him."

"Yes, but even if you do, the fact that you lied on national TV puts you in a terrible position. You saw what Jedidiah did to you today. It will be a thousand times worse in court, especially when you knowingly commit perjury on the witness stand. And now that I know you lied, I won't suborn the perjury. I won't tell on you because this is a privileged communication, but I won't put you on the stand and ask you questions when I know in advance that your answers under oath will be lies. And even if we did somehow prove that Simonson faked the video, Jedidiah would still get you to admit that you lied about Simonson, which is defamation, or to perjure yourself if I put you on the stand. It's a no-win, Nattie."

I feel awful. "So what do I do?"

"Take the deal. Lying to Roderigo on TV was defamation, but Simonson will sign a document releasing you from that. You haven't committed perjury until you lie under oath. So don't do it. Take the deal."

I replay the events of the last few days in my head. Chica in Lupe's bail hearing, artfully parrying the judge's pointed questions to protect her client and put her in the best possible light. Gary, shielding me from the serpentine Hightower, who was endeavoring to ensnare me in his coils. That is how I see myself in ten years, but it will never happen for me now that I'm expelled from State. No law school will touch me! But there's still a chance for me to have my dream come true if I do what Simonson wants. I hate the thought of giving into that bastard, but I did tell lies about him on national TV. It's only fair and just that I recant those lies in the same venue. My mind is made up.

"Gary, call Hightower and tell him I'll take the deal."

"OK. And I'll call Roderigo's people to set up the show."

"I'd like to do it here in town if we could."

"I'm pretty sure Roderigo will jump at the chance to have you and Simonson on the same stage no matter where it is," Gary says.

Later, I'm in the parking deck, sitting in the Z-car. I've no idea who the mysterious Emmaleigh is — another of Simonson's victims, a reporter waiting to ambush me, or a crazed fan (yes, I have fans now!) who will do God-knows-what if I meet with her. Well, there's only one way to find out. I punch her number into my phone.

Her voice is tentative. "Hello?"

"Emmaleigh? This is Natalie McMasters."

"Oh! You called! Can we talk?"

"That's what we're doing."

"I mean, can we meet?"

The events of the last couple of weeks have taught me to be a little more cautious. "That depends. Why?"

"I need to talk to you about what Fred Simonson did to me. I can't do it over the phone."

"Why not?"

"I just can't!" Her voice nearly breaks into a sob, but not quite.

"I guess I can meet you. Where?"

'My place?"

Bad idea. "I'd like to be a little more public. Can we get coffee or a drink somewhere?"

"I don't think so. I don't know if I can talk about this without crying and I don't want to do that where people can see."

"I can understand that. Is it okay if I bring somebody else along?"

"Who?"

"A guy who works with me. His name's Danny."

"I don't know…"

"He's a good guy. He won't judge you." I hope.

"I don't know if I can do this in front of a guy."

My patience snaps. "Look Emmaleigh, I've had a really lousy couple of weeks. People have been doing all sorts of nasty shit to me, so I'm not going to meet privately with somebody I don't know from Eve without backup. The two of us can meet in public or at your place and I bring Danny. Pick one."

The phone is silent for so long I think she killed the call. I'm just getting ready to shut it down when she says, "Okay. My place, with Danny."

"Where is it?" She gives me an address in the student quarter not far from where I used to live with Kwan and Fields. "When?" I ask her.

"You can come any time. I don't go out much."

Danny parks his pickup in front of Emmaleigh's house a couple of hours later. Emmaleigh looks a few years older than me. She's nearly 6 feet tall and has long straight hair and a sallow complexion that accentuates her gauntness. Her face would be pretty if it wasn't engraved with so many anxiety furrows. Her house is a typical student hovel with mismatched furniture, hardwood floors etched with termite channels, sheets on the widows for curtains and the tang of marijuana in the air. She shows us to her living room and waves us to a battered sofa covered with blankets.

"You can sit there," she says. She sits on a large floor cushion, facing us.

I introduce myself and Danny even though she knows who we are, just to have something to say. I know this is not going to be an easy conversation for her.

"Natalie, I want to thank you so much for coming forward about Simonson. It took tremendous courage for you to talk about what he did to you on national television — I could have never done that! It made me feel ashamed that I didn't have the courage to speak out too."

I wonder if she'll still feel that way after she sees the next broadcast I do with Roderigo.

"How did you get involved with that sleezeball?" I ask her.

"I'm a grad student in the English department. Women's studies. My thesis project explores erotic writing as literature — does it have any social value at all, or does it simply demean women by turning them into sex objects? You can imagine that such a subject could lead to some lively discussions and after one of these, Simonson called me to his office and told me that someone had filed a Title IX complaint saying that I'd created a hostile environment."

"And let me guess," I say. "He told you that he could make it go away if you did some things for him."

"Essentially. I don't hold old ideas about sex — I used to like it with the right person and I liked experimenting. But I don't like to be coerced. Nevertheless, I thought that if all it was going to take to make this go away and save my career was a blow job now and again, it was a small price to pay. After all, I wasn't going to be at State forever."

I glance at Danny as she's speaking — he's tight-lipped and his ears were crimson. He is somebody who holds old ideas about sex.

"So what happened?" I ask her.

"Well, it wasn't just a blow job now and again, or even a fuck. The more I gave into Simonson, the more he wanted and I came to realize that it wasn't about the sex for him, it was about the power. He made me get naked and play with myself while he asked me questions about things I had and hadn't done and when he got an inkling that there was something I didn't want to do, that was the next thing he'd ask for. Then when we were finished, he would make me tell him how I liked it. If I said I didn't like it or he even thought so, we'd do it over and over again until I said I did like it."

"Why didn't you tell him to shove it after he made the Title IX thing go away," Danny asks. I glare at him. Who told you that you could speak, man?

She won't look at him. "Because he never did make it go away. He intimated that he could swear a complaint at any time — it didn't have to come from someone else. And he was the one who did the investigating, the one who convened the hearings and the one who reported to the dean. I had no recourse at all!" Tell me about it, Bae!

"How long did this go on?" Danny asks.

"It's been about a year, since last fall. He asked if I'd ever had sex with a woman and when I said no, he made me do that. Some of the women were prostitutes and some were other students he was extorting. Sometimes he'd participate and sometimes he'd just watch or make a video. And of course, he threatened to upload the video to porn sites or send them to my family."

God, I so want to destroy that fuckwad right now!

"There was one woman in particular who was his partner, I think. They'd make me do threesomes and they'd dress up in leather, tie me up and treat me like their slave. They'd beat me if I didn't do everything they said, or if I didn't do it fast enough..."

Her complexion has become two shades whiter, her eyes are protruding and her mouth still hangs open when she stops speaking. A line of drool seeps from one corner. She's becoming seriously unglued.

"Emmaleigh, it's okay, you don't have to..."

"No! I have to tell somebody! One night they tied me naked over a chair, my arms tied in front and my ankles to the chair legs. Then men came in one by one and did me from behind, any way they wanted to and I couldn't see who they were! My God it hurt! And Simonson was filming everything. His lady-friend told me they were selling me on the Internet for ten dollars a pop, except for the winos who they'd let have me for free. They wouldn't even untie me to go to the bathroom. I cried and I begged for them to stop, but the woman just laughed, "Oh now you're getting' just what you deserve, shug!" she said.

Shug? No, it couldn't be! I turn to Danny and he looks like somebody just kicked him in the nuts.

"What did this woman look like?" asks Danny.

"She was thirty, thirty-five. Kind of plump, blonde hair..."

"And she called you shug?"

"Mostly she called me way worse things. But I remember exactly what she said because I hurt so bad..."

'Okay Emmaleigh, you can stop," I tell her. "You don't have to say any more right now. But would you consider going to the district attorney..."

"No! I can't! I can't get up in court and tell everyone what I let those people do to me! I trust you, Natalie. You're strong — I heard what you told Roderigo. You can stop them from doing this to other women."

How in the fucking hell am I supposed to do that if I'm going to apologize to him on national television?

Chapter 23.

We're both silent as we head for my place in Danny's pickup. I don't think either of us really believes that Diane was Simonson's partner and Emmaleigh's abuser.

While it's not terribly common, "shug", which is short for "sugar", is a Southern term of endearment analogous to honey, dear, or bae that's used in certain parts of the state. I heard it a fair bit growing up in Fayetteville. And Diane is so not the only frowsy middle-aged blonde on the State University campus.

I address the elephant in the pickup. "You know, we could go back there, show Emmaleigh a picture of Diane and clear this up way fast."

"It's not Diane," Danny says too quickly. "Besides, I don't have a picture of her. She never gave me one."

"What, you guys never took a selfie?"

"Nope."

Now I can't leave it alone. "Well then, what did you do when you were together," I ask him.

His ears are glowing like the tail lights of the car in front of us. "I told you before. Went out for drinks, mostly. Listened to country music and played pool and darts."

"And…"

"And none of your business, Nattie! I don't ask you what you and Lupe do together, though I guess most of the country knows that by now."

Where the fuck did that come from? I'm not going to hit him back — that's what he wants to shut this discussion down. "All I'm asking is that, when you had sex with Diane, did she ever give you the idea that she liked the kinky stuff?"

"No!" he says way too loudly. I don't believe him. I think she does like it, I think they did it and I think he's embarrassed about it.

Danny drops me off at the townhouse with a perfunctory goodbye. I think about driving over to University Hospital to take a quick pic of Diane on my cell, then sending it to Emmaleigh. That's not a bad idea. I can check on LeBrowne at the same time. The loss of the 3M office really hurts — with our database access there, I could have had a driver's license photo of Diane in five minutes.

The same nurse as last time is on duty at the Burn Unit. She glances up from her computer screen and smiles in recognition. "Lookin' for your friend Mr. Ellis, hon?"

I nod.

"He's not here anymore."

My gut is suddenly hollow. "He's not…"

"Land sakes, no, hon! He's been transferred."

"To where?"

She turns back to her monitor. "Well let's just see…" The mouse circles on the desktop pad. "There it is. They took him over to Tubman yesterday."

"Tubman?"

"Tubman Sanitarium. It's a long-term convalescent facility associated with the hospital. We keep the beds in this unit for the patients who need acute care. The fact that he's been transferred means he's doing well enough not need our services anymore."

"That's excellent!" I say. "Hey, is Diane Beasley around?"

"Hon, Diane hasn't worked in this unit for months."

"Huh?"

"It can get pretty stressful here. She transferred out to take a less demanding role. She's lead nurse for the oral ketamine trial down the hall."

It takes a second to register. "The what? You mean the CL…"

"Oral CL-581. It's a new oral formulation of ketamine that will be a boon for our burn patients if it proves out. That's why Diane got interested in it."

Ketamine! In my mind I see Diane coming down the hall from the trial ward towards me and Josh Russell the last time I was here, wearing a long-sleeved shirt under those hideous puppy scrubs and latex gloves. She was wearing long gloves again on that day at 3M when Danny read her out for insulting me. To hide the cat scratches she got when she was cutting on Xin Niu, no doubt. It's a good thing that I had to leave the Ruger in the car because of the enhanced security in the hospital lobby, or I'd go down there and shoot her down where she stands.

I give up on the idea of trying to get her pic, because I'm sure if I see her, I'll go off on her. What I need to do is get my shit together, then talk to Danny. He is so not going to want to hear this. But we need to get some solid evidence that Diane's in this with Fred Simonson and I'll need his help with that. That bitch is going down!

I'm suddenly way worried about LeBrowne. I'm also convinced that Diane had something to do with his sudden attack the other day, although I don't know what she did. She could have been lying to Danny when she told him that nothing was found wrong with the IV meds, although you would think that the hospital investigation would have discovered whether there was. Then I remembered something — I gave LeBrowne a drink of water just before the attack came on. He had a look on his face like he'd stepped in something after he'd finished his drink. I'd chalked it up to the pain from his burns, but now I'm not so sure. Maybe they should have given him a blood test for ketamine.

I'm sure the security at Tubman is not as tight as it is here. Maybe I'd better get over there and warn LeBrowne.

Back in my car, I google the Tubman Sanitarium on my phone. It's only a few miles away, in the center of a large green area on the map. I remember now, I've driven by that place a thousand times on the highway, never knowing what was there. I set my nav system for the address on my phone and take off.

A brass plate on a red brick column in a posh residential neighborhood marks the entrance to the Tubman Sanitarium grounds. I drive through the open gateway, which is flanked by two large black cast iron gates with spiked tops bent inward, to keep the inmates in, I expect. There's a guard shack with a modern gate just inside the old gate, but there's no guard and the gate is up. I drive about another quarter of a mile on a windy two-lane road that runs uphill through a hardwood forest. I'm the only car on the road, so it's hard to believe that I'm just a couple of miles from downtown. The road ends on the hilltop, where I exit the woods onto a circular driveway in front of a huge red brick castle that would easily occupy an entire city block. It even has a battlement running around the roof four stories up. Many of the windows are barred. There's a nondescript silver sedan parked right in front of the main stairs, but a sign that says *Parking* directs me around the side of the building. Hmmpf! Some people think they're so special they can park anywhere.

There's a modern parking deck around the back. Signs that say *Reception* lead to the front of the building where I find double glass doors at the top of the stairs, which lead into a modern lobby. A series of balconies overlooking the lobby are accessible by curved staircases that coil upwards on either side. The lobby is lit by a skylight that lets in the afternoon sun and the natural light is augmented by modern, wall-mounted fluorescent bulbs. The place still smells like a hospital though, reeking of iodine and bleach.

A counter divided into multiple niches segregates a large reception area under the balcony from the rest of the lobby. There's not a receptionist in every niche, but I spot one who's free and ask her if LeBrowne Ellis is a patient here.

She gives me a puzzled look, then says "Just a minute, please." She retreats to back of the reception area and I see her pick up a phone.

I'm beginning to get the idea that something is wrong here. I turn to go back outside and I see Detective Russell hurrying down the stairs. I briefly consider trying to duck him, but he looks right at me as if he knew I was here. The receptionist? She called him?

His face radiates anger as he approaches. "McMasters! Where's Ellis?"

"What?"

"Not what," he grates. "Where did they take Ellis? You're in on this!"

"In on what?"

Maybe it was the look on my face that convinced him that I really didn't know WTF he was talking about. "Your pal Ellis is missing from his room," he says. "The sanitarium called the cops and the case was passed to me. Then I find you here. What am I supposed to think?"

"I don't know what you're supposed to think. I came here to see a sick friend. Is that against the law?"

"Get smart with me and I'll run you in again."

"I'm not getting smart with you, detective. I came to see my friend and you tell me he's not here. Then I guess I have no reason to be, either. I'll just bounce, unless I'm being detained?"

He thinks about it, then he says, "No. Get out of here before I change my mind."

I go while I can. Dammit! Besides seeing LeBrowne, I wanted to nose around a little and see if I could find out any more about what happened to patient X. Now I'll have to leave that to Danny or Kidd.

I get back to the Z-car in the parking deck and open the driver's door, but before I sit I notice a dark object on the front seat. WTF? It's one of those old-fashioned flip phones. I had one in high school — thought they had gone out of style years ago. I pick it up, flip it open and power it on.

Why would someone leave this in my car? Obviously, to get in touch with me. But why not just call? I can think of only one reason.

I bring up the recents list. The phone has received a call from just a single number. I press the button to call the number back.

"A'ite?"

"LeBrowne? That you?"

"Yep."

"Where are you?"

"You don't need to know. I jes' left you this burner if'n you need to talk. And I hear tell that it was you got the medics to me so quick t'other day. They said I'd have bought it but for you."

"So I guess you owe me again."

"Guess so."

"How did you get out of Tubman?"

"My homies. Nobody pays any 'tention to a nigga in scrubs. I knew I was dead if'n I stayed there."

He's right about that. "Look, you just lay low and get well. We'll figure out who's doing this and deal with them."

"Jes' let me know if'n you need help dealin' wit' 'em. The Legends will be there."

The phone goes dead.

My mind is whirling on the drive home. It's way sus that Lebrowne was transferred at all so soon after damn near dying in the Burn Unit. I wonder if that was more of Diane's work. I'll have to call Danny when I get home and hope he's gotten over whatever was eating him this morning.

I have quickly come to accept that it's Diane who's behind everything that's been happening over the past few weeks. But why would she do something like that to me? I didn't even know Diane Beasley existed until she showed up looking for Danny at 3M that day. Truthfully, I've always thought it was damn strange that he would hook up with somebody like her. That is, unless she took advantage of him in a weak moment. Never underestimate the stupidity of a horny guy if alcohol's involved. Danny once told me that he doesn't believe in one-night stands and I believe him. That means that he's got a connection to Diane, as much as I hate that thought.

But if Diane's really behind all of this, WTF did I ever do to her? And how am I ever going to get Danny to accept that she's involved?

I make a sudden decision and turn the car on to a different path. There's something I've been putting off, but now it's time to commit. Then I can head for home.

When I pull into the parking lot at the condo complex, I notice Lupe's car in the space next to mine. That's way strange — she's not due home from work for another couple of hours. When I get inside, I know immediately that something's wrong. The lights aren't on in the kitchen or the great room and there's no aroma of freshly cooking food. I find her in our bedroom, lying on her back on the bed in the dark with the curtains closed.

"What's wrong, sweetie?" I ask her.

She snaps on the bedside light. "Come here and see."

I circle the bed to her side. She's now sitting up with her feet on the floor. She opens the drawer in the bedside cabinet and removes something from it, which she offers to me.

It's two little glassine bags, stamped with a caricature of a skeleton in a top hat. Each one contains a small amount of a white powder.

"Is it drugs?" I ask her. She knows I won't do them and to my knowledge, she never has either. "Where did you get this?"

"In my locker, at work."

WTF!

"I almost did not see it," she goes on. "It was all the way at the bottom, where I put my shoes."

"So where did it come from?"

"I do not know. It is not mine."

Does anyone else know your combination.

"I do not think so."

Shit, that doesn't matter. If you know how, you can defeat one of those cheap padlocks that everyone uses in minutes. We used to do it all the time in high school to see what embarrassing things we could find in somebody's locker. Or even more likely, someone could have pushed those little envelopes through the vents in the locker door, where they would have fallen just about where Lupe found them.

One of the things that Lupe's bond is contingent on is that she's not charged with a felony. If that happens, her bond can be immediately revoked and she can be jailed. It's only a short step to deportation from there. A phone call to the cops or ICE by the one who planted the drugs would have taken care of that.

She puts my thought into words. "Maybe the bad person who is trying to hurt you did this."

Suddenly I'm terrified! A vision of our front door bursting open and a blue-clad SWAT team streaming into our home like storm troopers invades my mind. "Lupe! We have to get rid of this! Right now!"

It's a short step to the bathroom. I throw the envelopes into the toilet and my heartbeat slows as I watch them circle the bowl and vanish.

Lupe's crying now. "*Cariño,* I am afraid!" she wails.

"Afraid of what?"

"That they will send me back to Mexico."

"That's not going to happen, bae. We're married now."

"But Chica said it is not automatic that they will give me a green card. And this bad person will try to get me in trouble again!"

I want to tell her that that's not true, but it would be a lie. I take a different tack.

"Even if they did send you back, you wouldn't be alone. I am your wife. I will go with you. The three of us could make a life in Mexico and work like hell to get back here legally."

"No!" she shouts. "You have no idea what is like there! There is no work and the *sicarios* are everywhere. They come to fuck you and you cannot say no! And you cannot be my wife there. If they ever find out we are *lesbianas*, it will be a hundred times worse! I cannot let that happen to you and Eduardo."

I made it worse instead of better. I think she's exaggerating because I know that gay people vacation in Mexico all the time, in places like Tijuana and Porto Vallarta. Gay marriage is legal in Mexico and there's an annual Pride parade in Mexico City. But Lupe is from a small rural town where homophobia still may exist and I've no doubt that she's had such experiences. I know that any more arguing right now is not going to help, so I take her in my arms, kiss her and shush her. "C'mon, sweetie. Let's get you cleaned up before Eduardo comes home. No sense in scaring him, too." She lets me take her into the bathroom and wash her face.

Later. After Eduardo has returned and Lupe is fixing dinner, I call Danny. He doesn't answer. I hope he's still not PO'd at me from this morning. I don't need drama when there's work to be done. I call Kidd instead and tell him what's been happening.

"You did the right thing with the drugs," he says. "Both Danny and I have enemies on the force, so I wouldn't expect a fair shake from the cops. I'll go to Tubman and try to find out what happened with LeBrowne. And did you ever check on patient X?"

"I didn't have time. Detective Russell was on me almost as soon as I got there."

"Then I'll do that, too. But don't hold your breath. And Nattie, give Danny a break. If Diane is involved in this, it's going to make him feel like a horse's ass. But he's a good guy and he'll get over it. Just give him some space."

"I will. Thanks."

So now I'm back to letting other people do the work again. I hate it.

Chapter 24.

It's Thursday evening. I'm backstage at the auditorium of a local TV station — the same one where they had the gubernatorial debate. Now I'm going to be on that stage with Fred Simonson and Roderigo. I'm here to apologize to Simonson for lying about him on Roderigo's last show, so I can resurrect my devastated college career. Maybe…

They're keeping me and Freddy apart until we actually meet on stage. That's a good thing, because it's going to take everything I've got not to start beating on him when I see him. He's sure to have that smug look on his face that he gets when he thinks he's won — "Smilin' like a pig in a dung heap", Uncle Amos would say.

My "handler" is a lanky, gay twenty-something named Stanley who's on Roderigo's staff. "Don't you worry, honey," he says. "You look damn fan-tastic! That crowd's gonna give you some loove!" Remember what I said about people who call me honey?

The crowd he's referring to is the several hundred people packed into the auditorium. Word is there's a few thousand more outside who couldn't get in. The TV station obligingly set up screens and speakers in the parking lots to accommodate them.

The faint strains of Roderigo's theme music penetrate the paper-thin walls of my dressing room. They had a TV in here so I could watch Roderigo's intro but I made them take it out. I want to experience as little of this travesty as possible. After this is over, I never want to be on TV again as long as I live.

Stanley touches his earpiece, then says "Righty-o!" He turns to me. "They're ready for ya, darlin'."

I get up from my chair and smooth my dress. Yes, on Gary's orders, I'm wearing a dress — a lacy white thing with a straight neck and skirt that falls to just above my knees, with a gold belt around my waist. I look like I'm going to a high school prom. My hair is down and I've got a necklace of fake pearls around my neck. Gary wanted me to wear a pair of white heels too, but I drew the line at that. I told him it was low-heeled sandals or bare feet. Guess which one he picked.

Stanley takes my elbow and leads me to the right wing, still backstage. I hear Roderigo outside, "Now America, let's welcome again that brave little lady, Natalie McMasters!"

Stanley gives me a push and I enter to thunderous applause. I wonder what their reaction will be when I've donned my sackcloth and ashes? The lights are so bright that the crowd is a roaring, nondescript background and so hot that wetness flows over my entire body under my dress. I walk past the towering carriages on which cameramen are mounted like gunners on some futuristic weapons platform. More cameras dangle from the rafters, tracking my every step as I make my way towards my inquisitor.

The stage is simply arranged. Roderigo is perched on a tall stool between two armchairs, with a small table holding a glass of water beside each one. He hops off the stool as I approach and extends his hand to take mine. He bends at the waist like an old-time courtier to kiss my hand and the crowd goes wild!

He leads me to my seat and waits for the crowd to silence, then continues. "And now, America, I must ask your respect and forbearance for our next guest..."

"Fuck that!" yells a female voice from the crowd. I can't see whether the heckler is being ejected, but I imagine so.

"It is a valued American tradition that the accused is always assumed innocent until proven guilty. We can do no less on Roderigo's show! America, please welcome Mr. Frederick Simonson!"

A few boos and catcalls mingle with the subdued applause, but I'm sure the audience's response would have been much more hostile had Roderigo not made his conciliatory plea. Simonson enters, wearing a charcoal grey suit and a dark tie instead of the usual, hideous orange and blue number. Apparently, Jedidiah Hightower had the same talk with him that Gary had with me.

Roderigo and Simonson shake hands and Freddy takes his seat. Roderigo mounts his stool and addresses the audience.

"I'm sure you're all curious why Natalie and Fred are here tonight, America. It's because Natalie called and told me that she may have misrepresented what happened between her and Fred..."

"No way!" from the crowd.

"Please! We'll hear from Natalie herself in a moment. She said that she may have misrepresented some things and being the principled and moral person that she is, she wanted to meet with Fred in this venue to explain to America just what happened between them that night." Roderigo turns to me, "So Natalie, what is it that you want to tell America about your encounter with Fred?"

I'd thought long and hard about just how I was going to do this. Gary wanted to coach me, but I refused. I have to do it my own way.

"Thank you, Roderigo. I want to say that when I talked to you last time about what Mr. Simonson did, I did not tell you the truth." I look at Freddy, who's grinning at me like I've just handed him a million bucks. I steel myself and go on. "In that interview, I said that Mr. Simonson sexually assaulted me. That was a lie. That never happened."

The crowd erupts in groans and boos. Roderigo hops off his stool and approaches the front of the stage with his arms held wide, like he wants to embrace the throng. "Please! Let her have her say!"

Roderigo turns to me. "All right, Natalie, you say that you lied to me. Why did you do that?"

"I may have gotten the mistaken impression during my interview with Mr. Simonson that he wanted me to trade sex for his dropping the Title IX charges against me. And I was angry that he was charging me at all because I did not deliberately release that video of me and my wife on campus. Someone else did! I wanted to hurt him back. That was wrong and I want to take this opportunity to apologize to him, if he'll accept it."

The crowd angrily growls again as I approach Simonson, my hand outstretched. He rises out of his chair and takes it, saying, "Of course I'll accept your apology, Natalie. I'm sorry too, that I didn't realize how distressed you were about that video that day. And I want to say here and now that I'm going to talk to the Dean about reinstating your enrollment at State, if you'll agree to participate in an emotional counselling program." The crowd applauds. Simonson squeezes my hand hard enough to hurt me before easing off.

The crowd has quieted, but there's still an uneasy rumbling in the room. Simonson tries to let go of my hand and sit back down, but I suddenly tighten my grip. Of course, I'm not strong enough to hurt him but I sure get his attention.

I raise my voice to be sure everyone hears me. "I may have lied about what you did to me Mr. Simonson, but I'd like to introduce some other people who won't lie about what you did to them. Will Ethyl Katz please come up here?"

Simonson goes white when he hears that name. He tries to disengage from me, but I won't him let go. He's surely strong enough to make me, but he doesn't want to make a scene on national television. A young brunette woman in jeans and a State t-shirt comes up on stage from the audience and approaches us. Roderigo extends his mike and says, "And who are you, young lady?"

"I'm Ethyl Katz. I'm a sophomore pre-vet major at State and Mr. Fred Simonson forced me to perform oral sex on him once a week for two whole semesters. He said he'd have me expelled if I didn't do it."

A gasp arises from the crowd, which then goes silent as death. Simonson is paralyzed in my grasp.

A cry of "Me too!" arises from the audience. Another woman takes the stage.

"I'm Susan Jones. I'm a junior and a music major at State. Fred Simonson raped me in his office multiple times. He said I'd be expelled from school and never achieve my dream of being a concert pianist if I didn't let him!"

Another "Me too!" echoes throughout the auditorium. I feel Simonson flinch like someone punched him.

Emmaleigh Calhoun comes slowly forward. Sobbing, she chokes out her horrible story about Simonson, the blonde woman and the chair. I let Simonson go as she finishes, because he's falling back into his chair and I'm not strong enough to hold him up.

The noise from the crowd is ugly now. Roderigo quells them again and "Me too!" rings out once more. WTF? I was only able to get Ethyl, Susan and Emmaleigh to agree to be here tonight.

A familiar blonde woman ascends the staircase at the side of the stage and comes forward. Roderigo extends the mike. "And tell America who you are, young lady."

"My name is Andrea Kiefer. I am a reporter for the *State of State* and a proud lesbian woman! Until I met Mr. Simonson, I had only been with women, never with a man. I wrote an article on lesbian love for the student paper that he said created a hostile environment on campus. He said he'd have me expelled if I didn't let him fuck me and take videos of other men fucking me!" She turns to Simonson, who's crouched in his chair like an evil, deformed dwarf. "I want to thank you for broadening my horizons, Mr. Simonson. I'd never have fucked a man in my life if it wasn't for you. I want to give you something to thank you for that."

She reaches into her jacket pocket. I think she's pulling a gun and apparently so does Roderigo, because he sends the stool flying as he bolts like a rabbit to the back of the stage. I flail for her wrist as her hand exits her pocket, but I'm on the wrong side and I can't stop her before she directs a stream of clear liquid from a small squeeze bottle into

Simonson's eyes, then plays it back and forth across his face like she's spray painting a car. I get hold of her and wrest the bottle away, getting some of the liquid on my hands and hers in the process.

A sound that never should be heard from a human throat arises from Simonson's gaping mouth. Both hands are clapped over his face as he rises from his chair only to collapse face down on the stage. His feet are kicking like a kid having a tantrum and his screams are ragged and unceasing. I soon learn why as rivulets of invisible fire begin coursing down my hands and arms where the liquid from the bottle ran. I snatch the glass of water from the side table and inundate one hand, then drop the glass on the floor as I try to switch hands to drench the other one. I see the second glass on Simonson's table and I grab it. I briefly watch Simonson shrieking and writhing on the floor, then I douse my other hand and arm with the contents of the glass.

Kiefer begins screeching too and runs for the wings, but some stage hands grab her and hustle her off. I hope for her sake it's not too long before someone gets her hands into some water.

My hands are still burning so I run to the backstage bathroom, holding my arms high like a doctor going into surgery so I don't contaminate anyone else. Sheets of skin peel from my hands as I rinse them and they feel as slippery as if they'd been doused in oil. Luckily, my dress has no sleeves so I'm able to soak my entire arms to neutralize the streams of corrosive liquid that ran down them, but nasty red streaks remain where it touched.

My mind is reeling. I can't imagine the depth of hatred that compelled Kiefer to take her revenge that way. She's not only crippled and disfigured a man for life, she's totally destroyed her own life too. A more disturbing thought arises. Did I do the same thing when I turned Nicky over to the Legends? Despite what I told Danny, I really didn't think that they were going to torture him — I thought they'd just kill him and be done with it. And I did try to turn him over to the authorities first. Would I have let the Legends have Nicky if had known what they we're going to do? No, I don't think so. I'd have found another way. True, I did act in self-defense. I know that Nicky would have killed me as surely as I know that the sun will rise tomorrow. And I thought then and still think now that he deserves to be punished for what he did.

When you kill someone, it changes you. Totally. To date, I've killed three people with my own hands. Like Danny said, that was combat. I did what I had to do to stay alive and I have to make my peace with that.

But nobody deserves what happened to Nicky, or what just happened to Simonson.

Eventually the cops come. Detective Russell is among then, so naturally, he accuses me of complicity, saying that I knew in advance what Kiefer was going to do when I invited her. Luckily, Gary is here too and he tells Russell to either charge me or release me. Russell opts for the latter.

The townhouse is dark when I finally get home. Looks like Lupe has wisely gone to bed. But when I come into the bedroom, she rolls over and snaps on the light.

"I'm sorry I woke you, sweetie."

"You did not. I could not sleep." She moves to sit on the mattress with her feet on the floor. "I saw the terrible thing that happened on TV. Then I worried when you did not come home."

"The police came. I couldn't leave until they let me go."

"They do not think that you had anything to do with what happened to that man? Mr. Simonson?"

"Detective Russell said he did, but Gary made him let me go."

"Gary is a good friend."

"Yes, he is."

She's quiet for a moment, then she says, "*Cariño,* I still think that the police will come for me soon."

"Bae, you can't think that way!"

"I cannot help it. I think the bad person who kill Xin Niu put those drugs in my locker. And they will do it again. ICE will find the drugs and deport me or put me in jail."

I don't respond right away because I think she's right, but I don't want to tell her so. I say, "I told you, I'm not going to let that happen. Don't you trust me?"

"More than anyone. But there are things that even you cannot do."

My phone plays Leon Kidd's song.

"What's up?"

"Nattie, when was the last time you talked to Danny?"

"Yesterday morning. We interviewed a witness. Why?"

"I've been trying to get up with him since yesterday and he's not answering his phone. I'm at his place now. He's not here and it doesn't look like he has been for a while."

It's suddenly very cold.

Kidd notices the silence on the line. "You still there, Nattie?"

"Yeah. Leon, you don't think that Danny might have gone to see Diane to find out if she was involved with what's been happening to me?"

"That sounds exactly like what he would do," says Kidd.

"Then we've got to find him. Fast!"

"I'll be right over," Kidd says.

Chapter 25.

Me and Lupe realize that there will be no sleep for us tonight. Lupe goes to the kitchen and begins brewing a strong batch of *café de olla,* while I change the white dress for jeans and a t-shirt. In a little while, the doorbell rings and I open the door to admit Leon Kidd. One look at his glum face tells me something's wrong.

"What? Did something happen to Danny?" I ask him.

"Not him. That girl that attacked Simonson…"

I supply the name. "Andrea Kiefer."

"Her. She's dead!"

"For real! How?"

"Killed while resisting arrest. I've heard that one before," he adds.

"Who killed her?"

"The cops. My source wasn't sure who specifically was involved."

"OMG! Will there be an investigation?"

"IA investigates every officer-involved killing, but no charges are brought in most of them. Likely the public will never hear the details."

I'm blown away. Part of me can imagine that crazy bitch going off on some cop, but they shouldn't have had to kill her to take her down.

Lupe comes over with a warming tray containing stoneware jugs of strong black coffee and milk and bowls of *piloncillo* and cinnamon sticks. There'll be no sleep after drinking that.

"We have bigger fish right now," says Kidd. "We need to find Danny. What do you know about what he was up to?"

"Not much. Last I saw him, he didn't say anything about his plans. But it would be just like him to go see Diane, to give her a chance to explain herself. Did you ping his phone?" Danny insisted that all of us install a location app on our phones, so the other 3M detectives can find any of us they need to.

"Yes." Kidd agrees. "First thing I did. It told me he was on the north side of town. I drove out to the area that the ping indicated and ended up on the highway. I didn't look for the phone because finding it there in the dark could have taken hours, but I'll bet it's lying on the side of the road. I went by Diane's place, which wasn't far from where the ping told me the phone was and it was dark. Pounded on the door in case she was in bed, but no answer. Called the hospital and she wasn't there either. So she's probably in the wind."

A vision of Danny lying dead in a ditch invades my brain. Stop it, Nattie! "We've got to find him, Leon!"

"So let's find him. Where do we start?"

I haven't got a clue. I start reviewing the case in my head, trying to think of anything that might help.

"Something's been bothering me ever since we found out that Diane might be behind what's happening to me. I'm pretty sure she killed Xin Niu because she had access to ketamine, but I have a hard time seeing her fire-bombing the Legends headquarters or the 3M office. She had to have help."

"Simonson?"

"I don't think so. He's a wuss — terrorizing some innocent coed is more his style." I tell him about the story that Kiefer wrote about me having ties to the Urban Legends. "Where would she even get stuff like that, Leon? Y'all didn't even know that I knew LeBrowne until I told you the other day. It had to come from Russell. Kiefer's story came out after I met him at the hospital, when I went there to ask about LeBrowne."

"So how would Kiefer be connected to Russell?"

"That's a damned good question." I remember what Kiefer said before she sprayed Simonson. "Kiefer said that Simonson made her fuck other men while he videoed it. What if Russell was one of those men?"

"That's from way out in left field," Kidd says.

"Maybe not. It provides a great motive for Russell to want Kiefer out of the way, especially since she was on a truthing binge."

"So how would Simonson have met Russell?"

"Cops come on campus all the time, for a lot of reasons. That's how I first met Danny. It's not inconceivable that Russell and Simonson crossed paths at State."

"But it's a real hard sell that a campus staffer who's screwing coeds would ask a cop to join in the fun," Kidd says.

I think for a minute. "Maybe it would depend on how they met."

"What do you mean?"

"Look. You've got a college administrator, a cop and a nurse involved in some kinky sex thing." I remind him of Emmaleigh's story about the raunchy Southern blonde that helped abuse her. "And a bunch of other guys besides. What does that sound like to you?"

"Some kind of bizarre swingers' club?" I just look at him. "I'll be damned," he says.

"And if these people were outwardly respectable and highly placed, they'd do almost anything to keep the truth from coming out. Like kill Kiefer, for instance. We're talking about forcible rape here, not just some kinky sex between consenting adults."

"Okay," says Kidd, "but even if I'll buy that, why pick on you? Do you think your boy Nicky may have been involved with these people?"

I consider his question. "I doubt it," I say finally. "Nicky was a loner at heart. Oh, he liked his sex all right, especially with young girls, but he never gave me any indication he was into group gropes."

"He could have provided drugs for their parties, maybe," says Kidd.

"Maybe. Or maybe he and Diane met when he was a patient on the Burn Unit and she was his nurse."

Kidd plays devil's advocate. "We don't even know that it was him on the Burn Unit."

"You're right, we don't, but it's likely that it was. The time is right and patient X's injuries jibe with what LeBrowne told me the Legends did to Nicky. Danny told me that Diane tended to get invested in some of her patients. That's why she eventually got used up and left the Burn Unit. Maybe she got invested in Nicky." I'm liking this idea more and more as I explain it to Kidd. "Believe me, Nicky had a way about him with the ladies. He could charm the pants off of you without hardly trying. Maybe he told Diane what the Legends did to him. Maybe he told her it was me that turned him over to them, conveniently leaving out the part about him murdering two families. Maybe he convinced her that I had to pay for what I'd done. This kind of revenge definitely sounds like something he'd do."

Kidd takes up the tale. "Then Diane, who knew Simonson from the sex club, recruited him to help. They got the video of you and Lupe off the Internet and put it on campus CCTV. Then Simonson used his position as the Title IX Coordinator to extort you for sexual favors. They probably had some really raunchy things planned for you at their orgies if you capitulated. Maybe for Lupe, too." He stops talking for a moment. "But where is Mr. Nicky now?" he asks.

I know the answer to that one. "With Diane. The Legends really did a number on him, Leon. Maybe he needs a full-time nurse."

Kidd shakes his head. "Talk about weaving a tapestry out of scattered threads. And even if it's all true, how does any of this help us find Danny?"

"I think Diane's got him. We find her, we find him." Alive, I hope.

"How?" asks Kidd.

"Can we ping her phone?"

"No. The person whose phone you're trying to locate has to have an app installed. The cops can locate a cell phone by other means, but it's against the law if we do it."

"And we can't ask the cops to find her because we can't trust them." A pause. "Then we have to find somebody who knows where she is."

"Who?"

"Another member of their little club?"

"Who?"

I replay the events of the last few weeks in my mind again. "The first thing that Danny and I checked out was how that video could have ended up on CCTV. We thought it was a dead end. But maybe we met the guy who uploaded it and didn't know it."

"Who?" Kidd says for the third time.

"A creep named Harold Upmann. He couldn't even look at me when we were talking to him. I put it up to shyness, but maybe it was something else. And you know what? Simonson made a video of my interview with him in his office, then doctored it to get rid of the parts that might incriminate him. He's a college administrator, would he have the skills to do something like that? I don't think so. But I'll bet a TV jock like Upmann would."

"So we go lean on this Upmann character to see if he knows where Diane is?"

"At least he can tell us where they hold their little sex parties and maybe who some of the other players are. It's a place to start."

A minute on my phone on the Internet gives me Upmann's address. I glance at the middle of the top of the screen. It's 3:30 a.m.

"How do you want to do this?" I ask Kidd. "Go over there now and wake him up?"

"Yes," says Kidd. "If you're going to terrorize someone, do it in the middle of the night."

A trickle of doubt invades a crack in the solid wall of my certainty. "What if Upmann really is innocent?" I ask Kidd.

"Then we're probably going to be charged with breaking and entering, assault with a deadly weapon and a few other unpleasant things. What do you want to do?"

I visualize Upmann's face at our last meeting. The way he wouldn't look at me, then the way he finally did. Yes, I decide. He's guilty all right.

"Let's get the son-of-a-bitch."

Chapter 26.

Harold Upmann lives in an apartment complex close to campus, which is mostly occupied by students. Figures. A teen who never grew out of his adolescent sexual fantasies. Kidd makes short work of the lock on the door with a couple of picks (I have *got* to learn how to do that!) then pushes the door handle down to open it, only to be confronted by a security chain. "Not to worry," he murmurs. He fishes in his jacket pocket and comes out with a rubber band, which he hands to me. "Here. You have smaller hands. Tie this around the top of the chain, then loop it around the door handle on the inside."

I do as he asks with some difficulty, then wiggle my hand back outside. He closes the door, then pushes the door handle down again and there's an audible Snap! from inside. When he reopens the door, the chain hangs limply, no longer keeping the door from fully opening. I see how that worked — pushing the handle down caused the rubber band to draw the chain along its track on the door until it reached the release point.

Kidd pushes the door open, waves me inside and BAM! I've committed a felony, just like that. I only wish it was the first time. The place smells like a cross between a locker room and a dive bar and is dirtier than either one. Clothes, magazines and other effluvia are scattered everywhere, making our passage across the living room treacherous in the darkness. We go down a short corridor to the bedroom at the back of the flat. The door is ajar and I can hear snores coming from inside. Kidd pushes the door open and we enter.

Leon Kidd is one of the sweetest guys I know. He's also a 6'2" black man who weighs nearly 300 pounds, has a bald head, a huge wart on his upper lip and looks like he was either a gangbanger or an NFL player in his younger days. If you're a pansy-ass white boy who wakes up in the middle of the night with Kidd looming over you, shoving his Glock in your face, he is your worst nightmare personified. And Kidd knows it.

He claps a hand over Upmann's mouth to cut off the scream and shows him the gun. "You don't want to do that, Harold," Kidd says. He removes the hand when Upmann's eyes indicate the crisis has passed.

"Whaa…, whaa…, whaa…"

"We just want to have a little chat, Harold. You tell us what we want to know and we're out of here. If you don't..." Kidd puts barrel of the Glock under Upmann's left nostril.

"What do you want to know?" he says. Then he sees me. "You!"

"We want to know all about your little orgy club, Harold," I tell him. "Oh, don't bother denying it. We've got some nice movies of you from the Internet screwing a girl tied to a chair, among others." That's a lie I thought up on the way here, but Upmann's wide eyes tell me it hits the mark. I knew it would! "We can send them to the papers, if you'd like."

"What do you want to know?" he says again.

"Oh, who else is in your frat, where you have your parties, that sort of thing."

"I can't tell you who's in it," Upmann says. "They'll kill me!"

"I'll kill you if you don't," says Kidd.

I can see Upmann struggling with it. Must be hooked up with some pretty bad dudes if he doesn't want to talk with that Glock in his face. I remember what's important here. "There must be someplace quiet you go to have your parties, Harold. Where?"

He doesn't want to tell me that either, but Kidd's Glock finally wins out. "Let me up," he says. "I'll draw you a map."

We do as he asks. He gets out of bed and leads us to the kitchen table where he draws us a map of an area outside of the city. "There's an old house back in the woods. You can't see it from the main road, so watch for a gravel driveway on your left."

"You can show us right where it is," says Kidd. "Get dressed. You're coming with us."

Upmann's mouth flops open like he's been kicked in the nuts. "No! I can't..."

Kidd is finally tired of him and opens a gash on his cheek with the front sight of the pistol. Upmann scurries down the hall to the bedroom, with Kidd following.

Great. Now we can add kidnapping to the charges. But it will be worth it if we find Danny!

We conduct the blubbering Upmann down to Kidd's car and set off.

The party house is about a twenty-minute ride from Upmann's place. I drive, while Kidd rides in the back with our reluctant passenger. We end up in a forested area near a state park. The yellow blotch of the headlights reveals that the center line on the two-lane asphalt road has nearly worn away and my passenger side tires continually slip off the road onto the gravel shoulder as I instinctively try to keep the car from drifting into the opposite lane. I nearly drive past the narrow road on the left as Upmann points it out. I'm glad he's with us — I would have missed that for sure without him.

The party house is a couple of hundred yards down the windy gravel road. The piney forest is a perfect screen — all sorts of nefarious activities could happen here with no one to hear the victims' screams. There's no moon, so the house is a hulking black mass against a Prussian blue sky. The windows are dark. The road leads around to the back, where we find an open area that could accommodate a dozen cars, easily. But none are here.

I stop the car and turn around to look at Kidd and Upmann. "It looks like nobody's here. What do you want to do?"

"They could have Danny tied up inside. Let's take a quick look."

"What about him?"

Kidd asks Upmann, "You got a key?"

"It's home. You didn't give me much time to get ready."

Fine. Let's add another count of breaking and entering to the charges.

"You'll find a couple of flashlights in the glove compartment, Nattie," Kidd says. "I'd rather not turn on the house lights and advertise that we're here to anyone who might drive up."

I find the flashlights, then hand one to Kidd. We get out of the car and walk to the back porch, with the pale pools of light darting around in front of us like ghostly animals startled out of their hidey holes. After we ascend the short staircase to stand on the back porch, Kidd says to Upmann, "I'm going to put this gun away, but know that I can run you down if you rabbit. You will not like what I do to you when I catch you." Upmann is so thoroughly cowed by Kidd that he nods his head nervously.

We enter the back door by the simple expedient of breaking a pane of glass in the back door, reaching through and turning the deadbolt. Like in many homes of this era, the rear door opens into the kitchen, which is vintage, not modern. But why do you need a contemporary kitchen in your orgy house?

Upmann leads the way into an area that likely used to be a living room/dining room connected by double doors, which have been removed to turn it into one big room. The flashlights reveal that the floors are littered with mattresses and futons, but there's also a weight bench and a vaulting horse, whose functions I don't even want to guess at. There are several mirrors on the walls and a couple of free-standing ones and I spot a sturdy straight-back chair that was likely the vehicle of Emmaleigh's defilement. Other cushioned chairs and sofas are also scattered about the room. Straps dangle from the ceilings and the flashlight beams glint off of a multifaceted mirrored chandelier that doubtless spins when the power is on. I spy several web cams mounted on the walls, much like the ones I used when I danced online as Kira Foxxx and there's a hand-held camera lying on one of the chairs. There are also four flat screen monitors mounted on the walls at strategic locations. I suspect at least one of them can be seen from anywhere in the room.

I ask Upmann, "Where's the computer?"

"Waaa…what computer?"

"The one that controls the monitors."

"There's a panel in the wall over there."

"Show me."

He leads us to a nearly invisible door in the wall that opens with the push of a button. Inside is a closed laptop. I flip it open and turn it on. A screen pops up:

Password: ? ? ? ? ? ? ? ? ?

I hate passwords! "Who's in charge of the computer?" I ask Upmann. He doesn't respond.

Kidd says, "I'm so tired of this guy!" He wheels Upmann around, grabs him by the throat and lifts his feet off the floor. Upmann kicks futilely for a minute until Kidd lowers him. Upmann coughs and retches when Kidd releases his grip on Upmann's throat.

"Answer the lady," Kidd says.

"Who's computer is it?" I ask again.

"Fred Simonson's." Of course it is.

Okay, I've probably got three shots at the password before it locks me out. Distasteful as it is, I picture Simonson in my head. I see that ugly tie.

I type O r a n g e a n d b l u e.

Password not correct.

I think again. I picture Simonson sitting at his desk in his office. I type C e n t a u r s.

Password not correct.

Maybe it should have been *centaur* instead of the plural team name. This is a real waste of time! It could be anything. But I've got one more try before I'm locked out.

I remember the first time I was in Simonson's office, when he showed me the sex tape. He typed just a few characters to activate his computer, no more than six or seven. I think a moment. Why not?

I type T i t l e I X .

The screen flickers to life.

Wouldn't you know it, he uses the same video software as Kira Foxxx did. I find the folder with all the .mov files, which are identified by initials and dates. There must be a hundred of them! I pick one at random and double click it.

An orgy involving easily a dozen people appears on the screen. Some are nude, some wear random articles of clothing and some are masked or hooded. There appears to be more men than women involved, though it's difficult to tell because the scene keeps shifting as the cameras change. The sex is both couples and groups, straight, queer and BDSM. I don't recognize any of the unmasked people, but I do a see a blonde woman who could be Diane, wearing a hood with her blonde hair streaming out behind, a leather corset and thigh high boots, riding a guy on the weight bench. There's sound, but it's mostly groans, shouts and screams. I pull up a couple more videos and they're about the same, although I think some of the participants may be different. I wonder just how many people are involved in this club.

I scan the .mov file names more closely. I find one identified with the initials elc. Emmaleigh something Calhoun? I double click it.

It's the video of Emmaleigh's degradation on the chair! It's a long video, nearly two hours, and many of the scenes appear to have been taken in real time. I can tell by the choppiness that the camera was turned off and on, so her ordeal must have lasted much longer. Watching it brings tears to my eyes and makes me sick to my stomach, but I click through it to see if I can identify any of the rapists. Wait! There's Upmann — got you, you sleezeball! The woman in the hood and the corset appears and I'm sure it's Diane, beating poor Emmaleigh with paddle and taunting her between assaults. I turn the sound up and recognize Diane's distinctive voice and accent. Got you too, bitch! Some of the assailants are masked, but there's something about one of them in particular. He's wearing more clothes than the others — he's nearly fully dressed. It's difficult to make out details on the small laptop screen, so I open another window and activate the flat screens on the walls outside, then leave the alcove to have a look.

The outside screens are easily 60" and there's little loss of resolution. The guy who's raping Emmaleigh is standing behind her chair with his hands on her hips. And he's wearing gloves.

Gloves? What kind of guy wears gloves to an orgy? I know — the kind who knows he's going to be taped and doesn't want his hands to be visible, of course. Because he's got a very identifiable birthmark on those hands. Josh Russell!

The vid doesn't prove its Russell but it strongly suggests it and it explains why he did his best to interfere with the investigation. Back at the laptop, I pull up the email app and send an email to myself with the .mov file as an attachment.

Kidd is calling me. "Nattie, come up here. There's something you should see." He went upstairs?

I pick another four videos at random and send them to myself, then shut down the computer and close the alcove.

I find a large L-shaped staircase in the front of the house that goes to second floor. I go up to the landing and call, "Kidd! Where are you?"

"Up here!"

I follow his voice and enter a room halfway down the hall.

Holy shit! My flashlight beam is playing around in a well-equipped home hospital room, complete with an electric bed, patient lift, IV stand and gas tanks. Kidd and Upmann are standing next to the empty bed, whose rumpled sheet and blanket suggest it was recently occupied. And I'll bet I know by whom.

"He survived," says Kidd.

I turn to Upmann. "What do you know about this?"

"Nothing! I swear! I've never been up here before in my life. Simonson and his wife said it was strictly forbidden."

His wife? Diane is Simonson's wife? Poor Danny!

"So this must be Nicky's bed. But where is he?"

Kidd has no answer. "Interesting as this is," he says, "it's not getting us any closer to finding Danny. I'm out of ideas. How 'bout you?"

I shake my head. I glare at Upmann. "I lied before about that video of you on the Internet, but I'm not lying now. I found the video downstairs that shows what you did to Emmaleigh Calhoun."

"They'll throw it out in court because of what you did to me to get it," sneers Upmann.

"You're right. But I wonder what Roderigo would do with it…"

"You can't do that!"

"Sure I can, Harold. Payback's a bitch. After America finds out what you did, maybe you'll find a job in South America somewhere. If somebody doesn't cut your nuts off first."

"What do you want me to do?" he whines.

"Go to the cops," says Kidd. "Identify as many of the people in the group as you can and testify against them. The first guy to rat gets the deal, you know."

"I'll give you a day to think it over, Harold." I tell him. "Then you're going to be a TV star."

We head for Kidd's car to drive back to the city. We did a lot of good here tonight, but we didn't find Danny. Now I wonder if we'll ever find him alive.

My phone starts playing. *Psycho*? I look at the screen. Why would she call me at 6 a.m.? I answer it. "Rebecca? What's up?"

"Hi, shug."

Chapter 27.

My heart is in my throat!

"I reckon you're somewhere you have no business to be, shug."

"What do you mean?"

"There ain't nothin' in that house that you need to concern yourself with."

How does she know where we are? The answer hits me like a slap in the face — both Danny's and my phone have the location app installed. But she called me on Rebecca's phone. She must have Danny's too!

"I've got a couple of folks here who've been inquirin' about you, shug. Of course my Danny's here, he's never far from me, in body or in spirit. But what do you think that nasty boytoy has gone and done? He's done taken up with another woman! I hope you know that I just can't have that!"

WTF is she even talking about? "Diane, if you've hurt Danny or Rebecca…"

"I haven't hurt anyone, shug. As a matter of fact, those two look like they're havin' a good time. A right good time!"

A banner pops up on my screen. *Rebecca Feiner is trying to Face Time you. Accept. Decline.* I hit *Accept*. Diane's face appears on my screen. She smiles broadly when she sees me on her screen.

"Look, shug! Now isn't that precious?"

The scene on the phone spins crazily as she reorients the camera, then two people appear on the small screen. I can see enough of the background to recognize Rebecca's upstairs office.

A naked woman is bent over the back of a cushioned chair with her legs spread and her ankles tied to the chair legs. Her hands are tied to the front legs so all I can see is the long black hair on the back of her head. A naked man is standing behind her, his groin pressed tightly against her butt. It looks like his legs are tied to hers and ropes extend from his wrists to encircle her neck. It's hard to see a lot of detail on the small screen but the man looks a lot like Danny. It is Danny! OMG! Diane, what have you done?

Kidd looks over my shoulder. I hear his sharp intake of breath when he sees the screen.

I can't even imagine how those two proud people must feel! But I know how I feel. Enraged.

I turn so my cell phone camera is pointing away from Kidd. Not because I don't want him to see what's on the screen. Because I don't want Diane to see him when she comes back on the screen.

"Shug, I think these two want you to come over here for a little *ménage à trois.* We'll expect you in half an hour. And you better come alone, or somethin' awful might happen."

The screen goes black.

I turn to run out to the car but Kidd grabs me by the shoulder. "Where you goin'?" He asks.

I glare at him. That doesn't deserve an answer.

"We need a plan, Nattie. We just can't go off half-cocked."

"My plan is to go over there and shoot that bitch multiple times."

"Good initiative, bad judgment. You don't even know who else is there. I'm going with you."

"She knows where we are Leon, she's tracking our phones. She'll kill them if I'm not alone."

"I'll drop my phone at my place. Then we'll go by yours so you can pick up your car. You go in first and I'll follow you. Got your Ruger?"

I pat my front right pocket.

"When you get there, you keep her talking until I can get in and back you up."

I give Kidd the lay of the land of Rebecca's place. "You'll have to park a ways back and come in through the woods," I tell him. "Diane can see the whole front driveway from where she is in Rebecca's office. You'll have to circle the house and go in the back door."

"Okay. I'm a Marine, Nattie. I've done recon before. Your job is to keep her calm until I get there. Don't challenge her or piss her off. Let her think she's in control."

That won't be hard. She is in control. For now, anyway.

We jump into Kidd's car and head out. After driving for about ten minutes, Kidd's voice comes from the back of the car. "Stop here a minute, Nattie." He says to Upmann, "Take your shoes and socks off and get out."

"What? Here? I can't walk barefoot!"

"That's the idea, Harold. Now get out before I make you leave your pants here, too."

Upmann complies, whining. Kidd gets out with him, shoves him in the ditch so he goes down, then gets in the front of the car with me. "That ought to keep him from alerting her until this is finished. Drive."

It's about 7:00 when we get to the townhouse complex after the detour to Kidd's place. As I jump out of Kidd's car, I notice that Lupe's car is gone. That's funny — she usually doesn't go to work this early.

"I've got to go inside a minute. Something's wrong," I tell Kidd.

The townhouse door is locked, as it should be if we're not there. The great room and the kitchen are dark and the door to our bedroom is closed. I cross the great room and put my hand on the bedroom door knob. I take a deep breath and open it, scared about at what I'm going to find.

The early morning light illuminates a small lump in the middle of our bed. A mop of dark brown hair is conspicuous against the background of the pink pillow. Eduardo! Then I see the envelope on the bed beside him. I pick it up. The flap is tucked, not sealed. I open it and remove a piece of cream-colored stationery and unfold it. It's covered in Lupe's precise handwriting. I read

Cariño —

Please do not be angry with me.
Today at work, I was in the ladies room when Katie came in and told me ICE was there for me. I think they find the drugs again! I run down the back stairs before they see me and come straight home. Eduardo is here, so I tell him that he should eat something out of the fridge and play video games and wait for you to come home because I have to go out again.
I am sorry but I take all of our money from the drawer. I cannot use my cards or they will find me.
Please know that I love you, my wife. I know that you would come to Mexico with me, but I cannot let you do that. There is no life there for you or our son.
Please do not look for me. Take care of Eduardo — he is American and he deserves a good life.
I am so sorry. Please do not be angry with me. It is for the best.
I will love you forever,

Lupe

I am going to be sick…

Kidd finds me a few minutes later, hunched over the toilet.

"Whaat!"

He helps me to my feet and I show him Lupe's letter.

"Nattie, I am so sorry!" He hesitates, then. "Maybe we should call the cops and tell them about Danny and Rebecca."

"No! Russell is in on this. I'm sure of it! Call the cops and they're dead. Go and wait for me outside. I have a couple of things to do, then I'll come."

I ring Mom in Fayetteville. Come on, pick up, pick up…

"Hello?"

"Mom, it's me. I need you to come here, right now and take care of Eduardo. I don't have time to explain."

"Nattie, what…"

I cut her off. "Please! Lupe's gone and I have to find her. Eduardo's asleep and he needs somebody here when he wakes up. Please come right away!"

I think she hears the desperation in my voice. "All right, Nattie. It will take me ten minutes to get ready, then I'll leave." A pause. "Are you OK?"

"No, I'm not OK. I'll tell you when I see you. Please just come and see to my boy."

I kill the call. I go back into the bedroom where my little son is sleeping like an angel. I tuck the covers around his chin and ruffle his hair.

OMG, Diane is so going to pay for this!

I go outside where Kidd is waiting. "Let's go," I tell him.

I'll remember this drive as long as I live. I can't stop the tears for the first five minutes, just thinking about Lupe. Then I focus on the rage that's building up in me and the hate. I envision Diane's body jerking as bullets from my gun tear into her. That stops the tears.

When we get to Rebecca's, I just keep going up the driveway while Kidd stops just off the main road. We talked about this — if Diane's monitoring my progress on her phone, we don't want to give her cause for suspicion if she sees me stop at the head of the driveway, then start up again. I drive slowly up the winding gravel road among the stately oaks until Rebecca's house comes into view. The morning sunlight glints off the mirrored windows on the 2nd floor of the A-frame. No sense in trying to be subtle. I pull right up to the front porch.

The front door is ajar. Nice of you to leave it open for me, bitch! The lights are off downstairs and it's quiet. I draw the Ruger from the holster in my front pocket and head upstairs. I have no delusions that I'll get to use it.

I step into the office and I see Diane seated at Rebecca's desk. The diffuse light of dawn illuminates Rebecca and Danny, bound to the easy chair in front of the floor to ceiling window. Diane's got a large, black semiauto pistol pointed at them. Both are gagged by a ball in the mouth secured with a strap behind the head. Danny's naked legs quiver under the stress of the bondage and there's a large loop protruding from his butt. Despite myself, I strain to see whether he's inside Rebecca or not. Knowing Diane, I assume so. She'd think it was funny.

"You can just toss that gun over here, shug," she says.

I expected that. It thumps as it hits the floor.

"It took you long enough to get here. I hope you weren't stupid enough to call the cops. I'll know."

"I know you would. I didn't."

"Smart girl. Go and sit on the couch and I'll tell you what's going to happen here."

I go over to the leather chaise. There's a pair of handcuffs on it.

"Put those on and sit down."

Kidd said to let her think she's in control. That's pretty easy — she is! I clip the cuffs on both wrists, not too tightly, then sit.

"Put your feet up and stretch out."

Uh-oh! This could be bad. But I have no choice, so I do as she says. I hope the semi-darkness in here will save me.

She lays the pistol on the desk and comes over. She tightens the cuffs until they're painful. "There, that's better." A wave of relief washes over me. As she walks back to the desk, I roll my legs off the chaise and sit upright. She picks up her gun and turns to face me, then frowns. "I didn't tell you you could sit up," she says.

"Why are you doing this to me?" I ask her. "You don't even know me."

"Oh, I know you pretty well, shug. Danny told me all about you. Everything I wanted to know."

"So you dated Danny just so you could find things out about me? Why? What did I ever do to you?"

She raises her voice. "You can come in, now."

I hear a noise from the corridor to the annex — a high-pitched whine like a dentist's drill. An apparition creeps into the room. It's a large, motorized wheelchair, very much like the one used by Stephen Hawking. A wizened figure squats within it, dressed in lime green hospital scrubs and white canvas shoes. With his leathery bald head, brown-and-red mottled cadaver's face and his hands drawn up in a clawed rictus, he looks nothing like the handsome man who made love to me two years ago. But it's Nicky, all right.

His hands move on the screen mounted on the front of his chair. A metallic voice emanates from a concealed speaker. "Hi …. Natalie …. it …. has …. been …. awhile".

"Take a look, shug. Take a good look at what those niggers of yours did to my beautiful boy. Then ask me why."

I stare squarely at Nicky. A few days ago, before I lost my heart, I might have been repulsed at the sight. Today, I feel satisfaction. I start to say so, then I reconsider. I need to keep Diane talking, not get shot.

"I didn't know that's what they were going to do to you," I say lamely to Nicky.

"He was gonna leave you for somebody else," Diane says, "and you just couldn't stand it. So you sicced your niggers on him to teach him a lesson."

"Is that what he told you?"

"That's what happened!" she snarls. I see a familiar smirk appear on Nicky's battered face. "Oh I know he did some bad things," she continues. "He told me he had to sell meth to get by. Poor thang! And it didn't bother you nohow, when you thought he was your beau."

I want to scream at her, *He murdered two families!* But I might as well scream it at the sky. Besides, would someone who could cut open a little cat and do what she has to Danny and Rebecca, two of the finest people I know, even care?

"Come over here, sweetie," she says to Nicky, "and show her what you've brought her."

The wheelchair squeals over to the desk and Nicky aligns it parallel to Diane, who reaches into the storage space below the seat and comes out with an object whose outline is easily recognizable. A blow torch!

Diane fumbles in a purse on the desk and extracts a disposable lighter. She turns the knob on the torch and I hear the hiss of the gas. She flicks the lighter and the blue flame ignites with a pop that becomes a quiet roar.

"Now who's first? You, Nattie? Danny? Rebecca?"

Nicky's hand moves on the screen. "Natalie …. first….".

"You have to have patience, shug. Let her watch her lezzie doctor get a makeover so she'll know what's in store for her!" She leers at Danny. "And I'm sure Danny will love it when she starts movin' around!"

Gun in one hand and roaring torch in the other, Diane gets up from the desk and steps toward Rebecca and Danny. I can't let this happen! I steel myself, leap up and charge her head down like a bull! The gun in her hand belches flame and a red-hot poker impales my thigh. I collapse to the floor like a broken doll.

Another gunshot rings out from downstairs, then a second. "That would be your rescuer getting what he deserves," says Diane. A chorus of yells, thumps and bangs comes up the stairwell. Diane looks alarmed, puts the flaming torch on the desk and runs to the doorway to look downstairs. It's now or never!

Ignoring the screaming pain in my thigh, I bend my knees and scrunch up to bring my right ankle to my cuffed hands. I draw the little revolver from the ankle holster with both hands, then aim it at Diane, fifteen feet away. The sting runs up my arms as the .357 bucks in my hand and I see a red rose blossom in Diane's side. She wheels and fires at me and I feel the hot wind from the bullet as it zips past my face. I shoot again and the recoil makes the gun jump out of my hands. Diane's pistol thumps on the floor as both hands fly to her neck, vainly trying to stop the gout of blood flowing from her throat. OMG! I nearly missed!

Still lying on the floor, I pick up the .357 again and aim it at Nicky. He's still smirking! His hand moves on the screen. "Do …. me …. favor …."

There's a commotion at the top of the stairs and LeBrowne bursts into the room, followed by two of his boys. Nicky sees him and turns ashen.

"Don't kill him, Nattie!" LeBrowne screams at me. "He mine! He killed my bruthas!"

Nicky Osman murdered his own father, his mother and his little brother, a fifteen-year old girl who loved him and her mother and father too. He's indirectly responsible for Kiefer's death and Simonson's maiming, the burning of LeBrowne's homies, the degradation of Danny and Rebecca and Xin Niu's agonizing death. And it's his fault that Lupe has left me! That I can never forgive. I should let LeBrowne have his revenge!

LeBrowne walks over to the desk and picks up the still burning blow torch. He brandishes it at Nicky with a gold-toothed grin. Nicky fixes his rheumy eyes on me and flails at the screen. The metallic voice rasps "Please....". I can see the wet stain blooming in his crotch in the strong morning light and imagine the terror welling up in his desperate umber eyes.

I can't do it! I point the .357 at the center of his chest and pull the trigger again and again until the hammer clicks on an empty chamber.

Chapter 28.

I'm sitting at the kitchen table with the yellow marbled top in the house I grew up in, like I've done countless times before. We had family dinner, my birthday parties and I did my homework at that table every night. My family is here — most of them, anyway— Mom and Uncle Amos, who's holding Eduardo on his lap. Leon Kidd sits across from me, a bandage still swathing his head. That big, black man has become family too. Neither Danny nor Rebecca are here, although they were invited. Some wounds take longer to heal than others. And of course, my wife is not here.

The occasion is Kidd's release from the hospital. He had an altercation with the late detective Russell at Rebecca's house, during which Russell clobbered Kidd with a pistol butt and fractured his skull. It turned out that the fracture was a fortunate occurrence because it likely prevented Kidd from dying of brain swelling before he could get medical assistance. But it was touch and go that first week.

My leg is encased in plaster from the hip to below the knee because the bullet from Diane's 9mm shattered my femur but it luckily missed the femoral artery or I would have bled out in short order. The docs at University Hospital pieced the bone back together and inserted a steel rod that is now a permanent part of my anatomy. When I was released a couple of weeks ago, there was no way I could care for myself and an eight-year-old boy in my townhouse, so Mom brought me to Fayetteville. The doctor said that the recovery time for this kind of injury is three to six months and that I was probably looking at the longer end because my injury was from a gunshot wound.

I haven't told anybody the whole story of what happened in Rebecca's house. Naturally, I had to tell the cops something, so I took the credit for killing Diane in self-defense and I blamed LeBrowne for killing Nicky with my gun. LeBrowne was initially furious with me for that but he did acknowledge that I had a right to kill Nicky too, although he thought his claim had more merit than mine. In the end, he told me it was okay to tell the cops he had done it because it would give him street cred.

"But you owe me now," he'd said.

"What's the bill," I asked him.

"You know when the time comes."

I'm way sure I don't like that.

They've been looking, but the cops still haven't found LeBrowne.

I tried to talk to Rebecca about what happened, but she said that she couldn't help anyone else until she could come to terms with what happened to her. Danny never came to see me while I was in the hospital, nor would he return my calls. I asked Rebecca if she had heard from him and she said no. So I made Mom take me by his place just to make sure he hadn't offed himself or something. I made her wait in the car while I went up and banged on his door. He didn't answer and I kept banging. Finally, I yelled, "If you don't open up and let me know you're OK, I'm calling the cops to knock your door down."

The door opened and he was there, dressed in a plaid bathrobe and sporting a week's worth of beard. I wasn't sure if was him or the apartment that smelled so bad.

"I'm okay, Nattie," he said.

"You don't look okay. Do you need to go see somebody?"

"I am. I've been to the VA once and I've got an appointment next week. I just want to be alone for a while until I sort things out." He hesitates, then, "Look, I heard about Lupe. I want you to know that I'm very sorry for you. If you want, when I get my head straight, I'll help you find her if you want."

"I'm going to hold you to that, Danny, so you better get well." I said.

Harold Upmann was found dead in his apartment, hanging from a ceiling fan. The next day it was on the news that the orgy house had burned to the ground. I made CD copies of the videos I'd sent to myself, put them in a safe deposit box and gave Gary a letter to be opened in the event of my death. I didn't recognize anyone in the videos, but I'm sure that facial recognition software would yield some interesting results.

Fred Simonson is alive, but he's a broken man, blinded, disfigured and a permanent resident at Tubman.

I'm still trying to get my head around Diane's total hatred for me. She must've taken pity on Nicky when he was her patient in the Burn Unit, and gradually fell in love with him as she nurtured him. After he was transferred to Tubman, she assumed total responsibility for his care and even moved him into her own home as her resident patient. I could just see him, day after day, pouring his poison into her ears like Rasputin, about what the Legends and I had done to him, and how he was the innocent victim of a shameless temptress who couldn't accept that he would leave her. After a couple of years of that, combined with Simonson's evil influence, the kinky orgies and a liberal dose of the drugs she pilfered from the hospital for Nicky, anyone would become unhinged. When I was being cast as a heroine in the news after the affairs with Randall Leighton and the strip club, she must have really gone over the edge.

State University sent me a letter and told me that, after due consideration, I was welcome to come back for the Spring semester. There was no mention of emotional counselling. I called the registrar's office and told them that I didn't think I could attend because of my injuries. They assured me that there would still be a place for me whenever I wanted it. So law school is still a possibility, except that I'm not sure that's what I want anymore.

What I really want is my Lupe. As soon as I'm healed, I intend to devote my every waking moment to finding her. If I do find her and she tells me that she doesn't want me in her life anymore, I'll try to honor that. But I sure as hell won't let her sacrifice her own happiness because she thinks she's ensuring mine. She could not be more wrong. If we're not allowed to live here and she won't live in Mexico, then we'll just have to find someplace in this sorry-ass world where we can live.

I said before that I was sorry about what the Legends had done to Nicky after I turned him over to them. Not anymore. Now I'm sorry that I had a weak moment and shot him instead of letting LeBrowne have him again. Nicky Osman took away my Lupe, the most precious thing in my life and the only one who really understood me. I'll never forgive him for that!

After Mom brings out a cake and we all have some, she says, "Nattie, I have another surprise for you. I'll just go and get it." She disappears and comes back after a minute with a shoebox, which she puts in my lap. I take off the lid and a little, tan Siamese kitten with a black nose and ears and the bluest eyes you ever saw puts his paws on the side of the box and mews at me.

"*El gato!*" shouts Eduardo. He jumps off Uncle's lap and runs over to scoop the little one out of the box. The kitten immediately begins nuzzling his chest and purring. It seems like ages before I can speak through the tears.

"Mom, you'll never know how much this means to me. But…"

She peers at me over her glasses at that word.

"… I hope you can keep him for a while. And Eduardo too. Because as soon as this leg heals, I am going to find Lupe." I address Kidd and Uncle. "Danny has already said he'll help me. I hope I can count on you two as well."

"You know you can count me in, girl," says Kidd.

Uncle has a strange expression on his face as he watches Eduardo, who's now on my lap cuddling his new kitty. "Well, I reckon you can count on me too, Nattie. I guess that's what family's all about."

— The End —

About the Author

As a kid, I started reading mysteries with the Hardy Boys, Ken Holt and Rick Brant, then graduated to the classics by authors such as A. Conan Doyle, Erle Stanley Gardner, John Dickson Carr, and Rex Stout, to name a few. I have written fiction as a hobby all of my life, starting in marble-backed copybooks in grade school. I built a career as a technical and science writer and as an editor for nearly thirty years in academia, industry and government. Now that I'm truly on my own as a freelance science writer and editor, I'm excited to publish my own mystery series as well.

Follow me on Facebook at https://www.facebook.com/3MDetectiveAgency/, on Twitter @3Mdetective, on Instagram at@3mdetective or email me at tom@3mdetectiveagency.com to get all the news about Nattie and her colleagues at the 3M Detective Agency.

Don't miss the next book in the Natalie McMasters series by Thomas A. Burns, Jr. — Trafficked! — Coming in early 2019

www.ingramcontent.com/pod-product-compliance
Lightning Source LLC
Chambersburg PA
CBHW020631250626
47154CB00008B/2631